'. . . The Heartstone Odyssey is both an admirable work of art, and a real contribution to the movement towards greater understanding and recognition of the cultures of India, Britain, and how they can develop and thrive together.

Anti-racist is too glib an adjective for this profound and magical epic, but its messages and resonances cannot fail to raise the consciousness of all who read it, or those who use it as source material for teaching.

Those of us who have visited Britain and India at once feel at home with the style, atmosphere and idiosyncrasies of the writing, and the finely drawn, charming characters. It is clear that Arvan Kumar has deep roots in both Britain and the subcontinent.

The story of the dancer, Chandra, has a special meaning for artists who seek to share their cultural heritage with others, but its theme is accessible and universal.

Literature, like music or other art forms, has a special ability, and a responsibility to change peoples appreciation of the world in which we live. The Heartstone Odyssey is a shining example of a book which can enable readers to look at their environment, and the people in it, with new eyes.

I am happy to have the opportunity of commending Arvan Kumar's book to children and adults of all ages, wherever they may live.

Pandit Ravi Shankar
Delhi, October 1988

'. . . The greatest strength of the book is in another area which has been sadly neglected by other children's authors. The story describes a world in which there exists a powerful and well co-ordinated anti-racism movement – much more powerful, that is, than many a young victim of racism is likely to be aware of today. This is something that we are still striving for, but the vision, in the meantime, will provide a source of strength and encouragement to many of our children.' *John Siraj-Blatchford, Dragons Teeth*

'. . . What particularly impresses me, especially in my line of work, is the way the story deals with racial conflict and provides the pegs on which children can hang their ideas about resolving conflict. Adults too often compromise with racial abuse and violence, and they often force children to do so to. The Heartstone Odyssey confronts what we sometimes call the real world with magic, mystery, danger and rescue, suspense and resolution in the most gripping and entertaining way, and it echoes the heart-felt needs of children for a world that assures them of justice, equality, freedom and respect. I want every school in the land to introduce its children to this story which is one of the finest ones I have ever read . . .' *R. A. German, Principal Education Officer, Commission for Racial Equality*

'. . . Some of the most influential animal characters in children's (and for that matter of adult) fiction – Watership Down's rabbits, Winnie the Pooh, Toad of Toad Hall – are about to face competition from the mice of Wellminster Cathedral and the old Eastwich Observatory.' *Uma Ram Nath, The Guardian*

'. . . This book has introduced children to the very real injustice that exists in our world. It has given children the confidence to talk about their own experiences.' *Headteacher, Manchester*

'. . . I have read it to large groups, much larger than I would choose – having over 100 in each. Despite this, the children love the story, are keen for each session to come round and are totally engrossed whilst I am reading. The children, especially the older ones, are very able to relate aspects of the story to present day local experiences.' *Headteacher, London*

'. . . The story has exceptional qualities. I was absorbed by its content and spellbound by its narrative. . . . It inspired me and gave me access to other people's lives, their hopes, their fears, their conflicts. It challenged attitudes and traditional views about people of different races, colour and religions in an unthreatening but powerful way. Stories of this type and quality rarely emerge. It matches the splendour of "The Lion, the Witch and the Wardrobe". *Headteacher, London*

'. . . The epic saga of the mice I have found to be beautiful and fascinating. The appeal to children from 7 to 70 is I believe irresistible. At the same time, this powerful tale gives an insight into many areas of life and provides very positive and worthwhile models. I am looking forward with some impatience to the next part of the story.' *Headteacher, London*

'. . . It is definitely an exciting adventure story with a strong feeling of gentleness underlying it all. . . . The writer deals with racism in a very sympathetic and subtle way. . . . The book stays with you. . . . In many epic stories of this kind, the action takes place in imaginary lands but here the saga is set in real countries.' *Junior School Teacher, London*

'. . . I am deeply impressed by what has been achieved in getting across a message of hope in a way that touches on some of the central problems of our society without endangering the project by provoking a hostile backlash.' *Rt. Hon. Anthony Wedgewood-Benn, MP*

'. . . Arvan Kumar's 'The Heartstone Odyssey' is an exciting tale which touches on the universal themes of justice and equality in a way that moves schoolchildren to commitment and eloquence. . . I recommend this story for its narrative quality and the capacity of the writer to motivate young children to discuss the age-old art of storytelling in a spirit of intense interest and enquiry.' *Michael Hussey, Senior Inspector Multi-Ethnic and Anti-Racist Education, ILEA.*

'. . . It is essential to make people aware of the bigotry and prejudice of racism, and to make them feel compelled to eliminate such primitive responses.' *Stuart Randall, MP*

'. . . I am sure it will do invaluable work.' *Julian Bradley, Head of Publicity, Metropolitan Police, New Scotland Yard*

'A splendid children's book. . . ' *Anatol Lieven, The Spectator*

'It is a rare treat indeed to read a book by a new author which leaves such a lasting impression on the reader. The story has the timeless appeal of a future classic, combining very successfully elements of folktale and fantasy with the very real conflicts experienced by many people in today's multicultural society. The book works well on two levels: firstly, as an excellent and enchanting story, and secondly, as a remarkably perceptive depiction of racial prejudice which many children will recognise. Children of all ages will enjoy the story, and be enlightened by the gentle but thought provoking message it has to offer. I loved the story and eagerly await the sequel! I would warmly recommend 'The Heartstone Odyssey' for the shelves of all public and school libraries.' *Youth Librarian and Secretary, Youth Librarians' Group*

THE HEARTSTONE ODYSSEY

ODYSSEY

CHANDRA'S STORY

ARVAN KUMAR

Allied Mouse

ALLIED MOUSE
PUBLICATION
INDEX – STORIES
Allied Mouse S 001
First Published 1988

ISBN 0 9513492 0 1

Published by ALLIED MOUSE Ltd, Longden Court,
Spring Gardens, Buxton, Derbyshire SK17 6BZ

Front cover illustration by Tony Moo-Young

Printed and bound in Great Britain by
BPCC Wheatons Ltd, Exeter
Member of BPCC Limited
Aylesbury, Bucks, England

First Printing 1988
Second Printing 1989
Third Printing 1990
Fourth Printing 1991
Fifth Printing 1991

THE HEARTSTONE ODYSSEY

CHANDRA'S STORY

This story is of and belongs to mice everywhere and in whatever land they find themselves. I say whatever land since you must understand, even if you do not know it already, that sometimes mice make very long journeys to wherever their hearts take them. The tale is also of a very sad young woman whose problem was the start of one such journey and her story too should be told even though, as is so often the case with people with problems, she does not always know how to explain herself very well. The mice found out and that was the beginning of the great adventure, so do read on because, if you turned round, there might just be a mouse sitting there hoping you will share their story and be their friend.

CHAPTER 1

The Park

It was a clear October afternoon and the autumn sun cast long shadows from the trees of Langley Park in the London Borough of Bromswood. Sitting on the grass at one side of the open space in the centre of the park was the figure of a young woman, her head bent forwards, and she was crying.

Her name was Chandra and she was a dancer, it was what she had always wanted to be ever since she had learnt her very first dance steps from her mother back in India. That had been when she was five and her family lived in the South, near Madras, but then two years later her mother died and her father had brought her to England. When she was older, Chandra learned that this had been so that her aunt, who already lived in London, could help look after her. At the time all she knew was that first she had lost her mother, then all her friends, and for a while it seemed the dance as well. Her aunt did not think that dance was a very respectable thing for a girl to do, especially since it meant being out late at classes, but Chandra had persisted. Dance was her love and her last link with her mother and she was not going to give either up if she could help it!

Eventually a teacher of Indian dance had been found and her father even paid for one of the beautiful silk and gold costumes, and replaced it when she got older and bigger. Finally, when Chandra had trained for many years, her teacher arranged her debut or first full performance called an Arangetram which was the way of acknowledging that she was now ready to work on her own and perhaps even teach others herself.

Throughout all the years of hard work, Chandra had never doubted that dance was what she wanted to do, not ever, until that day when she sat so very sad in Langley Park in the afternoon sun. In the morning Chandra had gone to the Bromswood Community Theatre and she had been so happy and excited, she always got excited before one of her performances and she had had a show that evening. Then everything changed, a notice had been pinned up on the theatre door:

'INDIAN DANCE TONIGHT - CANCELLED'

Chandra went straight away to find the manager, a grey-haired, chubby man from East London, from Bromswood, he had always been so kind surely now he could help. She could still remember his words,

'I'm sorry love but I had to do it, we had two more threats to the hall this morning - and someone tried to break in last night, there's just people round here that don't seem to like anything foreign.'

'But I'm not foreign, I live here too!' Chandra said trying, not very successfully, to keep her voice steady.

'Yes but you know what I mean, there's them round here who it seems that if they haven't seen it all before then they just don't know what to do. Next before you know it they goes and says stupid things and does them as well. Look, I wouldn't normally take this much notice but the hall lost a lot of money last year and if there was any trouble, Council might close us down. Then no one could do things. I really am sorry.'

The manager had stood there his hands turned outwards almost in a plea for understanding. Chandra had understood; to her the hall was as good as closed already. Everyone in the area knew of the attacks on Indian people in the street and on their homes, on anyone in fact whose skin spoke of a different land even if

2

they had been born there. You couldn't really forget the people who did such things, their messages of hate were on every wall. To most people it just looked messy but it was different if you knew that they were meant for you. 'Kill all Pakis' was clear enough and that was written three times in letters a foot high in Chandra's own road alone!

So now they had decided to stop her show as well, and it had worked, and there was nothing she could do. She just walked away carrying the bags that held her costume, jewellery and flowers, walked down the road of old terraced houses some brightly painted, others crumbling, to the park, Langley Park, where she now sat alone, or at least she thought she was.

Then Chandra heard a very small, very quiet, but quite distinct sound of someone or something sobbing in the bushes behind her. Diverted for a moment from her own troubles, she went quickly over to the shrubs and pulled aside the stems nearest to her. There, cradled in the leaves between two branches was a little light brown mouse with big dark eyes and long whiskers, a little mouse crying its heart out. Not knowing quite what she was doing, Chandra reached down and ever so gently lifted the mouse out of the bush and, sitting down again where she had been, looked at the tiny creature huddled on the hand she held out in front of her and wondered what she could do to help.

Now a very strange thing was about to happen to Chandra, a strange thing which might happen to anyone if they are lucky enough, Chandra was about to have a conversation with a mouse. If that seems odd to you, just ask yourself something, do you really know that mice can't speak or have you just never tried, and then if they could talk to you but you haven't tried, is that the fault of the mice or you?

So in the park Chandra sat looking at the mouse, the mouse that seemed to be the saddest animal she had

3

ever seen, and suddenly because it felt like the most natural thing to do, spoke to it, but very quietly though, so as not to frighten something so small.

'Please tell me what's wrong.'

The mouse slowly stopped crying and looked at Chandra with those huge dark brown eyes,

'I'm sad because you're sad,' the mouse said.

There was then a pause whilst the mouse just sat and looked at Chandra as if desperately willing her to cheer up so that it could be happy again. Then the mouse almost seemed to smile and spoke again,

'But if you cuddle me then I would feel better, and because I feel better you will feel better too. My name's Hugbundle by the way.'

Slowly, wondering if this was really happening to her, Chandra cradled the little mouse in the palm of her hand. The mouse wrapped its front paws round her first finger and rested its head on her thumb. There it lay for some minutes whilst Chandra gently cupped her fingers round it to make it feel safe until the sobbing stopped completely and the smile Chandra had thought she had seen earlier really was there all the time. Chandra also felt an even stranger thing, it really had been true, now the mouse was happy again she did feel better. So she sat in the autumn sunlight which seemed warmer now, just her and a mouse called Hugbundle, friends for what reason she was not quite sure.

Hugbundle sat up and climbed from Chandra's hand to the branch of a tree that hung down beside them. Hugbundle was very careful to sit in a patch of sunlight that fell on the branch in order to keep warm. If you ever have dealings with the mice you will find that keeping warm is very important to them and they will always try and search out the hottest place.

Hugbundle wanted to know all about Chandra, where she came from, her friends, and very soon found out that Chandra was a dancer. After they had been talking

4

for some minutes, however, Hugbundle suddenly sat up and looking very serious and straight at Chandra asked her why she had been so upset. Chandra told Hugbundle about the performance and what had happened and, as she spoke, Hugbundle looked sadder and sadder. When Chandra finished it seemed as if the mouse might start to cry again. Chandra leant forwards and trying to sound as kind as she possibly could said,

'What's wrong?'

'The more you tell me about your dance the more beautiful it sounds and I so want to see it and now I can't,' sniffed Hugbundle, a picture of absolute misery again. For almost a minute the mouse just sat dejectedly on the branch, she didn't even bother to move to stay in the sun.

Then to Chandra's amazement Hugbundle leaped up and jumped back onto her hand where she hopped around in excitement.

'You did say that some of your dances were about the moon and the stars didn't you?'

'Yes,' said Chandra.

'Well I think that you should give a show tonight anyway, and I know a place to do it - they'd all love to see you and best of all I could come too!'

Hugbundle was now jumping about on Chandra's hand more excited than ever.

'Yes but where?' Chandra asked.

'At the observatory of course!' cried Hugbundle in delight.

This left Chandra wondering just what the link between talking mice and something as scientific and complicated as astronomy was.

Still, Chandra had only known one talking mouse, and that had only been for ten minutes so she felt that she must still have a lot to learn, which she soon did. When Hugbundle calmed down enough to answer questions properly, she explained to Chandra that it was not

5

just people who looked at the stars but that they were a very special interest of the mice as well. Hugbundle told Chandra that for many years, not far from where they were, there had been a very special observatory used by people but in which there had also lived many mice who watched and learned from what they did. Then, in what had never made sense to the mice, all the astronomer people suddenly left and although they took a few of the telescopes with them they left many more behind. The place then changed, it was called a museum and many, many people wandered around it by day, which was very silly because there weren't any stars then, no one looked through the telescopes, which was very sad, and the mice had not known what to do.

Over the years though they had learned much and some of them, the astronomer mice, knew as much or even more about the stars than the astronomer people. One or two of these mice knew so much that they were called the professor mice and tended to be old with white fur and grey whiskers. The mice decided to take over the observatory. It was not difficult since no one went there at night now anyway and they continued to use the telescopes that had been left behind.

Chandra guessed that Hugbundle was talking about the Old National Observatory at Eastwich. It was true though, the scientists had moved to a new location out of London and the old site had been made a museum. It was strange to Chandra that she had never realised till then how sad it would have been if nobody ever used the telescopes again.

Hugbundle was really happy again now,

'Yes I'm sure that all the astronomer mice would love to meet you, what's the time? Let's go there right now.'

'Well it's 5.30,' said Chandra.

Hugbundle, who previously could just not stop talking sat silent for a moment as if she was trying to find a way of putting something, then she said,

'No not that sort of time, that's silly, I meant what's the sun doing?'

'Oh,' said Chandra trying to sound as if she should have known,'Well it's just about to set.'

'Good,' said Hugbundle,' do you think we could get to the observatory before it's completely dark?'

Chandra sat and thought for a moment, remembered that a bus went to Eastwich from the park and not knowing quite what she was doing or letting herself in for said,

'Oh yes, I think we could do that.'

Chandra opened her smaller bag and Hugbundle sat in the top amongst the flowers that Chandra wore in her hair with her costume. From there Hugbundle could hide with just the tips of her ears showing or could peep out at where they were going. Chandra, who was worried about how one should introduce a talking mouse to anyone they met, was relieved that no one on the walk to the bus stop or on the bus itself seemed to notice Hugbundle. Hugbundle nestled down amongst the flowers, but very carefully so as not to crush any of them, and seemed perfectly happy looking at everything they passed on their journey.

Chandra got off the bus at Eastwich and walked through the park and up the hill which led to the old observatory. It was dark but to the West there was still a faint orange glow in the sky, the colour then changing to a light blue, a dark blue and then deepest black as you looked higher. The sky was full of stars and outlined against these on top of the hill was the old observatory. As they climbed towards it they passed a huge tree which loomed up out of the darkness and seemed strangely alive that night, magic was in the air.

Slightly out of breath, Chandra reached the top of the last and very steep part of the slope and stood at the outer iron gates of the observatory. These were however shut and locked. Through them there was an open court-yard with several very old buildings on three sides. No lights or others signs of occupation were however to be seen anywhere. She put down her bags and held the smaller one open to help Hugbundle to climb out. Hug-bundle jumped down, looked round excitedly and said,

'Don't worry just wait here. I'll be back soon, very soon...' and with a quick wave of her paw Hugbundle scampered off under the gates and across the courtyard into the darkness.

Chandra stood in the cold clear night air and wondered what would happen next. She hoped that Hug-bundle would not expect her to climb over the gates that barred her way and which seemed to grow larger and more forbidding the longer you looked at them. She glanced at the notice board set into the wall beside her, it said that there were no admissions after five. She looked at her watch, it was nearly seven. From there her gaze wandered to look down the hill and to the docks and houses beyond. A thousand tiny lights shone and to Chandra danced before her as she studied the broad expanse of the East End of London, her home. Then she turned away quickly, remembering how unwelcome she had felt there only hours before and her heart was heavy.

Chandra's sadness did not however have time to take hold for, at that very moment, she looked behind her and could not believe what she saw. There was a line of tiny lights coming up the side of the hill, out from the trees below, across the grass and towards the observ-atory and the lights were moving! Chandra crouched down to watch, fascinated. As the nearest light came closer, she could make out that it was a mouse carrying a tiny lantern. Behind was another, and another, and another each carrying a lantern or a candle. The mice went straight towards the observatory, under the gate and to a small hole at the side of the main door. She looked back and still the line stretched right down the slope to the trees.

Chandra stood there amazed and would not have moved for hours if she had not been startled by a small but very excited voice behind her.

'I'm back and we've brought you something.'

There stood Hugbundle and behind her were two other mice struggling to carry what for them was a huge key. Despite its weight, they smiled up at her and squeaked together 'Hello!' Quickly to help them Chandra bent down and took the key pressing her hands together in front of her in the Indian greeting and bowed to the mice. Then she tried the key in the gate – it fitted!

Letting herself in, Chandra closed the gate behind her but when she turned to look at the observatory, her heart almost stopped in wonder. The whole courtyard was filled with mice each holding a lamp, they had come to light her way and welcome her. Between them they had left a path right up to the observatory door. A tear ran down from Chandra's cheek as she stood there not knowing what to say. For what seemed like hours she did not dare to move in case the spell was broken. Then Chandra felt a small but firm tugging at her skirt, it was Hugbundle who whispered, 'It's all right go on.' Chandra's confidence returned, again she pressed her hands together in greeting only this time it was to all the mice and bowed. Then it seemed that every mouse started chattering at once as if the silence of their special welcome was difficult to keep a second longer. They called to each other and as Chandra walked up the path many shouted out to her to say hello, some even jumped up and down so that she might notice them. As Chandra moved towards the heavy door into the observatory, even with the magic of that night, she scarcely guessed at the adventure that lay before her and the mice who were to become her friends.

CHAPTER 2

The Observatory

When Chandra reached the door of the observatory, preparations had already been made to let her in. Two of the more daring mice inside the building had climbed up and, after some difficulty, managed to pull the key out of the lock letting it fall to the floor. It was then dragged and carried out through the hole the mice used to come and go. This had been done by two more mice who now stood waiting to hand Chandra the key.

Once she was let in, Chandra, despite the adventures she had already had that day, could hardly believe her eyes. Several mice, all carrying candles, led her along passageways and up some steps to a large central room or hall. Around the edge of the hall, which was nearly circular in shape, were a number of very old telescopes, many made of brass that had been polished until it gleamed in the light of hundreds of lanterns. These the mice had arranged, it seemed, in every available nook and cranny bathing the whole hall in a soft, warm yellow glow.

At each telescope that faced out of a window there was a scene of intense activity. The mice had placed long ladders just strong enough to take their weight up against the telescope so that they could climb up and look out through the eye-piece. Apart from the mouse, or often two mice huddled together at the top of a ladder actually looking through the telescope, close by would be a group of two or three others sitting by a lantern with very small note-pads writing down details of what was seen using quill pens made out of feathers. When Chandra asked later why they used the quill pens, the mice told her that they came from the geese that lived on or visited the lakes and big river nearby. The mice only used the smallest feathers, they could not hold the larger ones, and it was these that the geese collected for them and gave in friendship for use in the observatory. In return, the mice shared their knowledge of the stars which the geese used to navigate by as they flew for days and days on the immense journeys they made far across the world even to the frozen wastes of the distant North.

By one of the telescopes there was an old mouse with white fur and grey whiskers who sat looking at Chandra and then called to her to come over and be introduced. Chandra went across and bowed very solemnly in greeting because she guessed this must be one of the professor mice that Hugbundle had told her about. The mouse spoke to her, still in the high pitched small voice of the mice that she knew, but this mouse had a slower, more considered speech that gave a feeling of calm authority.

'Hello Chandra and welcome to our observatory.'

'Thank you,' said Chandra, 'I am honoured to be your guest.'

'No, the honour is I think ours,' said the Professor mouse,' but such talk can wait, there is something that you must see - it is very exciting.'

The Professor mouse beckoned Chandra towards the telescope and she bent down and looked through it. There was a perfect image of the moon just risen, it was truly beautiful with wisps of cloud at its edge, but it was only the moon.

'It's beautiful,' Chandra said, 'but I don't think that the moon is a new discovery.'

The Professor mouse sighed but smiled kindly at Chandra,

'I will forgive you because you saw first the beauty and because in part you cannot help share the impatience of men for the new. It is an impatience that I too have but it must never close your eyes to the old. I do not think you would see me as much of a friend if I would not speak to you a second time because I already knew you. The moon is my friend. I am sad when she is not there and I welcome her when she comes, that is how I got my name - Professor Watchmoon.'

Chandra suddenly felt very sorry for having dismissed something simply because it was known and hoped she had not hurt the mouse's feelings. Almost as if he knew what she was thinking Professor Watchmoon said,

'Come, do not be so sad, there is still time, sit with me a while and let us enjoy the moon together. Anyway, how could I be angry with one who shares my name.'

Chandra started at this but the mouse went on,

'Oh yes I know, Chandra, and that means moon in the language of part of India doesn't it?'

Chandra nodded for Chandra does indeed mean moon not in Tamil, the language of the very South of India today but in Sanskrit, the ancient and mysterious language of the region. Chandra knew some Sanskrit because although it was very difficult to learn, it was the language in which all the history of her dance was written.

Chandra and Professor Watchmoon spent the next hour together gazing at that beautiful moon as it rose in the sky and it was with a very genuine sense of loss to them both that it finally disappeared behind a thick heavy bank of cloud.

Professor Watchmoon then looked at Chandra and said,

'Don't look as though the moon has gone forever, she always comes again and anyway, if what I know of you already is true, you could bring her back right now.'

Chandra looked puzzled.

12

'You are a dancer aren't you?' asked the mouse.

'Yes,' said Chandra unsure of what might follow.

'And you sometimes dance of the moon?'

'Yes.'

'Then please dance for us now and bring the moon back for us.'

Chandra sat there in wonder that the little mouse from whom she had already learned so much wanted to see her dances, the most precious thing she had. She was to have little choice though, the other mice had been listening and they all crowded round her calling up excitedly, 'Oh yes please, for us now,' and, 'You must. We'd love to see it,' and many other things, all at once so you couldn't make them all out.

The mice led Chandra to a smaller room where she could get ready and put on her costume. They left her candles to see what she was doing, although since they were mouse candles they were very small and a great number had to be brought in for her. When she started to unpack her costume, the flowers for her hair and most of all her magnificent gold dance jewellery, there was great activity amongst the mice who scampered around looking at everything not just once but several times squeaking to each other in excitement. They would have stayed if Chandra had let them but, when she was ready to start her preparations, she gently began to shoo the ever excited and chattering mice out of the room. Finally, she closed the door behind them having made them promise not to come back in by any other passages and holes they might know.

Then Chandra sat down at the large desk she was using as a dressing table and started to put on her make-up. It was only after about five minutes that she noticed the small brown nose with whiskers and two little ears poking up out of the flowers.

'I told you all to wait outside,' said Chandra impatiently.

'What, even me?' said Hugbundle climbing out of the flowers, 'you must want someone to help.'

Chandra was going to say 'No' but Hugbundle looked so hopeful, sitting there with her head on one side and smiling that, 'Yes,' is what came out. They worked together for over an hour and Hugbundle was in fact a great help as far as her size would allow. Chandra put on the costume of beautiful red silk with mauve and gold trimmings herself but then Hugbundle sat on a pile of books and painted on Chandra's eye make-up, even though the little mouse could only just hold the brush. When she had done it Chandra had to admit that it looked better than it had ever done before. Hugbundle also helped to tie the jewellery and flowers into Chandra's hair and then at last they had finished. Hugbundle stood back and said nothing for a long time.

'It's beautiful,' she sighed.

'Thank you,' said Chandra, 'but we had better go and find the others, they've all been waiting for us.'

Chandra opened the door and they made their way back to the main hall, Hugbundle sitting on top of the large tape recorder to play her music on that Chandra carried in her bag for emergencies. Even she had never thought it might be used for anything like this though.

As Chandra entered all the mice gasped and clapped their paws together in excitement, they had never seen anything quite as grand before. And so Chandra danced for the mice in the centre of the great hall of the observatory whilst they all sat round the edge - on the floor, on the window sills, on the ladders and even on the telescopes, all watching her as she moved by the light of the candles. Chandra did dance of the moon and the stars and of the temples in India and of the animals, she even knew a special dance gesture for mouse. She told the mice stories and danced them and every time she finished all the mice clapped and sometimes even cheered until she danced again.

14

Finally, when Chandra was not sure she could dance any more, Professor Watchmoon got up and all the other mice were silent. The Professor turned to Chandra and said,

'Thank you, I do not know the words to say what I want to but I hope you will come again and be with us if you will allow us to be your friends.'

'Allow you,' panted Chandra,' I do not think I deserve that doubt but I will be back if you will allow me.'

Then all the mice started clapping again and the sound of their applause drifted down the corridor as she slipped back to her room to change. Outside it was getting light and she glanced down at her watch on the table, it was nearly 5 o'clock. Chandra started to hurry. 'What if someone came?' The mice could disappear easily enough but she would be caught. As quickly as she could Chandra packed her things, tidied up the room, and slipped quietly down the passage into the hall with the telescopes. The mice had gone and so had the ladders and the lamps, it was as if nothing had ever happened there since the museum had closed. Then Chandra heard a key turn in the lock of the outside door and heavy footsteps and she was afraid. There was nothing for it, she would have to pretend she'd been locked in the night before when the museum closed and had had to spend the night.

Chandra could feel the beating of her own heart as she walked down the passage towards the entrance. As she turned a corner she came face to face with a man in uniform, the nightwatchman, and Chandra let out a stifled scream of fear and surprise.

'Hello Miss,' said the nightwatchman, 'I'm sorry if I gave you a fright. Let me carry your bags, the Professor's waiting for you outside.'

'Thank you,' mumbled Chandra and not knowing what to do followed the man wondering which Professor he might mean. She need not have worried however.

15

There on the bench in the full rays of the newly risen sun were Professor Watchmoon, Hugbundle and three other mice. The Professor was talking to a middle-aged Japanese man with glasses who was wearing a track suit and jogging shoes. Before Chandra reached them, the man turned and ran slowly off down the hill to the park.

'Ah thank you Fred,' said Professor Watchmoon as they approached, 'Chandra let me introduce you, this is Fred the nightwatchman.'

'Oh, hello,' said Chandra still nervous.

'Yes Fred's very sorry to have missed your performance but he hasn't been coming in recently, his wife's been ill and he likes to stay at home and take care of her so we promised to look after things and call him if anything happens.'

'That's right,' said Fred, 'and I'm very grateful to you as you know.'

He looked round at all the mice who smiled.

'I hope your wife is better soon,' said Chandra.

'Oh I'm sure she will be,' said Fred,' but we're none of us getting any younger are we and then it's the cold weather you know.'

Chandra nodded.

'Anyway I'd better get on,' and with that Fred went back into the observatory to get ready for the day's visitors.

At the bottom of the hill the Japanese man joined a tall woman with blonde hair also in jogging clothes and together they began to run slowly around the edge of the park. As they turned to start they waved to Professor Watchmoon who waved back, even if it was unlikely they could see him from so far away.

'Who's that?' asked Chandra.

'Oh that's Dr. Yamamoto from Tokyo and Laura Pepard, she's Professor of Astrophysics in Chicago. They're over here for the big astronomical conference this month.'

16

'And you know them?' asked Chandra with some surprise.

'Why not?' said the Professor, 'I'm going to the conference too, there's always room for someone small at the back. But enough of that, we've got other things to discuss now. Chandra, I have learned something of what happened yesterday and we may be able to help, but I want to check some things, do some research and do some thinking. Can you come back again tonight?'

'Yes,' said Chandra, 'what time?'

'The same, 8 o'clock to you, the time of moon rise to me,' said the Professor.

'I'll be there,' said Chandra, 'and thank you.'

'Don't thank me till we've achieved something,' said the Professor, 'but at least we can try.'

The mice and Chandra sat in silence for some time warm and happy in the sun.

'What are you thinking, Chandra?' asked the Professor.

'I was thinking about the moon, what it would be like to go there.'

'Yes I can understand that,' said the Professor, ' and yes, I think you would like it.'

'You've been there!' gasped Chandra.

'Oh yes,' said the Professor, looking a little embarrassed and shy, 'I went with the Americans on Apollo 15; there really is always room for a mouse somewhere, even in a small spaceship. Come tonight and I'll tell you all about it and show you some of my moon rock.'

With that the Professor jumped off the bench, waved and ran off with surprising speed for his age across the courtyard and through a small hole into the observatory. The other mice wished Chandra goodbye and made off towards the trees where she had seen them come from the previous night. Hugbundle stayed with her.

'Shall we go home?' said Hugbundle.

17

'You mean you want to come with me?' asked Chandra.

Hugbundle nodded and so Chandra lifted her back into her bag, in amongst the flowers, and together they walked back down the hill and out of the park in the morning sun.

Unseen by Chandra or Hugbundle, they were watched from some bushes by a large dark brown rat which, after they had gone, ran off as fast as it could in the opposite direction. Its name was Smirkmuzzle.

CHAPTER 3

Eastwich At Night

Chandra took Hugbundle back to her flat which was the bottom half of an old house. Only once they were inside did they both realise how tired they were. Chandra made Hugbundle a bed with two silk scarves on a cushion and then she climbed gratefully into her own; at once they were both asleep.

By mid-afternoon, the sun shone through a gap in the closed curtains and a shaft of light fell on Hugbundle's face. The mouse stirred, stretched out a paw to the warmth and slowly woke up. Hugbundle looked round the bedroom, saw that Chandra was still fast asleep and so very quietly started to explore. First she went and had a look in the bags with Chandra's dance things, just to check everything was all right. Then she climbed out and up onto a table in the centre of which was a basket of beautiful flowers with a card beside them. Hugbundle peeped round the cover of the card and read the message:

'To Chandra for a brilliant performance'

It must be from one of Chandra's shows thought Hugbundle who, now feeling even closer to the flowers than she had done, climbed up into the basket and up one of the stems and sat right in the middle of the bunch. She sniffed each one in turn for any scent, some were roses and smelled wonderful. After she had investigated every flower, Hugbundle climbed down and went over to the window sill where there was a patch of sun as the light fell between the curtains and sat looking at the garden. A small area of grass was surrounded on each side by trees and shrubs and at the front there was a flower bed with bricks at the edge to keep the earth in. Hugbundle started to feel sleepy again in the sun and she began to doze. Then, the sun was gone in an instant as if someone had just switched it off as a huge head towered over Hugbundle, a monstrous orange head with green eyes and horrible sharp teeth. Hugbundle shrieked, fell back off the windowsill, scrambled across the floor and up the blanket which hung down at the side of Chandra's bed. With one jump she was under the covers and hiding beside Chandra frantically poking her arm with her paw.

Chandra woke to see Hugbundle making signs for her to be silent and pointing desperately at the window. She sensed her muscles stiffen and her back go cold. Was someone trying to break in? Was it a burglar, or worse? Chandra was afraid. Very slowly and quietly she slipped out of bed, pulled on her dressing gown and tiptoed over to the window. Behind her Hugbundle could just be seen peeping over the top of the bedclothes and trembling. Cautiously and with her heart thumping in her chest, Chandra pulled back the curtain.

The ginger cat from next door still sat outside looking in and in a moment Hugbundle was gone, all that could be seen was a little lump under the blankets. Chandra tapped sharply on the glass and the cat ran off but it took some time to persuade Hugbundle to come out again. It was only after a promise of some cheese for their very late breakfast as well as Chandra's assurances of her safety that she finally emerged.

After they had eaten, the dancer and the mouse sat together and watched the news on television. Somewhere in North London a black man had been attacked by a gang of youths and had been severely beaten. Witnesses had heard them shouting about their victim's colour and yesterday did not seem so very far away again.

Chandra and Hugbundle slipped out of the house and caught a bus back to Eastwich. It was dark and remembering the news Chandra's throat tightened as they entered the park. She knew it was not safe to be there alone that late but she had to reach the observatory. Chandra walked quickly. Somewhere to their left a twig cracked and she thought she could hear someone breathing. Then she saw a figure outlined against the sky coming towards them. Chandra began to run Hugbundle clinging tightly to her coat. A cloud that had been covering the moon slipped away and the park was bathed in a ghostly silver light; Chandra froze. Two men were closing in on them from either side, their faces hidden by woolen scarves, and they carried sticks. Chandra did not run on again though. In front of her the path was blocked by a line of huge dark rats sitting back on their hind legs. The rats were smiling, their yellow teeth glinting in the moonlight; in the centre was Smirkmuzzle. They were trapped.

Then, from behind, there was the sound of a van screeching to a halt at the park gates. A door slammed and headlights picked out the scene in even more terrifying detail. A whistle blew, footsteps ran towards them and, as a dog barked, the rats' smiles turned to terror and they fled into the darkness, the men with them. A figure in a police uniform ran up and stopped at Chandra's side. With him was a large police dog, Rex, whose eyes still scanned the grassy slope in the hope of a better chance to chase one of the rats again.

'Are you all right?' said the policeman.

'Yes,' said Chandra, her voice shaking.

'Well this is not a very sensible walk you're taking, you'd best come with me.'

'Excuse me but in case you were wondering, I'm all right too,' said Hugbundle in her squeaky voice, but in the excitement no-one seemed to notice so she kept quiet.

'Parks at night just aren't safe,' the policeman went on,' especially for a .....'

'A woman and an Asian,' Chandra cut in as he hesitated.

'Well yes since you put it that way, and don't say anything. I know it shouldn't be but it is. Some of us are doing what we can but there's not a lot to go on.'

They had reached the van. Rex climbed in the back and Chandra got in the front with the Sergeant, Hugbundle sat on her shoulder looking out.

'Where to?' asked the policeman.

'The observatory,' said Chandra, then adding quickly since she knew that no-one was supposed to go there at night, 'I've just got to drop some things off, through the letter box you know.'

She knew it didn't sound very good but to her relief the policeman didn't ask any questions. He just mumbled almost to himself,

'Ah, I thought so.'

As they drove round the back streets to the observatory from the other side, Rex leant over and gave Hugbundle a big wet lick. This was just to show they were friends and that he wanted Hugbundle to know that he didn't think that she was a small rat or anything that might be chased. Hugbundle smiled back nervously and then spent the rest of the journey rubbing her whiskers to try and dry them off.

The policeman parked the van at the back of the observatory building and Chandra got out, Hugbundle still sitting on her shoulder.

'Thank you,' she said.

'That's all right Miss,' said the policeman, 'but will you do something for me?'

Chandra stiffened, nervous again.

'Will you tell the Professor that Sergeant Randel sends his compliments but perhaps, in the future, if he is inviting special guests late at night he could let me know so I could keep my eyes open. Good night.'

With that he drove off and Chandra and Hugbundle were alone again.

CHAPTER 4

Central Nosey Store

Chandra let herself into the observatory using spare keys Fred had given her that morning. Inside, a mouse with a lantern was waiting to guide their way down the passage to the main hall. In the hall there were fewer mice but great activity nonetheless. The atmosphere was much more serious than the previous night and although a few mice turned to say hello or wave as Chandra entered, none left their work for long. Not wanting to disturb them, Chandra whispered a quiet hello to all of them as she was led through the hall and up some stairs higher into the building. Finally they reached a small attic, so low that Chandra had to bend down, all round the edges of which were stacks of tiny books and papers and notepads, some piled up on the floor, others on shelves. In the centre of the floor was a thick carpet and to one side a real fire, in the small scale of the rest of the room, of coal and logs blazed cheerfully. By the fire, at his desk, sat Professor Watchmoon. The desk was covered in papers and scraps of notes all in different handwriting. The Professor looked tired and a pair of gold-framed glasses slipped down to almost the end of his nose.

'Hello Chandra,' said the Professor looking up, 'come and sit by the fire.'

Chandra and Hugbundle made themselves comfortable on some splendid red velvet cushions and warmed themselves in the cosy heat from the flames. Chandra told Professor Watchmoon about what had happened in the park and as they talked the Professor looked more and more serious. When Chandra finished her account and gave him the message from Sergeant Randel, he sighed and stared into the fire for some moments before speaking.

'I'm sorry Chandra—Things are worse than I thought and yes, I should have taken more care. A rat by the name of Smirkmuzzle was seen in the park this morning and that should have made me suspicious. Smirkmuzzle is not particularly dangerous himself but if there's something rotten going on, you can bet he is mixed up in it somewhere, helping out. Chandra, things have gone far enough and something must be done but only you can decide if you are the person to be part of it. You could walk away and leave it for another.'

'No,' said Chandra, 'I don't want to walk away and even if I did I'm not sure that I could. Some things follow you wherever you go, not just Smirkmuzzle.'

'I thought you'd say that,' said the Professor, 'but you had to be able to choose for yourself.'

'And me, I'll go too,' said Hugbundle, 'I'm sure,' and Hugbundle was sure, sure that she did not want to be left behind more than that she wanted to go, adventures made her nervous.

'Yes, of course,' said the Professor, 'and you won't be the only mouse but more of that later. Well, if you are both sure then I suggest you make yourselves comfortable because I have a lot to tell you, especially you Chandra. Since you have not been our friend for very long, you must learn of some of our ways.

'Throughout history mice have been known for two things, we get everywhere and we get into everything. Mice were the first mammals on the earth and our oldest ancestors saw the passing of the dinosaurs, some even say we helped them on their way. Since then, we can be found in every country and on every ship going between them. In all that time and in all those places we have

25

seen a great deal but usually without ourselves being seen and even if we are spotted no-one takes much notice anyway. When King Charles II who founded this observatory held secret meetings with his Generals the room was always searched for spies. If anyone had been found hiding they would have surely been arrested and tried for treason. Nobody however looked under the table and saw the mouse sitting there, or behind the curtain, or by the fire, or anywhere that we might have been, anywhere that we were. Being nosey by nature over the years we have tended to take an interest in the doings of men, apart from anything else they knew how to make better cheese than we did, and being nosey a lot of what was seen was written down. I am afraid though that this is where the problems start. Firstly, what the mice took an interest in was not always what history or subsequent generations might have wanted to know. For example, whilst the details of Napoleon's interrogation after his capture following the Battle of Waterloo remain a mystery to historians everywhere, I know that somewhere there is a detailed record by a mouse of what he had for breakfast right down to the last crumb. We can tell you nothing of Gandhi's thoughts in the year before Indian independence however much you, Chandra, or anyone else might want to discover it, but we could provide a diary of every afternoon nap he took in 1946. So the interests of the mice are not always the interests of others and then there is a second problem. Mice are in general amongst the most disorganised animals on earth, we can never put things where we can find them. Our scholars have been banned from all the major libraries in the world simply for putting books back in the wrong place every time. As to our own arrangements, in each country there is a place where the records of everything the mice have seen is kept, it's called the Central Nosey Store, but don't think of it as a reference archive as you know it. It's just a heap of notes

26

and scraps of paper in a room or a cave or, like the one in London, in a cellar. Then, every now and again, someone comes and throws some more notes on top of the old and that's it. They're secret in a place that only we can get to, but they are more fun to browse in than do any serious research. They even wanted to put my astronomical records in the London store once,' the Professor waved his arm about the piles of notes in the room and shuddered, 'but I soon put a stop to that.

Anyway Chandra I mustn't go on about our strange ways to you for ever, as I told you this morning I wanted to look some things up and I did. I've got some very interesting references here to events that might concern you and somewhere the store had to have more. So I went down there this afternoon with a team of helpers and we had a rummage until we got back to about the early 19th Century. After a long search we came up with a very little, but a little, that was of help.'

The Professor waved a paw at the scraps of notes on his desk.

'I've put this information together with what I already knew and it is this story I must tell you now, however incomplete. Almost two hundred years ago a mouse arrived in this country by ship, a sailing ship, from somewhere a very long way away and somewhere which was very hot, or at least we think so because the mouse found here very cold. The mouse had come on a special mission and was carrying a fragment of a great gem with special powers, the Heartstone. The text that I have does not make the purpose of the journey clear. It is vague and says that the fragment of the gem was brought to escape some great sadness where men of a different land had travelled to a place and done much harm. It was brought here to try and undo part of some sinister wrong but that is all I could find. Having reached these shores the mouse travelled with the fragment of the Heartstone for a long time all over the country. Then, finally, when the mouse was very old and near the end of his life, he sought shelter one cold night in a great cathedral which was being repaired. In particular one of the huge stained glass windows was being replaced with new glass of an incredible colour and design. All that winter night the mouse looked at the partly finished window and how the starlight fell on it. The following morning the mouse made friends with one of the workmen and the fragment of the Heartstone was set into the window in place of one of the pieces of stained glass. Such a small stone however would never have been seen or noticed again except that it was not just put in any part of the window. The fragment was positioned so that at every full moon at midnight the moon's rays would strike it and send shafts of wondrous light shining all around the cathedral. The pattern was not always the same since the moon was not always in the same place, but the magic was that at every full moon, but only then, the experience could be seen.

There was however a special beauty that only happened rarely. About every seventy years the moon strikes the stone in a very special way and the beams of light are not just silver but become a colour beyond any ever seen before on earth, a clear translucent blue which those who have seen it have only been able to describe as a blue fire. There is a prophecy that the third night of the blue fire will be the start of a great adventure to try and undo some of the wrong that brought the Heartstone here and the prophecy says that this will be the night when the mice shall come with the moon.

The stone and its light has always been one of the great wonders of the mouse world and at every full moon the cathedral is packed with mice at midnight who have come to see the show. This of course though makes the prophecy confusing and no-one has ever quite understood it. It says that the third night of blue fire will be the night when the mice shall come with the moon and

28

yet they have come every night of the full moon for over one hundred and fifty years. Chandra, it is my belief that the prophecy refers to you. Your name means 'moon' and you would come with the mice. However, before I can ask you to accept this and that it is linked to you and what has happened last night, I have to be sure of one thing and I must ask you to wait until I have the proof I want. That will be some time tonight.'

The Professor looked exhausted and no-one spoke after he had finished. They all sat there thinking their private thoughts and staring into the flickering images in the flames of the fire. It was not until nearly half an hour had passed that there was the sound of a mouse scampering up the stairs from below. One of the astronomer mice dashed in and handed the Professor a wad of notes and observations. The Professor picked up his quill pen and began to make rapid calculations. Then he drew a line under the last of his figures and looked up, straight at Chandra.

'The information from the store was incomplete but, using what there was, we have been making some special studies tonight. Based on these it is my belief Chandra that the third night of the blue fire will be with the full moon this month and that is in six days from now. Your story and the prophecy at least belong to the same time.'

Chandra's mouth fell open and beside her Hugbundle gasped.

'If you still choose to Chandra you must now fulfil the prophecy and see where it leads you, more I cannot tell you.'

'Professor,' said Chandra, 'if the prophecy does indeed refer to me then you have already played your part and there is no question that I shall go and go at once.'

'And me,' said Hugbundle.

29

'Very well,' said the Professor, 'It is decided for good or ill, but you shall not go alone. Still after what happened earlier you had best not leave till the morning. We will find you somewhere to sleep.'

Professor Watchmoon led Chandra and Hugbundle down a passage and into a very old bedroom with a sloping ceiling. In the corner was a four-poster bed and the covers had been turned back. Chandra thanked the Professor who turned to go. As the fatigued, stooped figure of the mouse reached the door she called after him.

'Professor.'

'Yes.'

'You haven't told me which cathedral.'

'No, no I haven't. Perhaps I'm getting too cautious about being overheard. It's Wellminster in Somerset but please be careful where you name it from now on, there are some by whom it would be best not to be discovered.'

With that the Professor was gone, to his own bed Chandra hoped, he had looked so tired. She also took his warning seriously, remembering that Smirkmuzzle could not be far away. Chandra climbed into the four-poster bed and tucked Hugbundle in beside her. At once she was asleep.

Chandra woke to the sensation of something or someone shaking her finger. She opened her eyes to see eight mice sitting on the bed, somehow they had carried trays with breakfast on them up for her and for Hugbundle of course. When they had eaten and Chandra was dressed, they went down into the main hall. It was just dawn with the first grey light of the day breaking through outside but the lanterns were still lit. In the centre of the hall was Professor Watchmoon now looking much better after some sleep and beside him were six mice with packages strewn about them on the floor.

'Ah, Chandra let me introduce you. These shall be your companions for the first part of the journey, meet

Honeymouse and Jasminemouse - they're identical twins so the only way you can tell them apart is one wears honeysuckle perfume, the other jasmine. Starwhiskers and Sunfur two of my best astronomers, Wanderpaws who has travelled most of this country and been to the cathedral before and Snuggletoes who is old enough to go on adventures, but only just, so this will be his first.'

Chandra bowed to all the mice who solemnly bowed back in Indian style, they had been practising. Then each picked two things from the packages around them, a cushion and a mouse-sized carrier bag containing a piece of cheese and a slice of chocolate cake for the journey, and so they were ready. All six of them and Hugbundle climbed into Chandra's shoulder bag and she picked it up and turned to go stopping at the door.

'Professor, won't you come?'

'No, I'm far too old for adventures and there's too much to be done here, but we may meet again before you think.'

So Chandra waved goodbye to the Professor and all the astronomer mice left behind and set off down the slope into the park. From her shoulder bag seven heads and seven pairs of ears stuck out of the open top looking at everything on their way. Mice like adventures.

CHAPTER 5

A Journey West

By the time Chandra got back to her flat the activity of the previous night had caught up with the mice who now lay curled up in a heap in the bottom of her bag, fast asleep. She carried them gently into the house and left them undisturbed in the bag on the table in her bedroom. Chandra then slipped gratefully into bed herself but she did not sleep easily; her mind was full of dreams of stars and cathedrals and prophecies, and of the danger she had seen in the park.

She woke some two hours later; it was mid morning. She looked into the bag, the mice still slumbered and Chandra wondered what their dreams were. Leaving them to sleep on, Chandra packed her own things for the journey and then found what food there was in the house to make breakfast. She went through expecting to see the mice still resting but they were all up now and repacking their own things inside Chandra's bag. Honeymouse popped her head out over the top,

'Hello, we heard you making breakfast.'

'Yes it's ready now,' said Chandra.

'Oh good!' chorused seven squeaky voices at once and all the mice jumped out of the bag onto the table and down onto the floor.

No one seemed to remember that they had had one breakfast in the observatory already, still, that had been a long time ago. As Chandra turned to go back to the kitchen, seven mice scampered along behind her.

Breakfast or lunch, and as the mice said, did it really matter, was a happy meal but was soon over. When it was finished final preparations were made and the mice climbed back into the shoulder bag. At mid-day they set off, Chandra carrying her own suitcase as well as the bag with the mice in it as she walked purposefully away from the house. The thoughts of the real nature of their quest had returned and she wondered how long it would be before she saw her flat again and what might have happened by then. Who could tell but at least there was one happy possibility, it might even include a show. At Hugbundle's insistence, her suitcase contained her costume, jewellery and a tape of her dance music. As Hugbundle had said,

'Just in case!'

As they left the house, a large black crow which had been sitting on the roof for some time looked down at them and then spread its wings and glided into the air.

Chandra walked quickly and soon they were at the local station where she bought a ticket to London. A train came almost immediately and soon they were on their way. The mice seemed to take it in turns to be on watch, a different head peeping out of the bag every time Chandra glanced down. Chandra wondered what sort of conference was going on inside the bag and what serious matters were being discussed. It was only later that the chocolate crumbs from the cake the mice had packed gave her the more practical answer.

With the mice busy, Chandra was lost in her own thoughts and so it was some time before she noticed something. It was strange that every time she looked out of the window there seemed to be a large black bird flying along beside the train, but high up. Who knew, it might even be the same bird and that would be odd. Still, she did not have time to wonder at such things, they had enough of their own problems to worry about.

When the train pulled into London Bridge station all the mice emerged, some brushing tiny flakes of chocolate from their whiskers. As Chandra walked up the platform seven heads swung this way and that taking in everything around them. None however looked upward to see the black crow sitting high above in the ironwork of the station roof.

After they had passed through the ticket barrier they were in the station itself. Two youths sitting on a bench spotted the mice and began to jeer,

'Hey darling, like your pets,' and

'Quick, someone get the pest control man,' and

'They'd look better in a cage. I'll go and find one.'

Chandra tried to ignore them and looked the other way. Wanderpaws however glared back and then disappeared inside the bag to reappear moments later with a sign made from a card he had wedged in a stick to make a placard like people sometimes carry at public meetings and demonstrations. Wanderpaws held this up defiantly and waved it at the youths, it read:

'WHAT'S SO FUNNY'

The youths, who as Wanderpaws had guessed did not know about talking mice, stopped in mid-insult and stared at each other,

'Trev are you sure that beer was OK?' one of them said and they sank down in unison on the bench hoping that no one had seen them.

Chandra walked on not realising what had happened but thankful that the shouts had stopped and they had been left alone. Crossing the station forecourt she followed the signs that led them outside and down some steps to the underground station where you could catch one of the tube trains which run under London. They wanted one which would go to Paddington Station from where they could get an ordinary train again that would take them to Wellminster. Chandra bought a ticket and

34

they went down a long escalator to reach the platforms deep underground. At either end of the platform was the tunnel from which the trains came and went and, from the safety of its darkness, a pair of yellow eyes watched as Chandra sat down to wait for the train. Bellow the eyes were some dirty grey whiskers and a long sharp nose, it was Smirkmuzzle.

The tube train stopped by the platform and the doors of the carriages slid open. Chandra with the mice climbed on board and found a seat. Then the doors slid shut and the train was off down the dark tunnel. To everyone they passed at the stations they stopped at on the way, it looked like another perfectly ordinary tube train. People do not look very carefully at things they are told are ordinary and they did not look very carefully at that train. Nobody noticed Smirkmuzzle as he sat on the buffer of the end carriage riding through the darkness and no one cared. Finally, the train reached Paddington and Chandra and the mice got off. Their path up from the underground platform to the main station was shadowed by small scratchy footsteps as Smirkmuzzle padded along behind.

Once they were in the main station Wanderpaws broke the silence in the party,

'Hey Chandra go over to that bench, we've got to plan something.'

Once they were seated Wanderpaws began to explain,

'Chandra you may think this is strange but it's very important, we want you to do something.'

'Anything I can,' said Chandra.

'We want you to buy us tickets, tickets to Wellminster.'

'And some chocolate biscuits,' said Snuggletoes but no one seemed to hear.

'That's going to be very expensive,' said Chandra, 'and I don't think you need them.'

'I'm afraid you may be wrong,' said Wanderpaws, 'but I don't want to waste time arguing, we'll miss the train. Please just do it for us, Jasminemouse get the money.'

'Not that silly stuff,' said Jasminemouse.

'Look it's not silly now,' said Wanderpaws, 'Chandra needs it to get us tickets and if it had been no use then the Professor wouldn't have given it to us to bring along.'

'Oh all right,' said Jasminemouse and disappeared inside the bag.

Seconds later she reappeared dragging a roll of bank-notes tied up with a ribbon,

'Is this it?'

'Yes,' said Wanderpaws, 'now give it to Chandra before anybody else sees it and Chandra, will you keep it safe for us?'

'Of course,' said Chandra, looking in some surprise at the money which was quite a considerable sum.

'I still think it's silly,' said Jasminemouse and Honeymouse nodded.

'Right, we'd better hide,' said Wanderpaws not taking any notice, 'everyone back in the bag and keep your heads down.'

So all the mice climbed back into the bag and disappeared from view. Chandra got up and went over to join the back of the queue at the ticket office. As she did so, two men walked over and stood in the line behind her. They had been leaning against a poster on the station wall and as they left it two words could be seen scrawled on its surface, 'WOGS OUT'. The ink was still wet. Beside the words was a crude drawing of a crow and beneath the poster sat Smirkmuzzle sniggering.

'Eight tickets to Wellminster please,' said Chandra.

'Eight?' queried the lady in the booking office.

'Yes eight,' said Chandra, 'I'm going with some friends.'

The ticket clerk punched out eight tickets and Chandra paid for them.

'Platform seven, the next train's in half an hour.'

'Thank you,' said Chandra and she set off to find platform seven.

'Two tickets to Wellminster love,' it was one of the men who had joined the queue behind Chandra.

'I'm not your love and that will be eighteen pounds fifty,' said the ticket clerk.

The train was already at the platform and Chandra found a quiet carriage and settled down in a seat by the window. She put the bag on the table between the seats and the mice climbed down and sat looking out. Other people got in the carriage but Chandra paid little attention to them and she was grateful that nobody took much interest in her, or the mice. Then a whistle blew and the train pulled slowly out of the station. Further down their carriage, the two men who sat facing them looked vaguely familiar but Chandra gave them little further thought.

About half an hour after they had left London the loudspeakers in the carriage crackled into life,

'Good afternoon ladies and gentleman, this is your guard speaking and may I welcome you on board the two forty seven to Bristol calling at Swindon, Wellminster and Bath. We shall be arriving in Swindon in approximately forty-five minutes and for those of you looking for refreshment, the buffet car is now open and is situated towards the front of the train, thank you.'

Chandra realised that she was beginning to feel hungry,

'Do you think that you could all hide whilst I go and get something to eat?' she said to the mice.

'That's all right there's no need for us to hide,' said Wanderpaws, 'we've all got tickets remember, don't worry about us we'll be OK.'

'Whilst you're there though do you think that you could get us some ice cream?' said Snuggletoes.

'A big tub and seven spoons,' added Honeymouse.

37

'All right but be careful whilst I'm gone,' said Chandra.

'Stop worrying,' said Starwhiskers, 'you haven't seen any cats on the train have you?'

'No.'

'Well there you are then, now go and get yourself a sandwich.'

'And the ice cream,' said Hugbundle.

In the buffet car, Chandra wondered how she was going to explain a request for one tub of ice cream and seven spoons. Fortunately she was in luck. As the steward handed her the food, he nodded towards a box on the counter,

'Spoons for the ice cream in there, help yourself.'

She did. Back at the carriage all was well. Five mice were looking out of the window and Starwhiskers and Sunfur were sitting with an old lady on the other side of the carriage. She was doing the crossword in a newspaper and they were helping her with the clues. The old lady had a full box of new pencils beside her, as she explained to the mice she kept breaking the points so some spares came in handy. As Chandra sat down and put the ice cream on their table, Starwhiskers and Sunfur scampered back and seven small expectant faces surveyed the tub. Then they all sat round the edge in a circle on the cushions they had brought from the observatory and began to lift out mouse sized mouthfuls with the spoons Chandra had collected. The spoons were of the flat wooden sort rounded at each end, a very useful shape for all sorts of things as Snuggletoes was about to discover.

'Tickets please.'

A man in railway uniform had entered from the next carriage, he was Asian, from India or Pakistan, or at least his family were; who could know where he had been born. The two men further down the carriage, the two who had followed Chandra onto the train at Paddington, deliberately slouched in their seats and put their feet on those opposite.

'Get lost Paki,' said one of the men, the other laughed.

'Tickets please and would you kindly take your feet off the seats,' said the inspector.

'Oh he wants us to take our feet off the seats does he,' said the man, 'Well look here we don't take instructions from no Pakis. Got it.'

The inspector was now half way down the carriage and had reached the two men.

'Tickets please and would you kindly take your feet off the seats thank you.'

One of the men reached up and grabbed the inspector's jacket, pulling him down.

'I told you Paki we don't take orders from your kind.'

The carriage was silent, everybody was listening to what was happening and yet nobody moved, most looked the other way. Starwhiskers jumped up but Sunfur put a paw on his arm,

'No, we've got the mission to think of.'

Snuggletoes could stand it no longer. Perhaps he hadn't been on adventures before but he wasn't going to sit and watch this. With one jump he was off the table across the carriage and beside the old lady.

'Can I borrow one of your pencils please?' he said.

'Of course,' whispered the old lady, 'but be careful.'

'No,' said Snuggletoes, he'd seen enough of being careful.

Quickly the mouse dragged the pencil back up on to their table. Nobody saw him, everyone was now watching the man and the inspector, the man showed no signs of letting go. Snuggletoes took a big scoop of ice cream from the tub and balanced the spoon across the pencil like a see-saw. Then he climbed up onto the edge of the tub and jumped down stamping on the end of the spoon as he landed. The ice cream flew through the air and hit the man straight in the face. He jumped back in surprise and let go of the ticket inspector. Snuggletoes stood glaring from the edge of the table,

'Now you leave him alone or else.'

He hadn't been on enough adventures to know that it's best not to say that until you have thought of an 'or else' but by then it was too late.

'Vermin, I'll get you for that,' said the man, 'and your Paki friends.' 'Well at least I've got friends,' said Snuggletoes, his voice not quite so steady now and hoping he still had.

The two men got up and began to lurch down the carriage.

'Quick,' said Starwhiskers, 'there's no choice now,' and he and Sunfur jumped back over to the old lady.

Sunfur got one pencil out of the box and gave it to her,

'Sorry,' he said and the two mice pushed the box over the edge letting the pencils spill out onto the floor. As the men rushed forwards, they slipped on the wooden shafts and fell in a heap shouting.

'What's all this!' a huge voice boomed from the end of the carriage.

Everybody, even the men, was quiet and turned to look. There in the communicating door, or rather filling the communicating door stood the guard, one of the largest men any of them had ever seen.

'Right you two down in the guards van with me and you get off at the next stop, now move!'

One of the men opened his mouth but then thought better of it. As they moved off down the carriage the other muttered under his breath,

'At least it wasn't the Paki who told us to do anything.'

'Oh really,' said the guard, 'Mr Chakraborty is my boss and I do what he and railway regulations tell me, and if you have any complaints about railway regulations or their implementation you had better contact the area supervisor - Mr Patel.'

40

When the train stopped at Swindon, Chandra and the mice saw the guard escort the men out of his section in the end coach, leaving them on the platform. As the train pulled away and their window passed the men, they shook their fists at the mice who were waving them goodbye. Chandra noticed a silver badge on the collar of one of the men's jackets, a silver badge in the shape of a crow. It was clearly visible, both the men had very short close cropped hair, and although she hadn't seen a badge like it before, it made her feel uneasy. Recently there had been a number of drawings of birds of similar shape beside the messages of hate against black and Asian people on the walls of Bromswood. The connection bothered her.

'Now about railway regulations,' it was the guard, he was back and standing by their seats and the table between, 'there just happens to be one about animals travelling in approved secure boxes.'

'Oh it's all right, they've got tickets,' said Chandra.

'Sorry that makes no difference, you wouldn't be the first crank that bought their pets a ticket to get round it.'

'Excuse me,' said Wanderpaws, 'but she only bought tickets because we asked her to, and we paid for them, not her.'

The guard sat down, very slowly.

'Well you are full of surprises aren't you,' said the guard, 'and I suppose you all talk too?'

He looked at the other mice who had gathered round, they nodded.

'And now must I forget what I had thought of as imagination and actually believe that one of you was making rude gestures at those two when I came in?'

Snuggletoes looked uncomfortable.

'You don't know anything about flying ice cream I suppose?'

The guard was looking straight at Snuggletoes whose ears were slowly turning red at the tips.

41

'Even if he does I don't think we should ask him, some things are best left as mysteries,' it was the inspector, Mr. Chakraborty, he'd come back into the carriage and sat down beside the guard. Snuggletoes nodded again.

'Yes it's more fun that way,' said Honeymouse trying to help.

'Are you going to punch our tickets?' Hugbundle asked Mr. Chakraborty, she was very proud of having her own ticket.

Sensing her hope and feeling of occasion, the inspector solemnly punched Hugbundle's ticket and those of all the other mice, each in turn.

'You are all going to Wellminster I see; holiday?'

'No we're going to see the H.......,' Snuggletoes was not given the chance to finish the sentence, Sunfur had placed a paw over his mouth from behind.

'We're going to see some friends,' said Sunfur, 'and see some of the sights,' she added trying to hide what Snuggletoes had given away.

'Yes that's right,' said Chandra also trying to help out, 'I've never been before and they're going to show me around.'

'I see,' said Mr. Chakraborty, 'or rather I don't see but see that it's better that I don't. Oh and don't worry about railway regulations. I'm sure that there is nothing to say that mice who buy their own tickets do anything but travel in the seats they have paid for like anyone else. Still we mustn't keep you but I have brought you one small thing, this,' and he pulled a fresh unopened tub of ice cream out of his pocket and placed it on the table, 'You seemed to have lost some of your last one.'

The train sped on towards Wellminster and the mice happily returned to sitting round the tub and enjoying their ice cream. Some miles away on a hill that could not even be seen from the track, two crows sat in a scraggy windswept tree, preening their long black wing feathers.

'So they need our help again,' said Croakwing.

'Yes,' said Screechfoot 'They want us to look for mice, mice in Wellminster.'

'But there's lots of mice in Wellminster.'

'Yes but not all together and with a woman, a foreign woman - one of those,' there was contempt in Screechfoot's voice.

'Oh one of those, well that will be easier. Tell me do we get some 'fun' with the mice?'

'Oh yes they've promised, but not at once. They want to 'talk' to them first,' Screechfoot laughed. 'Except one, the young one, we can have him as soon as we can get him, so long as we do things slowly. Very slowly.'

'Oh we can do things slowly all right,' said Croakwing, 'what's the hurry? After all you should never rush a good thing should you, it's such a waste.'

And with a rustle of feathers in the raw wind the two birds swept up into the darkening sky and flew with rushing wingbeats towards the distant spires of Wellminster.

CHAPTER 6

Wellminster

It was four fifty when the train pulled into Wellminster Station. Chandra and the mice got off and stood on the platform and waited until the carriages slipped by as the train left to continue on its journey. From the end coach Mr. Chakraborty and the guard waved goodbye as they disappeared into the distance and calls of good luck drifted back from them to the party on the platform.

All the mice climbed back into the bag and, whilst six small faces kept watch, Snuggletoes disappeared deep inside to find somewhere comfortable to have a nap. All his adventures had made him tired. Chandra found a taxi and asked the driver to take them to the cathedral. It was only a short drive and they arrived just as dusk began to fall on the city. The cathedral stood outlined against the sky and as the light faded, its spire seemed to reach up to try and touch the thin wisps of cloud that drifted above it. Chandra put down the bags and wondered what to do. Their plans to go straight to the cathedral had been all very well but now they did not know anybody and she did not feel inclined to just stop one of the many people who were passing by. Even the ones wearing the special robes of the clergy and cathedral staff all looked so busy and preoccupied.

'Chandra, don't look so nervous,' it was Wanderpaws, 'even if people have to have everything organised in advance, we don't. Just go and sit on the bench over there and I'll go and sort something out.'

They didn't reach the bench however; Chandra had only covered two paces when a small but unfamiliar voice stopped her in her tracks.

'Hello.'

It was a mouse.

'What's your name?'

'I'm Chandra, who are you?'

'Candletail.'

'And I'm Wanderpaws and these are my friends Honeymouse, Jasminemouse, Sunfur, Starwhiskers and Hugbundle. Later you can meet Snuggletoes.'

When Wanderpaws mentioned Snuggletoes, he shut his eyes and put his head on one side and then pointed downwards to show Snuggletoes was asleep.

'I'm very pleased to meet you,' said Candletail, 'and welcome to the cathedral.'

The formalities over, the meeting continued in what Chandra had begun to realise was typical mouse fashion. Candletail ushered them over to a seat in an alcove cut into the side of the cathedral, right into the stonework, and they all sat down. In the alcove it was surprisingly warm and cosy. They were sheltered from the wind and the great stones of the cathedral seemed to have retained at least some of the warmth of the final rays of the sun that had fallen on them. This was the West side of the building and later, Chandra found that there were similar alcoves on the East side that the mice used in the morning when the sun was rising.

Candletail wanted to know all about them and where they had come from and where they were going. Wanderpaws did most of the talking and told most of the story, but not quite all, and that included leaving out the Professor's calculations for the coming full moon. Since Candletail was a cathedral mouse, Wanderpaws did tell her that they had come to see the Heartstone though. Candletail was especially interested in Chandra being a dancer and made Chandra promise to show her the costume later. As they were talking a young man in a long robe walked past, he was a curate and Candletail called out to stop him;

'Hello Martin, can you spare a minute?'

'Yes of course, what is it?'

'Meet Chandra, Wanderpaws, Hugbundle, Jasmine-mouse, Honeymouse, Starwhiskers and Sunfur, oh and later you can meet Snuggletoes but he's asleep. They're visitors and I was wondering if some of the guest rooms in the old rectory were free?'

'Yes I think so but let's go over and check, I'm going that way now.'

'Thank you,' said Chandra, 'but I hope it's not going to be any trouble.'

'Not at all,' said Martin, 'we like having visitors. You'll find that Wellminster is a little different from most cathedrals. The Bishop's a bit unconventional and believes in doing things his own way, and that includes hospitality. If Candletail has invited you to stay then somewhere will be found, don't worry.'

They had reached a beautiful old building with ivy growing up the walls beneath which ancient beams could be seen in between the areas of white wall. Martin pushed the door open. Inside, the hall was comfortable and cosy with lots of thick rugs on the floor and a vase of flowers in the window. Martin picked up a well-used book from a table and opened it;

'Yes, that's no problem. There's a free room for tonight. Perhaps you would like to take them up Candle-tail. I've got to dash off and arrange the evening service but would you all like to join me for dinner later on?'

'Yes we'd love to,' said Chandra.

'Great, see you later. Candletail will show you the way, my cottage is just down one of the side streets. It's not far.'

With that Martin turned and slipped out of the rectory and back towards the cathedral.

46

Candletail led them upstairs to a very cheerful and snug bedroom on the second floor. Its windows looked out on the Cathedral and the courtyard in front of it and the sound of a church choir drifted across to them, the evening service had begun. In the corner a real fire had been lit, almost as if they had been expected, and the whole room was already warm. All the mice, including Snuggletoes who had woken up, immediately sat round the fire and held up their paws to the heat from its flames. Candletail promised to come back later and scampered off, presumably to spread the news of their arrival, at least to the other cathedral mice - they would be sure to want to know. Chandra sat with the mice by the fire and thought to herself that Wellminster really was different. Although nobody had ever said or done anything nasty in the past, she had always felt very much an outsider at churches. It wasn't that she was simply not a member of the congregation, thousands of people visited churches and cathedrals just to see and be there without joining in with the worship. It had always seemed to have something to do with being Indian as if a different culture meant that she must be a very strong member of another religion and therefore hostile or at least too different to be trusted. It was silly, she was no more an active Hindu than most of her neighbours were regular church goers but in the past, whenever she had met someone from the church, it had felt that they always assumed she was. Then they treated her with great care and that meant keeping her at a distance. Chandra had never been sure what they were frightened of. Even if she had been a strict Hindu her faith allowed her to worship anywhere dedicated to God, including churches, and whatever your background God was meant to be the same wasn't he. Not that Indians were any better when it came to welcoming others at their temples, if anything they were worse! Perhaps that's

47

where it all came from, but Wellminster was different. Here, anybody could feel at home.

To the North of the city, Screechfoot and Croakwing used the last minutes of daylight to extend their search. Swiftly and silently they wheeled over the streets, gardens and houses looking for any sign of Chandra and the mice. Only when it was too dark for them to see did they stop and seek a place to rest for the night. Finally they settled on some bare trees at the edge of a park,

'Tomorrow, perhaps tomorrow.'

'Yes there's always tomorrow, we'll find them in the end. After all who's going to stop us?'

'No one, that's the beauty of it all isn't it. Good night, good night till tomorrow.'

Back in the rectory, the mice and Chandra had got really warm by the fire. Then Candletail rushed in, she was out of breath and looked as if she had run a long way.

'You're quite sure that your name is Chandra are you?' panted Candletail.

'Well I should be by now,' said Chandra, 'That's what I've been called all my life!'

'Yes of course, silly question,' said Candletail, 'it's just that if it really is then you must come at once, there is someone you have to meet, it's all so exciting!'

'You mean when the mice shall come with the moon,' said Wanderpaws.

Candletail gasped in amazement.

'That's right but how do you know about that?'

'Oh just something that turned up in the Central Nosey Store,' said Wanderpaws, trying to sound ordinary.

For a moment Candletail looked disbelieving, then a smile of understanding spread across her face.

'It's the Professor isn't it, I thought you left something out earlier on, and this has his paw all through it.'

Honeymouse and Jasminemouse nodded.

'Well never mind, please come, come right now, there's a mouse, a very old mouse, he's part of the Heartstone story and he lives here. He's waiting for you and I've never seen him so happy in all his life.'

Candletail led Chandra and the other mice back across the courtyard and round to the side of the cathedral. There a small door stood ajar and a warm yellow light spilled out from it onto the paving stones outside. The party went through the door in single file, Candletail leading, and into the cathedral itself. The building was huge and the great roof towered way above their heads, almost lost in the shadows of the night. All around them there were arches and columns each with its own graceful curve and place. In the centre of the main aisle which ran up the middle of the building stood the oldest mouse that Chandra had ever seen. His fur was snow white and his face was wrinkled but not ugly. He bent down to lean on a small stick held in one of his front paws. It was Moonbeam Stonekeeper.

'Welcome, welcome to Wellminster, my family has waited a long time for you and I am honoured that it should fall to me to be the one to greet you,' said the mouse.

'Thank you,' said Chandra, 'we are honoured to be greeted by you and to be your guests.'

'And greetings from the Professor and the observatory,' said Sunfur.

'And from me,' added Hugbundle.

'I know you have travelled far and have already had many adventures,' said Moonbeam Stonekeeper, 'but I wanted to meet you tonight. You see in many ways my whole life, and I have been lucky that it has been a long one, has been dedicated to waiting in case you should come. So I hope you will forgive my impatience but I wanted to see you as soon as I heard. Candletail was the bearer of strange but great news indeed.'

49

'There is nothing to forgive,' Chandra replied sensing that they really were part of a mystery that was about to unfold, 'if your family has waited for us for so long then how could we delay our meeting even for one hour longer.'

'Come walk with me, I will show you something.'

Moonbeam Stonekeeper turned and slowly led Chandra and the other mice up the aisle of the cathedral towards the altar. Their footsteps echoed round the deserted building and no one spoke fearing the sound that a voice might produce would shatter the stillness of the place. Just before they reached the altar, Moonbeam Stonekeeper turned off to their left and they stood facing an immense stained glass window which towered above them, almost to the roof. Although it was dark and the glass could not be seen, small segments gleamed in the reflections of the lights and candles that still burned in the cathedral. That was not all, each of the watchers felt a sense of power and wonder, there was magic in that place. Still nobody and no mouse spoke, each was lost in their own thoughts, and each had been drawn to a tiny flicker of brilliance high up in the window where a ray of light from a distant star had fallen on something. As they looked at it, all in turn felt the strangest thing. It was as if that flicker was part of themselves and mirrored in some small way what they were and what they were feeling. Then it was gone.

'The stone knows that you are here,' said Moonbeam Stonekeeper, 'I saw you feel it.'

'Yes but what is it?' whispered Chandra, 'it almost, well it almost touched me.'

'That even I cannot tell you and the fate of my family and the Heartstone has been linked for over one hundred and fifty years. I think that no one will ever understand the stone and that is probably as it should be. Don't ask questions, just be. Be here and be with it, let it be with you.'

The old mouse, Chandra, and all the other mice stood silent for a minute gazing upwards at the point that had gleamed high up in the window. Then Moonbeam broke the stillness.

'There are things that must be found and fetched now that you have come, things that have been stored for many decades in preparation for this night. If I may have your help for a moment I must then leave you and we will meet again tomorrow morning, Candletail will show you where. Now please come with me.'

Moonbeam Stonekeeper led them over to one side of the window and to a section of stonework in the wall just above the floor. The gaps between the stones had been filled with the dust of centuries but if you looked carefully you could see an irregularity in their lines as if a small piece had been removed and then put back. At Moonbeam's request, Starwhiskers and Sunfur brought a candle over to the place and by its light he began to scratch at the lines with his stick. After some minutes a larger gap than the rest appeared at one side of the small stone.

'Now this is where I need your help, I might have moved this once but that was a long time ago. Help me, we must prise this stone out.'

Chandra bent down and gently began to lever the stone outwards with a small penknife that she carried. Suddenly it gave way and swung open but it had not simply been wedged in place, it was a door and it hung on small but perfect hinges holding it to the rest of the wall. The mice gasped and crowded round whilst Moonbeam stood back to let them satisfy their curiosity. By the light of the candle, they saw a tiny mouse-sized passage leading back into the giant stones of the cathedral. The floor of the passage was covered in dust and it looked as if it had not been used for years and years. On the passage's walls tiny lanterns hung from hooks waiting to be lit and, at its end, a flight of steps curved away to the left and downwards into darkness.

'Have you been down there before?' Chandra asked Moonbeam.

'Yes, but many years ago. My parents took me just as their parents had done years before. They showed me so I would know, know what to do if the prophecy was ever fulfilled in my lifetime, and now that time has come. I must go, and please, close the door behind me. The entrance should not be left unguarded. Don't worry, I will be able to open it from the inside and there are other exits.'

'Shall I come with you?' said Starwhiskers.

'No, it's my destiny and my duty, I shall go alone, but I will see you all tomorrow.'

With that Moonbeam Stonekeeper took down one of the lanterns in the passage and lit it from the candle. Then he set off slowly along the passage, leaning on his stick as he went. They watched him go until he reached the end and disappeared down the tiny flight of steps. After that they closed the door as he had asked and made their way slowly out into the cold night air.

Candletail took them across to Martin's cottage and together they had a very happy time and a wonderful meal, Martin was a very good cook. They stayed late and talked and swapped stories and tales with each other. Some of the funniest were Martin's accounts of things that had happened at other churches he knew, they usually concerned vicars who took things, especially themselves, too seriously and then ended up looking rather silly. All the time that they spoke, however, neither Chandra nor the mice could quite get the Heart-stone out of their minds, it almost seemed to be calling to them. Thoughts of Moonbeam and the passage also came to them and they wondered where he had gone to and what it was he had to find. Finally, they all agreed it was time to go to bed and Candletail took them back to the rectory. This was only after they had all thanked Martin for the marvellous food and he had promised to show Honeymouse and Jasminemouse the secret of his chocolate cream sauce.

Back in the rectory they all went straight to bed and were soon asleep, Candletail having arranged to come and wake them the following morning. Throughout the night, their dreams were punctuated with the image they had seen of that tiny glimmer of starlight on something high up in the stained glass window in the cathedral. They all felt somehow different but none of them yet realised that nothing would ever be quite the same again. Over to the North of the city, Screechfoot and Croakwing slept less peacefully, but they too looked forward with anticipation to the day to come.

CHAPTER 7

Moonbeam Stonekeeper

It was long after dawn, and after the first rays of the sun had crept through the curtains and into the room where Chandra and the mice slept, that Candletail returned to wake them. She did not explain what was to happen next but simply waited until they were ready and then took them downstairs to where a breakfast had been prepared and lay waiting for them. Mice rarely attempt anything serious before breakfast. Then Candletail led the way as they all walked across the cathedral courtyard towards another old building on the other side of the square. A brass plate by the door read:

Bishop's Palace

and they all went inside.

Screechfoot and Croakwing were getting tired of the North of Wellminster.

'Let's go South, there's nothing here,' said Croakwing.

'I wouldn't say nothing, we saw that child drop its packed lunch on the way to school and lose it, that was fun.'

'Fun or not that isn't what we're here for. Mice, mice with one of those. Remember?'

'And we still get to have the young one at once?'

'Yes they promised, but only if we find them first. They might have sent for Smirkmuzzle to search as well or hadn't you thought of that.'

54

'Come on then, let's see what's South before he gets there,' and with that both birds turned and flew with the risen sun on their left as fast as their wings could carry them.

Chandra, Candletail and the mice had been shown into an old book-lined study. At one end of the room there was a large desk, also very old, which stood in an alcove beside a bay window so that it caught the morning sun and looked out across the garden. Behind the desk sat the Bishop of Wellminster, a friendly looking middle-aged man who was beginning, as his wife sometimes pointed out to his embarrassment, to go bald. A dog collar and purple shirt identified his position. The Bishop was not however the only occupant of the study, nor was the desk solely his. On it sitting on a red cushion and with his own papers propped against a tiny book-rest was Moonbeam Stonekeeper.

'Welcome to Wellminster,' said the Bishop as he stood up to meet them, 'even if I am probably the last to greet you. I hope you had a comfortable night?'

'Oh yes thank you,' replied Chandra, 'Candletail and Martin have been taking great care of us, more than we deserve.'

'That I doubt,' said the Bishop, Honeymouse and Jasminemouse nodding as he did so, 'but if it is the case then it's our pleasure and you mustn't try to stop us'.

Honeymouse nodded again.

'Still you haven't come here to exchange idle gossip and you haven't really even come to see me, it's Moonbeam who's got something for you. Sit down, make yourselves comfortable.'

Chandra and the mice all found somewhere to sit, Chandra in a large armchair with Hugbundle sitting on its back behind her, Candletail on a stool with a soft top, and all the rest of the mice amongst the cushions on a sofa which just happened to be in the sun.

55

'Yes Moonbeam's as much a part of Wellminster as I am,' the Bishop continued, 'more so in many ways. It's not just that his family have been here a lot longer than I have, Wellminster has become a very special place but I don't think that it was always that way. When the Heartstone came here it changed more than just things for the mice. I don't understand but it gave something to everyone and sometimes I still feel that it does.'

Chandra remembered her own feelings about how different Wellminster was and began to wonder if that too had been the Heartstone at work.

'But the Heartstone is not part of my business here, not officially anyway, the church isn't quite ready for talking mice yet let alone their treasures so Moonbeam over to you, I think this is your day, not mine.'

Moonbeam Stonekeeper did not show any signs of tiredness, despite the adventure which must have lain before him down the tunnel. He still looked old, as old as he had done, but he had not changed. It was almost as if he was beyond the reach of the world and its hurts and strains now, at least age had given him that.

'Thank you,' he said to the Bishop, 'and thank you all for coming. My name, as you already know, is Moonbeam Stonekeeper and, as I have told you, my family has been at the cathedral for many, many years. We are known as the Watchmice since we not only watch over the stone but also watch out for a party of travellers whose coming was written of almost two hundred years ago. I believe that you are those travellers and that with your coming, the mission of my family is nearly at an end and I know that the Professor has said similar things to you before you left London. Neither of us can ask you to accept such a claim simply on trust however, I must tell you a story and all that I know and then only you can decide. First though, I must warn you of the possible dangers and ask of you a promise. If you accept my story and choose to follow the path it will suggest, then there will be risks involved. I know that you have already confronted some of these simply by coming here and don't think that they finished when you lost those men on the train. I'm sure that even now they, and their friends, are looking for you. Secondly, whether you accept my story or not, do I have your solemn word that you will keep the details of what I have to tell you secret unless you have to reveal them as part of your quest should you choose to begin it.'

Everyone in the room was very quiet as Moonbeam looked from one to the other in turn. To everyone's surprise it was Hugbundle who spoke.

'All of us have already had a hand or a paw in getting this far, even me. I think we are all ready to go on with something we've become part of and if there are risks, yes if there are risks, we'll have to think of something when they happen won't we and I promise to keep any secret I can.'

All the other mice and Chandra nodded.

'Very well then, it is time at last that I should tell my story,' and with that Moonbeam began.

'People and mice have lived alongside each other and shared this world for many years, yet in all that time there has been very little contact between us. We do not always understand the doings of men and they certainly do not always understand us. In particular, men do not take care to protect those things that are precious to us, even sometimes our homes. The Heartstone was a great and mysterious gem which was one of the most renowned legends of the mouse world, partly because of what it did and partly because no one had any idea where it came from. Mice have always liked mysteries. The stone was kept in a cave in the South of India and there it lay in peace for many years, many years up to about two hundred years ago. I cannot give you an exact date, mice are not very good with calendars and our records have no named year for what happened. The cave in which the stone was kept was not directly open to the surface but could only be approached through a maze of passages and smaller chambers. The entrance to this underground world was a closely guarded secret, it is not just now that we have had to fear the attentions of others such as the rats and crows. The secret was how-ever known to the mice who came from all over India just to see the stone and be with it. I say be with it since, although it is almost impossible to describe, the stone was not something which you simply looked at, how-ever beautiful. Any mouse that came into its presence was to feel a very strange thing, the Heartstone seemed to know how you felt and to reflect those feelings to you so you were never lonely. If you were sad then it was sad with you, if you were happy then it shared your joy. Music has always been very important in India, especially the South, and one mouse of that time wrote that the Heartstone was like standing next to a huge drum when it was being played, when it beats you know your own heart beats stronger.

Being a mouse cave although it was very big to us, to most animals and to people it would have been very small. Not only was it small but it was not very deep in the ground, in fact it was only just below the surface, and that was to be the beginning of the tragedy. Things in India were changing. The people there had always had their fights and wars but they had never taken them that seriously, or at least they never seemed to get any-where or do too much damage. Then, a new group of men arrived on ships. They were lighter in colour and although the place did not really suit them they seemed far more organised and they stayed. They said they came from Great Britain, not that that meant anything to the Indian mice or even the Indian people, at the time they had never heard of it so it had to either be very small or a very long way away or perhaps even both. But as I said, these new people were very organised and very sure of what they wanted. The mice did not keep track of what happened but suddenly they realised that the new people were in charge and running things. Everything was very different from what it had been and the mice did not like a lot of what they saw. Most of all they hated the soldiers that the new people brought. They all wore bright red tunics and had horses pull huge guns on great wheels all over the land. When these guns were fired, the whole ground shook and there was no peace for the mice anywhere. Then one day the disaster happened. One of the great guns was being pulled across the countryside and was taken over the place of the Heartstone cave. Its massive wheels broke through the roof of the cave and many of the side chambers collapsed. No one with the gun noticed what had happened, they just went on their way, but the mice were distraught.

For three days hundreds of mice dug frantically to get to the stone and rescue it. Finally, one of the digging parties broke through into what was left of the main chamber and there they stopped in horror. The wheel of the gun had gone right over the stone and had shattered it into several pieces. It lay on the open earth and almost seemed to bleed into it. Who knew if this was the stone itself speaking or its reflection of the feelings of the mice round it. Despite the hurt that the whole cave now spoke of, the mice kept digging until all the fragments of the stone were recovered. Then the mice had to decide what to do. Those from the North said that the soldiers in red coats did not do so well in the mountains there and that they could not pull the great guns up the steeper slopes. All the mice agreed that somehow, however impossible it seemed, the pieces of the Heartstone, all of them large and small, had to be taken North into the mountains for safety. Only one mouse disagreed, and that was my very distant ancestor. He said that although he was not quite sure why, he knew that simply running away was not enough. The wrong that had come to the land had to be challenged, even if that meant fighting it in its own place. The mouse, his name was then Sandrace Firefoot - he was a message carrier, later he was to become Sailvoyage Stonekeeper, the first of the Watchmice - said that a fragment of the stone had to be taken to the Great Britain the new people had spoken of and that he would do it.

So plans were made. Sandrace packed a small fragment of the broken Heartstone in a piece of the softest silk. The cloth was an off cut from silk woven by the people who made the fabric for the beautiful sarees of the South. They were friends with the mice who helped them by using their small paws to work in the tiny threads of gold that were added into the silk for decoration. In return, the mice got the pieces of spare cloth and used them in their homes or as bedding when they went on long journeys. So Sandrace set off with his piece of the Heartstone towards Madras, the nearest port, to find a ship going to England. That was all he knew. Behind him he left the main group led by another famous mouse, Swiftclimb Palmgazer, one of the best lookouts there had ever been. Her task was to try and find a way to get the rest of the stone North but at the time Sandrace left, no mouse knew how they were going to do it, it seemed such a daunting enterprise.

When he set off, everybody knew that there was little chance that Sandrace would ever be able to return. Mice never like to say goodbye forever though and so, however unlikely it seemed, plans were made so that they could meet up again. Swiftclimb promised that as soon as she had found a way of moving the stone North, she would send details to Sandrace so that he could follow if he ever came back. When Sandrace had almost reached Madras a strange thing happened. Out of the haze of the heat of that day there came an elephant and it made its way straight towards Sandrace. As it approached he saw that it was carrying something in its trunk and so he waited. The elephant asked him his name and when it was sure who he was gave him what it was carrying, two sets of documents rolled up and tied with cloth. One remains largely a mystery to this day. The other was a note and some drawings from Swiftclimb. She, some other mice and the Heartstone were being carried by another elephant towards a temple. That elephant was one of those who lived in the temples of the area and therefore this was not surprising. The elephant had however only known the elephant name of the temple, a name which the mice did not understand. There were many shrines in the region and it could have been any of them. So Swiftclimb and the elephant drew Sandrace a map and made some notes so he could understand it which they hoped he could follow at a later time if he came back. They had then encountered a second elephant, the one who had found Sandrace, who had almost appeared from nowhere. They had thought themselves alone but then they had turned round to find the elephant standing there, watching them. This particularly bothered Swiftclimb because of her skills as a lookout. She was sure that nothing, especially an elephant, could have crept up on her unnoticed. It was all very strange but the second elephant had promised to try and find Sandrace and give the map to him. Having little choice Swiftclimb had trusted the strange elephant with its miraculous powers of silent approach and had given it the map, the directions and a note. In that note, Swiftclimb explained what had happened and promised that they would leave more directions for Sandrace at the temple they were going to when they set off again on their journey North. It was not only Swiftclimb that found the messenger elephant strange however. After it had given the two sets of documents to Sandrace he thanked it and turned to go. Then something made him look back but the elephant had gone, just disappeared! They had met on open ground and there was no place for anything to hide, even a mouse, let alone an elephant. It had just vanished into thin air.

Still there was Sandrace with his packages and he reached Madras and did indeed find a ship that was going to England. Even I can only guess at what happened to those documents. The parcel from Swiftclimb has never been found and as far as I know, Sandrace was the last to see it, except for the map. The notes to explain it and without which it means nothing are gone. Sandrace, by the time he arrived in this country was in possession of certain prophecies about the Heartstone in the future. These we know and they are believed to have been part of the second package, wherever that may have come from. The rest of that second package has also been lost, but I am getting ahead of myself, I must tell you what happened when Sandrace reached England after a long sea voyage which must have been an adventure of itself. From now on though I shall call him by his later name, Sailvoyage Stonekeeper, as is fitting with the tradition of my family.

The ship Sailvoyage had found docked in the port of London and from there he made his way to the city itself. We can only imagine what a shock it must have been to a mouse that had lived all his life near Madras. Those days were before India too began to build large town developments as the West understands them. One thing we do know since it appears repeatedly in Sailvoyage's account, is that he found London and England very cold, very cold indeed. For some weeks, Sailvoyage, carrying the fragment of the Heartstone, wandered the streets wondering what he should do. He certainly did not like much of what he saw. The city in places held great beauty but everywhere he went, he encountered the same feelings and way of doing things which he had seen do so much damage in India. Worse, he heard talk of India and its people but could not make any sense of what was being said, it was all so wrong. How was it that this country which had taken such an interest in his could understand so little? Sailvoyage was becoming a very sad mouse and there were only two things which kept him going. Firstly, there was the Heartstone itself, at least he never felt completely alone, and secondly there were the cathedrals. Remembering how he loved the temples, Sailvoyage looked for them in London and found the cathedrals instead. He spent hours going from one to another where he would sit and watch everything around him. He especially loved the stained glass windows and the lights and candles, the candles in particular since they were not only nice to look at as their flames danced and flickered but also you could sit close to them and they were so warm. It was in one of the cathedrals that Sailvoyage met Lavenderwhiskers, a mouse from London. She was the first friend that he had had since he arrived and one day as they sat by an especially large and friendly candle, he told her his story and showed her the Heartstone. Lavenderwhiskers and Sailvoyage decided that there was too much wrong in London at that time for the Heartstone to stay there and that they should take it far out into the countryside. Remember in those days transport was not so easy and what they were talking about was quite an adventure. One night they hid in the back of a stagecoach that was leaving London to head West and they came to Bristol.

Sailvoyage and Lavenderwhiskers were to wander all over England for many years and they were very happy together. There is no full record of where they went and it is possible that they reached Wales and Scotland as well. They took the Heartstone with them everywhere, always hoping that they would find what it was that they should do. When they were both old and grey, they decided to return to Bristol where they had gone first. By this time they had had many children and one of them, Stonechild Stonekeeper, had travelled with them. As he grew older Sailvoyage got more restless, he had after all come on that long journey to do something and he knew that he could not live forever. It had seemed important to take the stone all over the country but they had done that and now there had to be an ending, or perhaps more than an ending. It was winter, both mice were beginning to feel the cold, and Stonechild was ill. They found a particularly cosy barn and made a nest in the straw where Stonechild began to get better, but only slowly. Somehow, Sailvoyage knew that he had not got long to live and that he must finish what he had begun. He and Lavenderwhiskers, perhaps they both knew what was going to happen, said their goodbyes and leaving her to look after Stonechild he set off into the chill of a winter's night to finish his mission. We do not know all the places he passed through but after some days, he came to Wellminster at a time when the cathedral was being repaired and a new stained glass window was being built.

Sailvoyage sat in the cathedral all night looking at the partly finished networks of coloured glass and remembered how he had loved them when he first saw them in London. The following morning, he made friends with one of the workmen and had the fragment of the Heartstone set into the window, high up towards its top. Somehow he then managed to send a message to Lavenderwhiskers who came with Stonechild as fast as they could. When they arrived, they found Sailvoyage tucked up in a warm blanket by a candle, the workmen had been taking care of him. He was happy but he was also dying and Lavenderwhiskers and Stonechild spent the rest of the day with him until he finally slipped away that night.

In the last hours they were to have together, he told them some very strange things, prophecies and stories. He said that they must stay in the cathedral until the coming full moon and then they would understand. He also told them that if they returned in one hundred full

64

moon's time they would see something even more incredible. He was speaking of the first night of the blue fire which I know the Professor told you about. He went on to say that what they would see then would only happen three times and that on the third occasion, the mice would come with the moon. Sailvoyage said that someone from their family should wait for that time to greet the travellers. In addition, they should give to them the things that he was about to pass on to Lavenderwhiskers to guard. Sailvoyage believed that his mission and his part in trying to undo the great wrong would only be complete when the travellers came and that it would then be up to them to continue the quest if they chose to. The prophecy also said that it would be the travellers who would return to London to continue the work there. Sailvoyage had never been back. It was predicted that the family of the Watchmice would last only till the travellers came and the task of the Stonekeepers was done.

Sailvoyage asked that he should be buried in the cathedral and showed Lavenderwhiskers exactly where it should be. The notes from Swiftclimb were to be placed with his body, not her letter but the directions to go with the map without which it meant nothing. Stonechild questioned this since they had been given the map itself to give to the travellers and it seemed that that would be no use without the notes. Sailvoyage however insisted saying that it was a protection until the travellers came so that no one else could find the map and use it. He promised that on the third night of the blue fire the travellers would find the directions, all they would have to do was wait.'

Moonbeam Stonekeeper sat back and looked round the room.

'And you think we are the travellers?' asked Chandra.

'Yes I do,' said Moonbeam, 'your name is too much of a coincidence and I have felt that the third night of the blue fire was coming close for some time.'

'There's something we should tell you,' said Sunfur, 'the Professor found some records and did some calculations. He thinks that it will be in four days' time with the next full moon.'

'Then truly the time has come,' said Moonbeam, 'my task is nearly over. Let me continue the story a little longer.'

Lavenderwhiskers and Stonechild did as Sailvoyage asked. He was buried in the cathedral and the directions for the map were buried with him without anyone reading them. No records of the place of the tomb were made and throughout the years no one has been able to find it. The two mice stayed in the cathedral till the next full moon and then alone they were to witness the first moon-night of the Heartstone. After that, news of it spread and then every full moon more and more mice were to come and see the wonder. When they came, Lavenderwhiskers would tell them Sailvoyage's story and soon news of what he had done, and what was happening in India, spread throughout the country. Lavenderwhiskers and Stonechild stayed at the cathedral and did not move on again. They did see the first night of the blue fire one hundred full moons later and they made the preparations that Sailvoyage had specified. So Stonechild as Sailvoyage's descendant was the second of the Watchmice. Later she had children and one of them was to take over the role. So it has been passed on from generation to generation by a male or female mouse right up to the present day. I am the last of the Watchmice and I have had no children but Sailvoyage, Lavenderwhiskers and Stonechild are my ancestors.

Stonechild built the tunnel that you saw last night beside the window. Each new Watchmouse has been taken down that tunnel so that they would know where to find things when the time came if it was their destiny to greet the travellers. That is where I went last night

66

and now I must give you these. Here is the diary of Sailvoyage which tells of his adventures after he landed in London.'

Moonbeam placed a tiny and battered cloth-bound book on the desk in front of him.

'Here are notes of what happened in India and the contents of Swiftclimb's last letter together with the prophecies I have told you about. As you will see they are in English and I believe that they were made by Lavenderwhiskers from what she knew of the story. Lastly, but most importantly, here is the map, the thing that it has really been my family's task to keep for you all these years.'

Moonbeam laid a small tattered piece of parchment out for them to see. On it there were no words, just lines, arrows and some figures. It was a complete puzzle and none of them could make any sense of it.

'Now if you choose to stay and accept the challenge of what might happen, you must wait for the third night of the blue fire. If you do not intend to take up the quest in whatever form it may have for you, then you must go at once. Ancient prophecies can have a strange power and they should not be challenged.'

'Oh we'll stay,' said Chandra, 'We'll stay, won't we.'

All the mice nodded.

CHAPTER 8

Four Days To the Full Moon

When Chandra and the mice emerged from the Bishop's Palace it was nearly one o'clock. As they wandered over towards the cathedral none of them spoke, all in their minds were still in that study listening to Moonbeam Stonekeeper. It had that sort of effect on you, meeting a mouse whose family had waited two hundred years for your arrival. Jasminemouse was the first to recover.

'Excuse me but isn't it lunch-time?'

All the mice stopped and looked at each other.

'Past lunch-time you mean,' said Snuggletoes, 'I don't suppose anyone's seen Martin around have they?'

'Isn't that him just going into the Rectory with a tray,' observed Hugbundle.

Seven pairs of eyes swung round to join hers to look and then eight mice scampered off at top speed across the courtyard leaving Chandra to follow at her own pace.

Over the next four days they were to have quite a few meals with Martin, all as good as the first. Some would have thought that even the mice would have got tired of chocolate cream sauce after a while but, as Moonbeam had said, people do not always understand mice very well. They saw Moonbeam almost every day. He now sat for most of the time in the cathedral by the window, or in the sun outside. He looked happy and at peace now that his task was over, perhaps it had been worrying him that he was so old and had no children whilst the travellers had still not come.

68

Screechfoot and Croakwing were not at peace however, not even with each other.

'Look Croakwing we've been North, we've been
South and now we've tried the East and West as well.
Why don't we go and look in the middle, by the
cathedral, it's the only place left.'

'We might have missed them, they don't have to be
there.'

'No but at least let's go and have a look.'

'No, let's go North again.'

'Why? Why not the cathedral? Are you afraid of something?'

'No not afraid, but the cathedral, it's not nice. I've
been there, you haven't, if you had you would know
what I mean.'

'What's wrong with it?'

'It feels funny that's all, especially when you fly round
it. There's a window on one side, it doesn't feel right.'

'Well it takes more than a window to scare me. I'm
going to have a look,' said Screechfoot, 'you go North
again if you want to.'

'Suit yourself but you won't like it and you won't find
them.'

'Why not?'

'Because it's a cathedral and she's one of those,
remember? They don't like cathedrals and we've always
got someone on hand to go and make them feel unwelcome.'

'What's the name of our person in Wellminster then,
let's ask them if they've seen anything.'

'I don't know.'

'You don't know, you don't know! But you're supposed to be in touch with all contacts in this region.'

'Well I don't know.'

'You mean there isn't one. Fool! That's where they're
going to be! And what's so special about Wellminster

that makes it about the only cathedral in the country without one of our people keeping an eye on it.'

'You go and find out, that's all I can say. I'm going North,' and Croakwing flapped off slowly back to where they had started their search.

Screechfoot approached the cathedral with care. No, she was not going to be frightened by any window but Croakwing had made her nervous, he didn't usually scare that easily. She made a cautious approach and landed on a roof to survey the scene from a distance. All seemed well but she could not see any sign of what she was looking for. Screechfoot decided she must go closer. Gliding up into the air on a gust of wind she let herself be carried over the building and past the spire. As she cleared the other side she felt it, something reaching up towards her and no it was not nice, not nice at all. She scanned the sky for hawks, she was a large bird herself but the last thing she wanted now was an argument with a buzzard. They were bigger and they always made Screechfoot feel uncomfortable. There were however none to be seen, the sky was clear, so it had not been the presence of one of those she had sensed. Screechfoot turned and swept back towards the spire. Then she felt it again, not a threat, not anything that could attack her, but a voice, a voice inside her head. It seemed to say go back, go back, you are not welcome here. It was a very hard voice to ignore, Screechfoot was not used to opposition, usually she was able to go about her murky business without anyone even asking questions. The unaccustomed resistance made her very uneasy and she turned again to make off over the town and recover. As she did so out of the corner of her eye she saw Chandra talking to Moonbeam as they sat in the sun and her dark heart jumped with pleasure. Good, she thought, I don't have to come back, now I'll go and see what is to be done.

On the second night after their arrival the Bishop gave a special dinner for them, for Moonbeam and it seemed all the cathedral mice and staff as well. That had been the day when a new curate, Simon, arrived and he hadn't had an easy first morning. It was not Simon's first post at a cathedral and he had at least some confidence that he knew what to do. His last position however had not been anywhere like Wellminster.

Simon got up early that morning to be able to go and have a look round and have some idea of where things were. The only thing that troubled him still was what he felt had been the undue silliness of the attempt to have a joke at his expense the night before. It was not uncommon for some trick to be played on new staff when they arrived at the larger churches, after all everybody had to work together and it was a way of getting to know each other. So Simon had half been expecting something and it had been no surprise when the other curate who had met him from the station, wasn't his name Martin, had started such an odd conversation. Simon had been on the receiving end of a number of such tricks already, and had produced a few of his own, but he really thought that this was one of the most feeble he had ever heard. Stories of talking mice indeed, what did they think he was, stupid? Still if they felt they had to do something fair enough but it had then really gone too far. Not only did the other curate keep up the ridiculous story but everyone had backed him up. Then when Simon had tried to enter into the spirit of the thing and have some fun as well they had all stayed deadly serious. He hoped he had not hurt anybody's feelings but a line had to be drawn somewhere and their smug comments of 'You'll see' when he had finally said what he thought of their story had not helped either. Still at least there would be no room for any such trivia today, now it was time for work and that was serious, serious for everybody.

It was these thoughts that filled Simon's mind as he walked over towards the cathedral. His good humour at the prospect of applying himself only to his new duties was not however to last. As he reached the East door, he had already checked that this was the one that would be open early, he heard a small high voice call out to him. He looked round but could see nobody, not even the small child he expected. Then there was the voice again. Simon looked down and saw a mouse. This was too much, somebody was letting pet mice go whilst someone else had found a rather dubious use for a talent for ventriloquism! Simon had seen ventriloquists, a person who can project their voice without moving their lips, on television but at least they had been able to make the voice sound almost human. Not like the one he had just heard, that had been nothing like it should be. Angrily he walked quickly on and into the building, he would sort them out later. Inside the door he saw another mouse watching him from the aisle but he tried not to even look at it and certainly did not stop to see if it talked, enough was enough. Going over to the main noticeboard Simon got out a card and wrote on it:

UNFORTUNATELY THERE ARE MICE IN THE BUILDING. IF YOU SEE ONE INFORM A MEMBER OF STAFF AND PEST CONTROL OFFICERS WILL BE CALLED.

Simon pinned the card on the notice board with some satisfaction and left.

'That's not very nice,' said Candletail looking at the notice, she was talking to her friend Dennis.

'No,' said Dennis looking up from washing his whiskers, 'and that's not all. He wouldn't even talk to me outside.'

'Hasn't Martin had a word with him?'

'Oh yes last night, but he didn't listen, thought everybody was joking.'

'Another one of those, oh well he'll learn. Still your team's going to do something about that I hope.'

Candletail pointed to the notice again.

'Don't worry, it's as good as done, you keep an eye on things and I'll go and get them.'

Dennis Doodlemouse was, as his name suggests, one of the cathedral mice who wrote all the signs and lettering that was needed. When these mice had time, they would hold a small brush in a front paw, or use a special pen that you could draw complicated looking letters with. That was called calligraphy and it looked very nice when it was finished and the Doodlemice always liked doing it. When they were in a hurry though or something was needed in an awkward spot, the Doodlemice would climb up and hold on with three paws, carry a bottle of ink or a small tin of paint in the fourth and write with it using the tips of their tails which they would keep dipping in the colour. There were four Doodlemice at Wellminster - Rainbowtail, Colourpaw, Whiskersketch and of course Dennis. Now Dennis is an unusual name for a mouse and some people who have got to know the mice and him have been particularly bothered by it. This is because they have tried to study the mouse names and work out a system for what is done. The funny thing is though that Dennis's name has never seemed to bother any of the other mice. When someone asked them about it, all they would say was:

'System, what system?' or

'What's a system?'

Anyway, very soon Dennis was back and with him were Rainbowtail, Colourpaw and Whiskersketch. They all carried tins of paint and small rope ladders which were rolled up. Dennis climbed up on top of the notice-board and the other mice threw the ladders up to him. He caught them, tied them on firmly and let them hang down to the floor. All four Doodlemice then climbed up the ladders and hung on whilst they started work on the notice with their tails. Very soon it read rather differently to the way Simon had left it. Now it said:

FORTUNATELY THERE ARE MICE IN THE BUILD-ING. IF YOU SEE ONE DON'T LOOK FOR A MEMBER OF STAFF, THE MOUSE WILL BE HAPPY TO SHOW YOU ROUND AND JOIN YOU FOR TEA AND CAKES AFTERWARDS. PEST CONTROL OFFICERS WILL BE CALLED RUDE NAMES.

The Doodlemice had worked quickly and their letters were not quite as straight as Simon's but on the whole the notice looked very presentable.

'That's better,' said Candletail when they had finished and five well pleased mice went off to find breakfast.

A few minutes after they had gone, Simon returned. He saw his notice, or at least what was left of it, at once and he was not very happy. This time they really have gone too far, he thought, and he hurried off to find the Bishop. He definitely wanted a word about what was going on. There was no one to ask at the Bishop's palace so Simon went straight to the study door and knocked. As soon as someone answered, he went in without paying any attention to the voice he had heard.

'Come in,' said Moonbeam Stonekeeper from his own place on the Bishop's desk, 'I think it's time we had a talk.'

So that was how Simon learned about the mice, after nearly an hour with Moonbeam it would be fair to say that for him too nothing was quite the same after Wellminster. By the time of the bishop's special dinner, everybody was friends and stayed that way even after some time later Simon found that the deputy assistant verger he had been asked to see urgently and had been looking so hard for didn't even exist, after all some small trick is usually played on new staff at large churches.

Simon asked the mice how he could make up to them for the horrible notice he had written. They all said it was up to Moonbeam and so they had gone to find the old Stonekeeper. It hadn't been difficult, he was by the window as usual, keeping warm in a patch of sunlight. Without hesitation, Moonbeam said that the one thing that would mean more to him than anything would be if Simon would organise a performance for Chandra in the cathedral. They did ask the Bishop but there was not much doubt what the answer would be, he loved the idea. So with everybody helping, a show was arranged for the night before the full moon. At Martin's suggestion some posters were even put up in the town so people knew they could come. That was to be the one note of sadness in the whole event. The morning of the performance, Simon came back from some shopping looking very serious. He wouldn't say what was wrong but hurried off shortly afterwards with all four Doodle-mice and they were carrying their paints and brushes. It was only later that anyone else learned what had happened. The same hateful slogans that Chandra knew so well from London had appeared on two of the posters together with a drawing of a crow. Nobody could believe that anyone from Wellminster had done it, everyone was sure it had to be the work of outsiders.

Hugbundle again helped Chandra get ready and it was a rather nervous mouse and dancer that crept out of the vestry where Chandra had changed and into the cathedral itself just before the show was to begin. They should not have worried however, the cathedral was packed with mice and with people including many from the town. Chandra danced in the space right under the great window which held the fragment of the Heartstone and Moonbeam sat right in the front watching her every movement. There seemed to be something about that performance that he wanted very deeply, perhaps it was the bringing of a dance from India and so close to his ancestor, Sandrace, that meant so much. Everyone loved the dances and, when they were over, the Bishop even

75

made a speech to thank Chandra for her efforts, Candle-tail watching to see that he didn't make it too long. When the bishop had finished everyone in the cathedral clapped and clapped until Chandra promised to do one more piece to end the show. Then, happy, those who had been her audience went out into the welcoming night and home. Only Moonbeam stayed behind, even Hugbundle had gone off to bed.

'Thank you Chandra, that was very important to me.'

'Thank you,' said Chandra still wearing her beautiful costume, 'but can I show you one more dance?'

'Of course I'd love to see it, but it's a shame that the others have gone, it would be too special just for me.'

'Oh no, not this one,' said Chandra, 'one day I hope thousands will see it but not yet. Till then it must remain a secret, our secret, and you should be the first to see it anyway.'

So Moonbeam settled himself on a pew and Chandra took up her position again at the foot of the window. She put a new cassette in the tape recorder that had been set up for her and the music and the dance began. Chandra did not explain what the piece was about, she said that Moonbeam would know and at once he saw the meaning. Chandra had put into dance the whole story he had told them of Sailvoyage and his coming to England and as she moved and the tale unfolded, a single tear formed in Moonbeam's eye and then ran down his ever so white fur. When she finished he simply said in a voice which trembled with his feelings:

'Thank you, now the story will never die,' and slowly he made his way out into the open air. Above, the moon was high up in the sky and it was nearly complete. Tomorrow would be the night of the full moon.

CHAPTER 9

The Third Night of the Blue Fire

The morning after Chandra's performance, everyone slept on late if they could, it had been well past midnight before most of them had gone to bed. That meant that everything round the cathedral was very quiet and peaceful. If anyone had gone inside the only sound they might just have been able to hear would have been the gentle snoring of one or two mice tucked up on cushions between the organ pipes. It was a good thing that the organist had been at the show as well so she didn't want to practice.

In Wellminster itself some of the shops opened late and everything was just that little bit slower than usual, many people from the city had been at the performance too. Not everyone was so content in reflecting on the previous evening however. In a field beside some of the last houses as you travelled out from the centre, two men and a woman crouched down in a corner trying not to be seen. On the hedge beside them perched Screechfoot and Croakwing and on the ground sat Smirkmuzzle.

'Well done Screechfoot,' said one of the men, 'you've saved us a lot of trouble, now this is what we will do. We have all got to go and see to something down in Bristol but we will be back tomorrow or the day after at the latest.'

'What's up,' asked Croakwing, 'more posters to work on?'

'No not much, just one of our friends down there has found out there's a black family trying to buy the house next door. We're going to go and help persuade them it's not such a good idea.'

'Yeah, let them go and live with their own kind,' said the woman.

'Further away the better,' added the other man.

'So,' the first man continued, 'you keep an eye on things here till we get back, cause a bit of trouble if you can, keep them on edge. But be careful, that cathedral's a funny place, none of our people has ever been able to stick it for long and some strange things have happened. Once there was some nigger family visiting and the Bishop himself would you believe was going to show them round.'

Smirkmuzzle, who had grinned at the sheer unpleasantness of the word 'nigger', looked puzzled.

'Why would a bishop want to show any of 'them' round?' he asked trying to inject as much contempt as he could manage into the word.

'As I've said this is a strange place and that could have been enough but in this case it was even worse. It was back in the early sixties when all the niggers in the American South were getting ideas of being equal and rubbish like that. This one called himself Reverend or doctor or something, claimed to be a preacher.'

'They should never have been allowed to call themselves things like that,' said the woman, 'they're not fit to be called Christian let alone Reverend.'

Behind her on the distant cathedral spire, the figure of Jesus, born as a Jew who she equally hated, looked on in silent rebuke as she continued.

'It's a shame things went so bad in America, I was always thinking I could go to one of the Southern States where things like them were kept in their place only then it all went wrong. Now 'they' have to have rights just like us, it should never have been allowed.'

'Anyway so what happened when they came here?' asked Smirkmuzzle.

'Yeah, that's what I was saying,' continued the man, 'the night before they were coming we arranged for somebody to put a few little messages on the walls, just to make them feel 'welcome'.'

At this the two others and Smirkmuzzle sniggered.

'It should have been an easy job, it was a full moon, plenty of light to work by. So there was our man with his paint spray and everything was fine. Then, just as he bent down to start, apparently it was by some big window, these shafts of light started shining all round his head. I think it all got to him a bit because he still swears that that light burnt the letters off the wall as fast as he could spray them on.'

'Sounds like he got scared and chickened out to me,' said the woman, 'then made up some stupid story to cover it up. Probably saw a policeman on his way down there or something.'

'How many have we got in the local force?' asked the second man.

'None. That's another problem,' replied the first, 'round here they're all like that cheat Randel back in Eastwich. We couldn't get anyone.'

'Don't know who they're supposed to be taking care of,' said the woman, 'where their 'duty' lies.'

'I'm glad they're not all like that in London,' the second man cut in, 'we'd have problems without a bit of help now and again.'

'Still that's just another reason to be careful round here,' went on the first turning to Screechfoot, 'you and Croakwing keep an eye on things till we get back and do what you can. We'll all meet up here tomorrow or the day after. Right?'

Everybody nodded.

'OK that's settled then, now we had better move.'

The two men and the woman stood up and stretched, then with Smirkmuzzle trailing along behind they walked over to a rusty battered van that stood in the entrance to the field. Eventually the engine started, belching black smoke from the exhaust as it did so, and they lurched off down the road.

The afternoon at the cathedral passed almost as quietly as the morning had done, everywhere there was a sense of expectancy that the main business of that day was to come only late into the night. At ten in the evening Chandra, the Bishop, Martin and Simon all gathered in the Bishop's study. With them were Hugbundle, Sunfur, Starwhiskers, Honeymouse, Jasminemouse, Snuggletoes and Wanderpaws. All the mice from the cathedral, including Moonbeam Stonekeeper, were busy preparing in the building itself and the Bishop had said that they should be left to do so, this was very much their night and even he would only be a guest when the time came.

As they waited, they talked quietly amongst themselves when suddenly they were interrupted by the sound of a vehicle braking sharply on the gravel outside. They all went through into the hallway and looked out of the window to see what had happened. Outside stood a dark green jeep with the letters U.S. Air Force written on the side. Behind the wheel was a young man in a flying suit, the sort worn by pilots of jet aircraft, and sitting on the front seat with a tiny flying helmet beside him was the Professor. They all rushed to the door to meet him.

'Hello!' said the Professor as they crowded round, 'you didn't really think I was going to miss this did you? Oh and meet Steve, he was kind enough to fly me down, trains are so tiresomely slow aren't they. We met whilst I was over at NASA for the moon trip. Steve was just a cadet then but now he's a full pilot and a very useful chauffeur sometimes.'

80

The young man smiled.

'Anyway, thanks again,' said the Professor turning back to Steve, 'and see you soon. Now take care and don't do anything I wouldn't do.'

With this, the Professor jumped down from the jeep.

'I thought you said take care,' laughed Steve and with a wave he swung the jeep round and drove off into the night.

'Why didn't you tell us you were coming?' asked Sunfur.

'Because then it wouldn't have been a surprise, and you would have probably just sat around doing nothing till I came. You forget I know you lot, never do anything someone else might come and do for you. Isn't that the motto.'

They all laughed.

'Now let's go back inside and you can tell me everything that has happened.'

It took about an hour to describe all the events of the trip since they had left London and as they all told their own little bits of the story the Professor listened intently, only interrupting to ask about details he was not sure of. They also told him of the full history of the Heartstone, their promise to Moonbeam allowed them to share it with someone as part of their quest and they were all sure that that included the Professor. On hearing about the men on the train and the crows on the way to the station, he looked very serious and asked them each in turn if they had seen anything in Wellminster. The details of what had happened to the posters for the show also worried him and he warned them all to be very careful since he was sure that danger was not far away. They did not have time to discuss it further or make any plans however since at eleven o'clock precisely Candletail appeared at the door of the study. She was carrying a mouse lantern, the sort Chandra had first seen at the observatory, and she beckoned to them to follow her out into the hall. There, lit and waiting, were more lanterns for each of the mice and full sized ones for Chandra, the Bishop, Martin and Simon. They each picked one up and made their way out into the cathedral courtyard; they were however not alone. From every direction lines of mice, all carrying lights, made their way towards the main cathedral door which stood open. It was like the procession into the observatory only much much bigger. Chandra soon gave up trying to count the mice but there had to be hundreds possibly even thousands. It was the procession of the full moon.

Not speaking, they did not want to disturb the magic and devotion of the scene, Chandra and the others joined one of the lines and made their way towards the door. Inside, the whole cathedral was lit up by the lights the mice had brought and by its own candles, hundreds of them, which had all been lit. On almost every pew and seat was at least one and usually more mice sitting there waiting. Some had brought cushions, others had lifted up the hassocks and sat on those, some seemed happy on the wood itself and still more mice were filing into the building. Candletail led them over to a pew which was on the other side of the cathedral to the Heartstone window; from it they could see everything, not only the window but most of the building as well, right from the main door to the altar and beyond. There sat Moonbeam Stonekeeper, his stick beside him, he looked up and gestured for Chandra and the mice, including the Professor, to join him. The Bishop, Martin and Simon slipped quietly into the seats behind, they knew that this was not to be their adventure.

At eleven forty-five precisely, all the mice turned down their lanterns until the flames flickered and died and blew out the candles. As the lights were extinguished the inside of the cathedral drifted slowly into a shadowed darkness, it was like being in some huge cave. Outside the gleam of the full moon could be seen as it rose in the sky and its light became the only one left as it crept into the corners and secret places of that world. Everyone and every mouse was silent, waiting. Outside, the cathedral clock struck midnight and still the minutes went by and nothing happened. Then slowly, almost imperceptibly at first, there was a glimmer high up in the window, a tiny spot of yellow gold light that stood out in the darkness. As the seconds passed it grew stronger, rays of light began to reach out towards the surrounding stonework. A gentle gasp and sigh of wonder rippled round the waiting mice and Moonbeam smiled. The Heartstone was speaking.

For all those present time seemed to stand still, but it had not, and as it continued the rays grew stronger and began to build up a pattern which shifted and moved, almost danced, around the building. It seemed that they were searching for something, or reaching out to someone, as they drifted across the watching mice or rested on one of the cathedral statues or the great gold cross on the altar itself. As those present watched the beauty and the mystery of that sight they became lost inside themselves. The light seemed to share your every thought, multiply your every joy and divide even the greatest hurt until in that sharing it lost any power it might once have had. Still the luminescent shafts were the yellow gold of their first appearance and still they drifted and swept round the cathedral. Then the full rays of the moon struck the stone. As they did so it began to pulse with light and its beams started to change. The edges took on tints and flashes of a pale and pure blue whilst their centre burned a flawless silver. The watchers held their breath and after a moment of hesitation that seemed like an eternity, it happened. All the light from the stone suddenly blazed forth a brilliant incandescent blue, a

83

blue fire which burned into the very soul of the building and everyone that was in it.

The congregation, for that is what it was, sat or stood transfixed. Even afterwards none of those present was able to find words to describe what they felt at that moment. You had either been there and understood, or you had not and then would never be able to begin to comprehend what had happened. Everyone who was there was touched by the stone and for them, their lives were never quite the same. None of them ever felt totally alone again, no matter what was to happen to them.

The light of the blue fire blazed out into every part and every recess, cranny and hiding place that even a building as large and old as Wellminster Cathedral held within it. Slowly though, after the first explosion of its brilliance, it began to form again into shafts of its radiance still keeping the appearance of the fire and the colour of the blue. One of these fell directly onto Moonbeam Stonekeeper. In its light he no longer looked old or frail and his white fur seemed itself to burn as he stood freely without the aid of his stick. Another beam began to sweep round the cathedral roof and then moved downwards until it struck the tip of a gold trumpet held in the hand of an angel captured as a statue high up on a wall. That beam was then reflected and cut down through the darkness round it to fall on a patch of stone at the base of a pillar, a patch of stone that was decorated in a gold paint, an embellishment that went back for years and decades. Next the two beams bent and united forming an arc from Moonbeam Stonekeeper to the pillar which flickered along its length for the minute that seemed like an age whilst it was formed. Then with absolute suddenness all the light was gone, snuffed out in an instant and the cathedral was plunged into a darkness which after the fire seemed blacker than the darkest night. Everyone was absolutely quiet, no one moved and not a word was spoken, but in the shifting silence that enveloped them all some were later to say that drifting in the air they had heard a tiny faint mouse voice, echoing as if it were a long way away;

'Come on Lavenderwhiskers, it's time to go now.'

Slowly, very slowly, the normal world crept back into the cathedral as mice fumbled in the darkness and re-lit the candles and the lanterns. Then, still with virtually no words spoken, all the mice and the Bishop with his curates slipped out into the night that waited for them. As the Bishop left he glanced at his watch, it was two o'clock. What had seemed like seconds or an eternity, it had to be one or the other, had taken two hours. Even he felt though he had been in a world where time as we know it was of little meaning. Finally only Chandra, Moonbeam, Candletail and the Professor with the mice from the observatory were left.

'I think it's time we went to look at that pillar,' said Sunfur voicing the thought they had all been sharing. They went over to the exact place where the beam had fallen and saw that it had burned through the layers of the ages to leave the bare fresh stone visible underneath. There was a faint inscription and Candletail held up a lantern so they could read it:

SAILVOYAGE STONEKEEPER 1838

At the edges of the stone with the inscription were cracks similar to those round the entrance of the Stonekeeper's tunnel they had seen on the evening they arrived. Sunfur and Starwhiskers climbed up and began to scratch away at them. After some minutes, all those watching could see that it was another doorway and finally with Chandra's help they managed to prise it open. Inside there was a small chamber but until a lantern was brought closer none of them could see any more than that. Sunfur scrambled down and stood

85

aside to let Moonbeam be the first to enter. The old mouse however did not move, he just stood there leaning on his stick, his moment of freedom from it had ended with the Heartstone beam.

'No, Sailvoyage may have been my ancestor but his tomb was placed and left for you, for the travellers, the mice that shall come with the moon. Please, unless you doubt yourself, you go in.'

Sunfur climbed back up and Candletail handed her a lantern. Then hesitating only for a moment, she stepped inside and as she did so the light she carried revealed a chamber hidden for over one hundred and fifty years.

Sunfur had entered what could only be described as a miniature cathedral except that there were no windows. Around her were perfect tiny pointed and rounded arches, just like those of the main cathedral itself, and above her head they curved together to form a faultless vaulted roof. At the far end of the chamber stood a stone casket decorated with carvings and inlays. On one side was inscribed SAILVOYAGE STONEKEEPER and on the other SANDRACE FIRE-FOOT. It was just like the ancient stone monuments for important people that can still be seen in old churches today. Inside, Sunfur knew Sailvoyage's body would have been laid to rest when he died. Behind the casket however were two sculptures which would not have been seen in any church. Sunfur had not been to India but she had seen pictures of the temples there and the incredible carvings that they contained. Behind the casket were two which apart from their size looked very similar in design. To the right was the likeness of an elephant only it was seated, almost like a man. This was carved in a dark stone whilst to the left was a figure dancing, standing in a pose that Sunfur thought was rather like one Chandra had used in some of her pieces. It had one leg raised and held at an angle in front of the other and the hands were

86

together with one palm showing outwards. The right hand pointed up and the left down. To either side of the casket, a candle had been placed in a holder and because it seemed the most natural thing to do Sunfur went over and lit both of them from her lantern. The chamber was now filled with a soft warm glow and behind Sunfur the others peered in from the entrance. Moonbeam smiled but he also looked sad at the same time.

Apart from the casket, the candles and the sculptures the floor was bare except for two packages and it was to these that Sunfur turned her attention. They had been laid one to each side of the aisle that led up to the casket and it was to the one on the left that Sunfur went first. For a mouse it was a big packet the outer wrapper of which was a square of faded yellow parchment. Pulling this off carefully, Sunfur found inside a second wrapping of cloth and a note in a flowing handwriting of human size that looked old fashioned. The note read:

'To a more courageous soul than I could ever be who deserves this far more than I.' Puzzled, Sunfur unwrapped the cloth and found inside a medal of the sort that is given to soldiers who have been very brave. It was old and slightly tarnished and the ribbon attached to it was rather faded but as Sunfur turned it over in her paws, she saw that there was an inscription on the back which was still clearly visible:

Lieutenant Giles Benson of His Majesty's Armies for Valour

'What do you think it means?' asked Sunfur turning to the others as she read out the note and the inscription.

'Even I do not know that,' replied Moonbeam, 'there are parts of this story that are still to be discovered and understood. I doubt if it will ever be fully told.'

'Perhaps we will find out one day,' said Hugbundle, 'something very special must have happened but I think you should leave the medal there, it was meant for Sailvoyage.'

Sunfur nodded and carefully re-wrapped the medal and replaced it where she had found it. Then she went over to the other side of the chamber and the second package. It too was wrapped in parchment and it had been tied up with a ribbon. This time there was a note on the outside though, slipped under the ribbon where it was knotted. Sunfur pulled out the note and unfolded it.

'For the travellers on their coming with my greetings and my blessings wherever fate may lead them'.

Sailvoyage Stonekeeper formerly
Sandrace Firefoot.

'I think it's for us,' whispered Sunfur.

'Yes it is and you should take it with you,' said Moonbeam.

'Sunfur carefully lifted the parcel and carried it to the entrance where she handed it to Starwhiskers who was waiting. It was gently lowered to the floor and then Sunfur herself climbed out of the chamber. All the mice stood at the entrance and bowed their heads in respect. Then Chandra slowly pushed the door closed again and Sailvoyage Stonekeeper was left to his final peace.

On the flagstones of the cathedral floor the mice crowded round the parchment and Chandra crouched down beside them. Honeymouse and Jasminemouse pulled at each end of the faded red ribbon and the knot came undone. Inside the outer role of parchment was another and pulling very gently at its edges the mice spread this out so they could see it. All the mice frowned, they could make no sense of the tiny writing that filled the page, even the letters seemed unfamiliar.

Then as Chandra bent forwards to get a better view she gasped in recognition.

'It's in Tamil! My parents' language.'

'Of course it would be,' exclaimed the Professor, 'these must be Swiftclimb's notes for the map, they were written in the South of India. Chandra can you read them?'

'I think so but I'm better at speaking Tamil than reading it and I'm rather out of practice.'

'Never mind, work out what you can and we'll try and make sense of it,' said the Professor, a tone of undisguised excitement in his voice.

'I'll go and get some paper so we can make some notes,' said Candletail and she scampered off to the vestry.

Chandra took the parchment and sat down on a nearby pew. All the mice climbed up on the back of the seat so they could see over her shoulder.

'Now let me see what I can make of it,' said Chandra, 'it's not simple directions or anything, there just seem to be the names of some of the stars and planets and dates and times.'

'Of course,' said Starwhiskers, 'these are astronomical sightings taken on their journey. If you link these up with the arrows on the map then you know the place from where they started and the direction they then followed. The figures on the map must be the times they travelled.'

'Quick!' cried the Professor, 'read out what is there and perhaps we can understand what they mean.'

For the next twenty minutes, Chandra translated all the observations listed in the document and Candletail carefully wrote them down, this time in English. When they had finished the Professor took Candletail's notes and sat down to study them. He scratched his head and looked worried.

'I'm not sure what I can make of these quickly, you see they all relate to sightings close to the Southern Hemisphere and a long time ago. I will have to look in some very detailed references and tables before they will mean anything. The sooner I can get back to the observatory the sooner I can get started.'

'Well even for you that will have to be in the morning. I think tomorrow's going to be a very busy day and perhaps we should get some sleep,' said Wanderpaws.

'Yes you're right, perhaps when I get older I will learn some patience but till then, everything is so exciting, it should happen quickly.'

Snuggletoes looked at the Professor in disbelief, perhaps they didn't share the same thought of what old was.

'Yes, perhaps you will,' said Moonbeam, the one mouse present who could have made such a comment, then he added with a smile, 'but somehow I doubt it.'

'Come on,' said Chandra, 'Wanderpaws is right we are all going to need to be awake in the morning. I think however incredible tonight has been, it is a beginning not an end and tomorrow is where we really start.'

At this Moonbeam nodded content that the quest had indeed passed on.

Candletail led the way and they all filed out of the cathedral. On the way back to the rectory, they stopped at the Bishop's palace and left Moonbeam in the study sitting at his place on the desk with some papers he wanted to read through one last time before going to bed. There was a blazing log fire that had been made up for him to keep him warm and it was from there that he wished them all good night and a peaceful sleep. They carried a picture of him sitting in the place where he had first told them the story of the Heartstone in their minds as they made their way to their own beds.

At four a.m. that morning Moonbeam Stonekeeper, the last of the Watchmice, fell asleep at his papers still warmed by the fire. It was a sleep he was never to wake from. The prophecy fulfilled he slipped quietly from this world. His long life had finally come to an end.

CHAPTER 10

The Stonekeeper's Farewell

Chandra woke just before one o'clock the following
afternoon. The memories of the previous night were still
with her, but somehow all did not feel well. She glanced
down and saw Hugbundle fast asleep on the pillow
beside her. She looked across the room, all the other
mice were sleeping as well, except the Professor who had
already gone. Back to the observatory with Candletail's
notes thought Chandra as she slipped out of bed quietly,
trying not to wake the others. She had been right, on a
table by the window was a note in the Professor's hand,
or rather in the Professor's paw.

> Dear All,
>   I'm sorry not to have said goodbye but it seemed
> such a shame to wake you. Have gone back to the
> observatory with the notes so I can work things out.
> Probably see you back in London but if not I will catch
> up with you later. Must dash, the helicopter's waiting.
>   Good luck
>   Professor Watchmoon

Chandra smiled to herself, trust the Professor to get hold
of a helicopter. She wondered if and hoped that he
would be able to make sense of the map. Although they
had not decided what to do, it seemed to be very important, perhaps the key to everything.

Chandra peeped round the edge of the curtain, pulling
it aside carefully so as not to let any light into the room
and wake the mice, and she looked out straight into the

face of Screechfoot. For a moment neither of them moved, then Chandra waved her hand sharply at the crow to drive it away. Any normal bird would have left at once but Screechfoot simply stood there watching. Then Croakwing flapped slowly down from a tree to join her on the rectory roof. In his bill he carried one of the smaller posters for Chandra's show. For a moment the two birds waited. Then, each taking one side of the poster in their beaks, they pulled on it till it started to tear. They kept pulling and tearing until the crumpled sheet of paper had been reduced to mere shreds. Chandra watched horrified, even she had never seen anything like it before. When they had finished, the two crows looked at Chandra as if they were laughing at her and then took off and disappeared over the city and into the distance. Even their departure however had a promise of return as a threat within it.

'What's wrong Chandra?'

It was Hugbundle, she was standing on the window-sill but inside the curtain so she hadn't seen what had happened. Chandra drew back from the window and sat down on the bed, Hugbundle with her. The other mice, awake too now, had realised that something was wrong and came over and joined them.

'There were two crows outside the window and they just sat there tearing up one of my posters,' Chandra said in a hushed tone.

Starwhiskers jumped over to the window and looked out. Then he turned back grimly and nodded.

'Right, where are they!' cried Snuggletoes leaping up and looking for something he could use as a missile.

Wanderpaws put a paw on his arm.

'Not this time, if we ever do find them all of us will have to be more careful than that, even you. They are dangerous, very dangerous, and after what you did on the train they will be looking out for you in particular. Even the Professor wouldn't take them on lightly and he certainly wouldn't just look for something to throw at them!'

Snuggletoes sat down slowly.

'That's better,' said Wanderpaws, 'you've still got a lot to learn about adventures and one thing is that we always try and come back from them with the same number of mice as when we started. If you go on this way you're not going to live long enough to see the end of your first and then we'll be short by one when we get home.'

Chandra reached out and touched Snuggletoes' shoulder with her finger, he looked up at her.

'Wanderpaws is right,' she said, 'but thank you. Thank you for thinking what you could do first and only about the problems later. That says a lot about you you know. There's not many people like that and they're special.'

The mice climbed slowly up onto the windowsill and lifted the bottom edge of the curtain. Together they sat in silence as they watched the fragments of the poster blown away by the wind.

Outside by the cathedral they met Candletail, she was very excited.

'Have you heard the news?' she said as she rushed up to them, 'Magicnose was at the cathedral last night, she was seen!'

'Who's Magicnose?' asked Chandra.

Candletail stopped short, just about to say something.

'You mean you don't know?' she asked with a tone of disbelief in her voice after a pause.

'No,' said Chandra shaking her head.

'Oh,' then there was another pause, 'well come over here in the sun and I'll tell you.'

Candletail explained to Chandra that Magicnose was a very famous mouse, not like the Professor for what he did or Moonbeam for who he was, but because she was so mysterious and so little was known about her.

Amongst the mice who all told everything to each other, not once but several times, this had been quite enough to attract attention but it was not all. Magicnose just seemed to come and go without any reason or any explanation. One day she was there, the next gone and you might not see her again for months or years. There were rumours that she went on secret journeys, perhaps even across the world, but without her stories which she never told, no one could be sure. Then there were the reports that she even spent time with the porcupines. Now porcupines are rather like hedgehogs only much bigger and with very much larger spikes that all stick out at the back. These spikes protect the porcupine very well and as a result they are able to go about their business largely without interference. People and animals leave porcupines alone and porcupines leave them alone. Rather as with the mice, the part they play in the world is not appreciated by people but unlike the mice it is largely their own fault. Porcupines are by nature very unsociable, not just with everybody else but even amongst themselves. If you have not made friends with the mice, you must ask yourself the question whether you have ever spoken to them and given them a chance but with a porcupine you could talk to it for a whole hour and be lucky to get an answer. Of course in England there are very few porcupines around and, being unsociable, they are trying not to be found but they are just as difficult to get on with even in countries where there are many of them. It was this combined with an apparent love of organisation and systems for doing anything which made the mice even more suspicious. The porcupines could be helpful, they were very good at technical things and solving problems, but getting their help could take hours or days and the mice were quite sure that they were best avoided. Apart from anything else, since they had little to fear from anybody they could afford to be rather noisy and sometimes kept the mice awake and they could be rather destructive. Candletail and the other cathedral mice had never seen a porcupine and were not sure they would ever want to but from what they had been told about them any association with them by Magicnose made her even more of a mystery.

'So there you are,' said Candletail, 'that's Magicnose for you and she's back, probably round here somewhere, but of course she might have gone again. Anyway I've got to go and tell Moonbeam, I was looking for him in the cathedral but he's not there so he must be over at the Bishop's palace. See you later,' and Candletail scampered off.

Chandra and the mice were still sitting in the sun when Candletail came back a few minutes later. At once they could see that something was wrong, very wrong, and Sunfur put a paw round Candletail's shoulder as with tears in her eyes she told them what she had found. Together they all made their way with heavy hearts to the study. The news had travelled fast and outside the Bishop's palace there was a large group of mice all speaking in hushed whispers and looking very sad. Inside they found, as Candletail had done, the body of Moonbeam Stonekeeper lying amongst his papers almost as if he was asleep. In that first glance though they were sure that life had left him, it was hard to say why but they all just knew somehow. Chandra said that she would not be long and slipped out and back to the rectory. She returned quickly and in her hand she held a square of the South Indian silk that her costume was made out of, she always carried some spare pieces in case a costume needed a repair. They wrapped Moonbeam's body in the brilliant red fabric and then Candletail and some of the cathedral mice carried him slowly through the crowd outside to the cathedral. There they laid the body beneath the Heartstone window and lit a circle of candles that they placed round it. Two mice took it in turns to watch over and be with Moonbeam. Chandra hoped that he would have liked the silk. It seemed an appropriate shroud for the last of the Watchmice, a family whose distant ancestor, Sandrace would himself have known the silk weavers of his own day from the very place that the cloth had come from.

In the study, Sunfur and Starwhiskers were carefully tidying Moonbeam's papers so they could be looked after and kept somewhere. As they came to what Moonbeam had been reading last, Starwhiskers stopped and looked up.

'Look at this,' there was still a great sadness in his voice.

Sunfur came over and joined him.

'It's a letter from Starfall Stonekeeper, he must have been one of Moonbeam's ancestors, to his daughter Heavenguard talking about the time when she was to take over as the Watchmouse. Now here's the important bit, look.'

Starwhiskers pointed to a paragraph in the letter and both mice bent over to see. This is what it said:

Lastly, be very careful with what is kept safe and hidden in the Stonekeeper's tunnel. When you are older you will want, like we all have before you, to explore beyond the first store. There is not only the map and the things with it. Other documents are stored in a higher chamber which are in a strange writing no one can understand. They may mean something to the travellers though and if they accept the quest they should be given them. On a pad on the desk Moonbeam had made a note; 'Tomorrow - the higher chamber, must I go there again to find them?' - it was almost as if he had been writing down his thoughts and something had been troubling him.

Starwhiskers and Sunfur looked at each other and then at Honeymouse, Jasminemouse, Wanderpaws, Snuggletoes and Hugbundle who had crowded round.

97

'I think we should go and find them, it's what Moonbeam would have wanted,' said Sunfur.

'Yes you're right,' said Chandra from the window where she was standing, 'but not yet, not till Moonbeam has been laid to rest somewhere.'

The other mice nodded.

It was late in the evening before Moonbeam's body was moved from the cathedral. Candletail and some of her friends had gone into Wellminster and bought flowers and a special plant with very large leaves. These leaves they had folded together very tightly so that they stayed in place and they had made a boat from them. This they had then filled with flower petals and onto that softest of bedding Moonbeam was lowered. Flowers were then placed round him and at his feet a single white lotus blossom was laid. Tiny candles were stood amongst the flowers and a mouse lantern was hung from the stalk of one of the large leaves where it curled up and over at the back of the boat and hung above Moonbeam's head. All this was done in the cathedral at the base of the window and in sight of the Heartstone. Finally, when everything was finished Candletail climbed carefully up onto the edge of the leaf boat and pulled back the red silk to leave Moonbeam's face uncovered so he could see the window one last time and his journey from it. Then she lit the lantern and the candles and climbed down. Eleven mice from the cathedral - five on each side and one at the bow - lifted the boat and carried it slowly out down the aisle and through the main door. There were eleven mice so that there was one for each of the planets and one for the sun and the moon as well. In front of the boat walked Candletail with a lantern. Behind came Chandra, the mice and the cathedral mice. All were also carrying lights. They made their sad way down the side of the building and as they passed the Heartstone window, a flicker appeared high

98

up and reflected down onto Moonbeam's face. In its light, his old features looked even more as if they were just sleeping peacefully. As the procession turned away from the cathedral the last direct link between the Watchmice and the Wellminster Heartstone was ended.

The direction that the procession had taken took them to a gate that led into the churchyard. At it stood the Bishop with Martin and Simon, their heads bowed as the mice passed. The boat was carried along a gravel path between the rows of gravestones and the shadows they cast in the moonlight. No one was afraid though. In Wellminster and with the Heartstone behind them all they felt was the shared sadness of so many past lives that, like all others, had had to come to their end. As they passed one grave, however, a gentle gust of wind caught the boat and the candle flames flickered in its breeze. There were some fresh flowers on the grave and from them a single petal was lifted up and, after drifting in the air for a moment, it settled with the others beside Moonbeam in the boat. The lights from the lanterns did not reach up high enough for them to read the inscription on the gravestone however, and nor did anybody look, so the letters 'In Loving Memory of Giles Benson - Lieutenant' remained unnoticed.

At last the leaf boat procession left the churchyard through another gate and found itself in the cathedral garden. A lawn sloped gently down to meet a curving lake that lapped its edges. From the other end of the lake a stream linked it to a larger river and Moonbeam's boat would have a clear passage to the sea. It was the water of the lake that had given Wellminster its name - the church by the well. The boat was carried slowly across the lawn and it was placed gently in the water. The mice crowded round it and all in turn reached up to touch the stern in a last gesture of farewell. Then the eleven mice who had carried the craft all pushed

99

together to send the boat out onto the lake to start its journey. It drifted out a few yards and then floated there lifting peacefully on the tiny ripples that broke the water's surface. The candles and the lights still burned and their reflected beams made a path across the water to the watchers on the shore. The whole scene was lit by the softest gentle silver moonlight from above.

After some time, the mice began one by one to extinguish their lights and then turn and go back up the slope towards the cathedral. Soon only Candletail, Chandra and the mice from the observatory were left and alone they watched the leaf boat still drifting on the lake with its lights burning clearly in the night. The Bishop quietly walked down through the garden to join them and together they gazed on the scene, none wanting the final separation of leaving the water's edge. Then something caught their attention from further down the lake. In the moonlight they could see a bank of swirling white mist drifting across the surface of the water towards them. The fog looked strange however. It was thicker than any of them had ever seen before and it travelled too quickly, too directly, to be anything other than most unusual. Unable to move the watchers waited as the wall of white cloud swept towards them. In seconds it had reached Moonbeam's boat and that was lost to their vision. Chandra wanted to cry out but found she could make no sound. Still the fog advanced, a great swirling white screen that enveloped and obscured all that it touched. Then it was around them. At once they could see nothing except the whiteness that enclosed them on all sides, they could hardly see each other. Hugbundle climbed up and hid inside Chandra's coat with only her head left peeping out and all the others moved closer together for protection.

With the fog all sound was lost, it was as if a blanket of silence had been drawn about them, and they did not even hear the cathedral clock as it chimed so close behind. All they were aware of was the gentle lapping of the waves at the water's edge and the rapid beating of their own hearts as they waited for what might be to follow. Then they heard it, a slow heavy footfall coming towards them. That was not the greatest sound however, with the steps came a deep rushing breathing noise of some great animal. The mice had never heard anything like it before but Chandra knew what it was and whispered quietly to the others in her astonishment.

'It's an elephant!'

They all strained their eyes across the water and around them to catch any glimpse of their strange visitor but still they could see nothing more than inches away through the all pervading absolute white fog. Then the sounds of the elephant's breathing grew less and seemed to recede. As they did so the white haze began to lessen. Suddenly, as if a curtain was being drawn aside, the fog drew back from the shore and left them as it had found them in the clear night air. By the light of the moon they were able to watch as the bank of mist raced back across the lake and into the distance. It took only seconds for the unveiling to reach Moonbeam's boat and it was then that they all gasped in wonder - it was empty! The leaves still held together and the craft still lifted and fell on the tiny waves of the lake, but inside there was nothing, nothing at all. The flowers, the candles and Moonbeam's body had all just disappeared. All that was left was the single lantern at the stern which still hung lit from the stalk of the leaf and which marked the place where the boat lay.

For some minutes they all stared at the boat and the lake without speaking, almost as if they expected if

101

they waited long enough that they would wake up to find everything as it had been. The boat remained empty however and finally Wanderpaws broke the silence.

'What was it Moonbeam said? There are parts of the story that are still to be discovered and he doubted if anyone would ever know all of it.'

'Yes that's right,' whispered Sunfur, 'perhaps no one would ever know it all.'

'Even so,' said Starwhiskers, 'I think that it's time that we knew more. We promised Moonbeam that we would continue the quest but so far we have no plans and no ideas what to do. Now we should have, but first we must see what else is in the Stonekeeper's tunnel.'

The others all signalled their agreement.

'Well there's no time like the present, let's go and have a look,' continued Starwhiskers, 'I'm ready if you are.'

There were more nods of acceptance.

So the party by the lake finally did leave Moonbeam's boat to make its journey down to the sea but, it was not with the sense of almost desertion that they would have felt before and because of which they had stayed so long. Moonbeam had already gone on whatever journey lay before him and they knew that he would now want them to start theirs. At the cathedral door the Bishop left them and wished them good night, as he had already said, this was not his adventure. So it was that late that night, the day after the blue fire, Chandra, the mice from the observatory and Candletail stood once again at the entrance to the Stonekeeper's tunnel. Having opened it only a few nights before it was easier than it had been and soon the door swung back to reveal the passage inside. Starwhiskers and Sunfur stood in the entrance and took down two of the lanterns and lit them.

'We may be some time,' said Sunfur.

'Yes I know but be careful,' replied Chandra, 'we don't know what's down there.'

'No, but we do know it was made by the mice and it has been kept by them. It should be safe,' Sunfur's voice however did not quite match her confident answer.

'Yes I know but take care anyway, remember what Moonbeam had written. Something frightened him, he didn't want to go to the higher chamber.'

Reluctantly, Sunfur nodded.

So, leaving the others looking in from the entrance, Sunfur and Starwhiskers started down the tunnel. It was only a short distance to the end of the passage that they had been able to see on the first night and then they stood at the top of the steps that led down to the left. They waved and disappeared down them and were lost from view.

CHAPTER 11

Closer to the Son

Starwhiskers and Sunfur followed the steps as they curved down and to the left. More lanterns hung on the walls which remained, like the outer tunnel, smooth surfaces of stone where the passage had been cut into the very fabric of the building. For a while neither mouse spoke, the apprehension in Moonbeam's note worried them and they did not know quite what to say. By the time they reached the foot of the steps, the curve had taken them through a full half circle.

'We must be facing back under the floor of the cathedral,' said Sunfur.

'Yes, we've probably been standing right above the tunnel and never known it,' agreed Starwhiskers.

Together the two mice held up their lanterns to reveal another short stone passage ahead of them. At its end there was a very old wooden door with big iron hinges and a large lock. Fortunately, however, they could see that it stood slightly ajar. Cautiously they made their way down the tunnel and gently pulled the door open. Inside there was a bare chamber still cut into the cathedral stone. The room was not particularly large and on first inspection had nothing in it. At least so far none of their unspoken fears were realised. A break in the layer of dust on the floor though showed where something had been recently moved.

'Look, that must have been where the map and the diary were,' cried Starwhiskers.

'Yes but that's not our problem now,' said Sunfur from the far end of the room where she was standing, 'take a look at this.'

A further passage led on from the chamber but in the light of Sunfur's lantern, they saw that almost at once it divided into three, two paths sloped upwards, one down.

'Which one do you think we should take?' asked Sunfur.

'The letter said a higher chamber but that still leaves two,' said Starwhiskers, 'there's nothing for it, we'll just have to try them both and see what happens.'

With Starwhiskers leading they started up the first passage. This too led round in a curve and, as they continued along it, it still took them upwards. They were hopeful. Suddenly though they were faced with the inside of a stone door, exactly like the one at the start of the tunnel by the window. Starwhiskers pushed on it and it swung open with surprising ease. They looked out from a mouse-sized opening behind the great altar and from it they had a clear view of the whole cathedral. Chandra and the other mice had fallen asleep waiting at the first tunnel entrance, their lanterns were still burning beside them.

'Shall we wake them?' suggested Starwhiskers.

'No, let them sleep. Let's go and try the other passage.'

The second tunnel however merely brought them out on the other side of the aisle, opposite the Heartstone window. Disappointed they returned to the room where the map had been.

'There's only one thing left now, higher chamber or not we're just going to have to see where this goes,' said Sunfur standing at the opening to the passage that sloped downwards.

'Nothing else we can do so let's get started,' agreed Starwhiskers and with Sunfur leading and their lanterns held high the mice stepped into the entrance.

The downward slope of the passage continued as it had begun at a fairly gentle angle but there were many turns and curves to both the right and left. Soon both mice had lost all sense of direction. After they had been walking for about twenty minutes, Starwhiskers suddenly noticed something on the wall.

'Hey, come and have a look at this.'

Sunfur, who was still in front, stopped and came back to see. On the wall were several faded drawings. There were a lot of strange shapes in them and Starwhiskers looked puzzled.

'Can you make anything of it?' asked Sunfur.

'No, no I can't.......unless, wait a minute. Don't you remember when Dr Gupta from Delhi visited the observatory to see the Professor, didn't he bring some photographs that looked a bit like this?'

'You're right. It was that old observatory, the one in India, what was its name now .... Jantar Mantar, that's it Jantar Mantar.'

'This could be important! We must tell the Professor, it might help him work the figures out if they were linked to sightings based on that observatory.'

Excited now the two mice pressed on with renewed speed. Still the passage led on until, unexpectedly they came round a corner and were at the foot of the longest staircase that either of them had ever seen. It stretched on up above them far out of the reach of the light from their lanterns and into the darkness beyond. They started up it but as far and as fast as they climbed, still the stairs seemed to go on forever, always reaching up beyond the limits of what they could see. Both Starwhiskers and Sunfur began to get tired and they were panting with the strain but they struggled on upwards; having come so far they were not going to turn back.

Finally, when they both felt they could go no further Sunfur stopped and rested.

'I know it said higher chamber but this is ridiculous,' she panted.

'Yes it is,' gasped Starwhiskers, 'I never knew mice ever built anything like this. I'm not surprised that only some of the Watchmice came up here, Moonbeam could never have made it with his stick.'

'I wouldn't bet on that, not if he'd really wanted to. Quietly I think he was a very determined mouse.'

'Yes, you're right, but it would have been quite a climb for him, perhaps that's why he was worried.'

The thought reassured them and it was with less fear that they continued onwards. Their lifted mood was not however to last long. Above them, just at the edge of the beams from their lanterns, they noticed something on one of the steps. A few moments later they could see it clearly and they both froze and stood trembling.

'Darkness joined,' whispered Sunfur.

A faint 'yes,' was all that Starwhiskers could manage in reply.

What they could see were two candles placed upside down with the tips of the wick at the top of each touching so that they formed a V shape. It was a signal that the mice used to warn of an evil place or somewhere of great danger. The meaning was simple, the lights -any sort of light would do, not just candles- upside down and unlit indicated the darkness of the place that light had not been brought to. The use of two showed the power and strength of the danger, hence the name 'darkness joined'. It was a warning that all mice knew and under-stood. Very few would pass beyond a point where it had been laid.

'What shall we do?' whispered Sunfur.

Starwhiskers hesitated for a moment.

'We must go on. Moonbeam knew the danger and he was going to come back wasn't he.'

'Yes I think he was,' said Sunfur, 'and that also means he thought it was important but from now on we must be careful as we have never been before.'

Starwhiskers and Sunfur nervously edged round the candles and then began the ascent of the steps beyond them. Neither knew what lay above and both their hearts were racing, the darkness joined sign was never left lightly. They climbed now side by side, there was just room on the stairway, neither wanting to place the risk of leading on the other. Slowly they crept higher and as they did so they began to feel a draft of cool air on their faces, they knew they must be nearing something. Then they saw the top of the stairs above them, they ended in a small stone landing and to the left was an arch that formed an open doorway. Through the arch all that could be seen was blackness but around its edge there were deep gouges in the stone, as if someone had tried to force an entrance. Then a sudden gust of wind blew out both lanterns and they were in darkness.

Instinctively, both mice huddled together for protection. If it had not been for the fear of falling on that immense stairway in the dark, they would have probably fled back the way they had come but now it held them where they were. Minutes passed and nothing happened. As their eyes got used to the gloom, they could see that in fact all was not black beyond the arch; through it there was a gentle glow, at least there was some light ahead of them. Cautiously, silently and as slowly and carefully as they could, they crept up the last few steps and peeped out through the opening. At once they both felt dizzy, they were looking down into the cathedral but from a narrow gallery only just below the roof. They had climbed all the way up inside one of the walls and now a vertical drop of what seemed like hundreds of feet opened up below them. There was no railing or wall to protect them and one false step would have left them to plunge downwards into the abyss below. Through the arch was a ledge which ran off to their left as it jutted out from the vast wall of the cathedral. The ledge was narrow, mouse sized, and would only allow them to pass in single file and on the outer side it remained completely open. After a short distance, the ledge continued on round one of the great pillars which reached right up from the floor and the back of which touched the wall itself. As the ledge curved round the pillar, it disappeared from view and they could only hope and guess that it continued on the other side. They could not be sure since beyond the pillar was a large recess and the ledge would have to carry on round its walls which they could not yet see. They knew however that the precarious route which they looked along was not itself the meaning of the warning. Mice are very good climbers and do not fear heights like people and it would have normally been thought of as quite adequate and safe for them if they went with care. Starwhiskers and Sunfur could see however that something had happened there, all along the ledge were the same sinister gouge marks they had noticed round the archway. The only comfort was that they did not seem very new, being weathered to the same colour as the surrounding stone. As they peered over the edge far below them, they could see Chandra and their friends still waiting for them at the tunnel entrance and still fast asleep. A very large part of both mice wished they were with them.

'Come on,' said Starwhiskers, 'leave the lanterns here, they're no good now they've been blown out and let's see what's round that corner.'

Hesitantly Sunfur nodded. The lanterns were placed just inside the arch and the mice crept out and along the ledge staying as close as they could to the safety of its inner wall. Even with that precaution, they had unwelcome repeated glimpses of the drop and the cathedral floor below. At last they reached the pillar and followed the ledge round it and into the unknown.

109

Both Starwhiskers and Sunfur jumped as they turned that corner and only their closeness to the wall saved them. Then they stood in fear and dread at the strange and awful sight that lay before them. Wedged in the narrow crevice created where the pillar curved away from the wall was the skeleton of a large bird, a crow, its bones coldly visible in the moonlight that filled the vault of the cathedral roof. The skeleton was upside down so that the neck and skull curved below it and rested on the ledge itself. The large bone of one wing was broken and the skull lay twisted sideways and upright in the position it had fallen back in after the neck had snapped. All along the ledge and round the pillar were the same gouge marks they had seen earlier. Starwhiskers shivered.

'Whatever happened here?'

'I'm not sure I want to know; this place feels wrong, something terrible took place and those bones, you can still sense the darkness in them,' whispered Sunfur.

'Still we must go on now, if we're careful I think we could squeeze past the skull and onto the ledge beyond,' said Starwhiskers.

Sunfur felt an icy chill pass down her back at the thought but agreed they had to finish what they had come for if they could. With infinite care the mice began to creep past the skull, on the inside with their backs flattened against the pillar. If at all possible neither of them wanted to touch the bone. The closer they got to it the more it seemed to still be alive, to threaten them. Finally they were beyond it and they both sighed with relief.

'I suppose no one has ever seen it from below,' said Starwhiskers.

'No, too high up and hidden by the pillar, it's only once you're up here that you'd know it was there,' agreed Sunfur.

The mice did not have much further to go on their quest. A few more inches along the ledge and an opening appeared in the wall on their left. Gratefully, they both ducked through it and pushed open a door that it concealed. Inside, they found old lamps but they still contained oil and best of all there were matches. In seconds the cheerful flames leaped upwards and revealed a mouse-sized room strewn with cushions and bordered on two sides by deep rich curtains that reached all the way from the ceiling to the floor. Everything looked rather old and was very dusty.

'I think we're here,' said Starwhiskers.

Sunfur went over to the longer of the curtains and pulled it back along the rail it hung from. Clouds of dust rose from it as it moved and uncovered a window with latticed glass which gave a view out over Wellminster as the initial grey of dawn broke the sky. It was the first time that any mouse had seen that sight for nearly forty years.

The first rays of that morning picked out the fragments of rock at the room's edge which had given the name to the crystal room, the retreat and the archive of the Stonekeepers. By the additional light they could see things more clearly. Something on the floor caught their eye and Sunfur bent down and picked it up. It was a crumpled piece of a newspaper, a cutting from a front page, and together the two mice spread it out amongst the cushions. The date was 1947 and there was only one main headline:

'DATE FOR INDIAN INDEPENDENCE
ANNOUNCED'

The paper was old and had yellowed but far worse it was covered in dark reddish marks. Despite the effects of the passing years, both mice knew instinctively what they were.

'They're blood stains,' said Sunfur in a voice that trembled.

111

Starwhiskers repeated the question that had bothered them both since they saw the top of the stairs.

'What happened here?'

It was something that neither of them could answer and nor did they find any clues in the search they made. The story of the dreadful events of one night in 1947 had only been known to Moonbeam and he found it so upsetting that he had never written it down. The secret had died with him.

It had been the day after the one, as the newspaper headline had said, when a final date had been agreed for India to become independent. The second world war was over and much attention had been given to what should happen in India and when the British would leave. The problem was often talked about and so when a date was fixed, it was the main news in all the morning papers. When Paula Benson opened her own newspaper at breakfast time, the headline was the first thing she saw. It immediately caught her eye, her great great grandfather had seen so much bad and suffered so much in India with the army that she was very glad that the link of empire with Britain would soon be over. His stories had stayed in her family throughout all the long years since he had been there. The news was so important to her that she was to talk about it often during that day, including outside in the garden with the local vicar in the afternoon. As they talked, neither of them noticed Scarfeather, the darkest hearted crow there had ever been, perched on a tree and listening to them. The news made Scarfeather very angry and, as he sat and watched them, a plan began to form in his cruel mind.

There was no moon that night, it was the day between the last of the old moon and the first of the new. Scarfeather did not understand Wellminster or the Heartstone fully but he had learned a little and he knew that the moon was important. As the afternoon wore on he also noted with satisfaction that dark cloud was spreading to cover all the sky. There would be no light that night from moon or stars and the Heartstone would be at its weakest. As dusk fell, Scarfeather flew towards Wellminster which was only a few miles away and made straight for the cathedral with the intention of doing as much mischief as he could. When he arrived, it was almost dark and unseen he slipped through the side door which stood open. Later, when everyone had gone he flapped up into the space of the canopy of the cathedral roof and looked down to see what he could damage or harm. As he flew in tight circles above the aisle, he felt the presence of the Heartstone but he was truly the darkest of the crows and he swept on through the air not heeding the challenge that reached out to him. Then something caught his watchful hurt seeking eye; above him and on a ledge close to the roof he saw a movement. Instantly he swung upwards and curved round to see Nightray Stonekeeper, the Watchmouse of that time, caught half way along the ledge from the stairway in the wall to the crystal room. Nightray was carrying a cutting from a newspaper about the news from India to put with other souvenirs and things that the Watchmice thought important in the collection they had made over the years and which they kept in the room. Scarfeather swooped down and pecked at Nightray who flattened himself as low as he could on the ledge and against the wall. Scarfeather missed and his beak left the first of the gouge marks in the stone that Sunfur and Starwhiskers had seen. As Scarfeather swung away, Nightray ran on down the ledge to try and reach the safety of the room. The crow was however too quick for him and the next dive found him still out and exposed in the open. As Scarfeather attacked, Nightray fought back with the only weapon he had, the candle he carried to light his way, which he swung at the great dark bird as it lunged towards him. The candle struck home and amazingly remained alight after its blow, it was however only a

113

mouse candle and was therefore very small. The worst damage it did was to singe some of Scarfeather's neck plumage but at least it made the bird jerk away as the flame neared its face. Despite this the second attack struck home, Nightray was caught by a slicing blow from the cruel beak of his assailant and he fell back bleeding onto the ledge and was lucky not to topple over the parapet and into the drop below.

For minutes that seemed like hours the battle was to continue. Again and again Scarfeather lunged down whilst Nightray tried to protect himself with his candle brandishing it in front of him almost like a tiny sword. Sometimes Scarfeather was deflected and would miss leaving more and more gouge marks on the wall, pillar and ledge with his beak. Other blows however found their mark and soon Nightray was bleeding from many wounds. Worst he was never given the chance or time to run for cover either back to the stairs or on to the room, he was trapped. From the window the Heartstone could be felt as a throbbing pain sharing Nightray's suffering but there was no light for it to feed on, it was powerless and Scarfeather remained stronger than its simple presence. It could not drive him back.

Outside, Nightray's son, Moonbeam, heard something of the noise of the fight and dashed inside to see what was happening. Horrified, the young mouse saw his father struggling to drive Scarfeather back and caught in that desperate position half way along the ledge. At once Moonbeam snatched up the nearest lantern and dived into the entrance to the Stonekeeper's tunnel. From it he ran down to the map room and dashed on into the tunnel leading to the stairs. Soon he was at their base and without a pause he threw himself upwards and into their ascent. On he raced never stopping up all that immense flight of steps even as his lungs burned and his legs felt they would crumple under him. Finally, he saw the top and leapt to the archway entrance to catch a glimpse of his father lying critically injured and now unable to defend himself farther down the ledge. Moonbeam shouted up in challenge to Scarfeather who was preparing to make his final attack. The call diverted him as Moonbeam had intended and he swung and lunged in his full fury at the archway entrance. His beak cut groove after groove in the surrounding stone as Moonbeam ducked back always just out of reach. Fortunately, the ledge was not wide or deep enough for the large claws and feet of the crow to gain a foothold and after two or three stabs at his quarry, Scarfeather was forced to drop back and out into the unobstructed air to regain flight before swinging in again for another onslaught.

It was in one of these turns that Moonbeam thought he had a chance to reach Nightray and drag him to safety. As Scarfeather dropped away from the arch, Moonbeam sprang through and out onto the ledge. He had however misjudged the speed of the crow and before he had even reached his father, Scarfeather was back and diving down to attack him. A blow from Scarfeather's beak caught Moonbeam on his leg and he collapsed sideways in terrible pain holding on to the ledge with his uninjured paw. His lantern fell and rested against the wall behind him. Scarfeather swept up laughing and then prepared to dive once more and kill Nightray where he still lay unable to move or help himself. The crow made one more circle in mid-air as if to celebrate his victory and then began to turn. Moonbeam watched horrified as the scene unfolded before him. Then, in what even he feared was a last and futile gesture of defiance, he reached behind, picked up his lantern and threw it with all his strength at the dark bird that tormented them. With his injury and exhaustion, the lamp fell hopelessly short and as it arched and plunged towards the floor below, his heart crashed with it. As the lantern tumbled over and over, the oil it contained spilled out and all caught fire at once making an orange flare that Moonbeam's desperate eyes followed downwards. It was all the light the Heartstone needed. At once it burned with that orange speck and then its hurt and pain scorched out as the air was filled with sheets of crimson flame. Scarfeather twisted sideways and upwards but he was blinded and could not see where he was going. Too late he saw the statue rush up from the surrounding blaze and his left wing struck it with the full force of his speed. The bone cracked and with one wing useless Scarfeather veered sideways and toppled over out of control. He dived helplessly to crash into the pillar at the ledge's turn where he flipped over catching and twisting his neck as he did so. It snapped with only the merest hint of resistance and Scarfeather's dark heart was still forever.

It was some minutes before Moonbeam was aware of what had happened. With the blaze of the Heartstone he had passed out and it was into a cold dark world that he awoke. He crawled back to the arch moving with great difficulty because of his injury and collected and lit a spare lantern that was kept there. Then, slowly, he made his way out along the ledge to where his father lay. Nightray made no sound but he was still breathing. Despite his own hurts, Moonbeam dragged him to the top of the stairs and then began to carry Nightray downwards and to help. Moonbeam's father was however not to speak again. Somewhere on those stairs life left him and it was only a body to mourn for that Moonbeam held when he reached the bottom.

Moonbeam of course at once became the Stonekeeper. He never fully recovered from the injury to his leg and from that day onwards he walked with the aid of a stick, the stick that later people thought was only because of his great age. Perhaps it was because of this or through having to take on the duties as Stonekeeper so suddenly and so young that Moonbeam was never to have that special friendship with another mouse and the children

116

that it could bring. So it was that he became the last of the Watchmice. After some days when he had recovered he made his way back up to the gallery one more time, the last visit he was ever to make. He took the newspaper cutting from where it still lay as it had fallen on the ledge and creeping past the body of Scarfeather he placed it just inside the door of the crystal room. Then he climbed, with difficulty because of his stick, back and down the stairs pausing only to leave the darkness joined sign near the top stone landing.

As Starwhiskers and Sunfur stood in the crystal room and wondered, there was no way they could guess at what had happened that night or even that it was Moonbeam who had been involved. To them, much of what they found was always to remain a mystery. They did however continue to explore.

'Let's see what's behind the other curtain,' said Starwhiskers going over to it.

He pulled it back releasing a further cloud of dust and revealed a number of shelves all piled high with notes and papers. They began to look through them.

'This is awful,' said Sunfur holding a very old page from a newspaper.

'What is it?' asked Starwhiskers.

'It's all about when some of the soldiers, like the ones in red coats who broke the Heartstone only later, fired their guns on a crowd of people who were holding a meeting. Hundreds were killed at somewhere called Amritsar.'

'When did it happen?' said Starwhiskers.

'Nineteen nineteen.'

For some time the two mice looked through the piles of documents. All were about India and most were from newspapers. Not every one was about bad things though although many were, and together they formed a sort of history about the time that the British had claimed India as part of an empire. The mice put the last cutting, the one about independence that Nightray had brought, with the others and the record was complete. Then, hidden behind one pile of the oldest notes, they found what they were looking for. Sunfur and Starwhiskers lifted down what for mice was a large rosewood box with beautiful gold patterns inlaid into the wood. The box had a lock but the key was in it and it turned easily. Then Sunfur lifted the lid and they both peeped over the edge to see inside. There were two things in that box; a role of ancient papers in the same strange writing as the notes for the map they had found in Sailvoyage's grave and a small square of silk cloth. The cloth was of Indian design and was like Chandra's costumes. It was a deep purple and gold and looked as if it had only been made the day before, the colours were so bright and clear. It was obvious to the mice though that no one had been up there for years and somehow, the cloth gave a feeling of being even older than that, although neither of them could say quite why they felt it. Puzzled by yet another mystery the two mice sat back and looked at the strange fabric. Then, with a certainty she could not explain, the answer came to Sunfur.

'It's the cloth Sailvoyage wrapped the Heartstone in!'

At once, Starwhiskers was sure she was right and they both looked at each other in wonder at what they had found. Taking the cloth and the documents, they both somehow felt that they should be kept together, Sunfur and Starwhiskers crept out of the crystal room and back along the ledge. Both mice again pressed against the wall to keep as far away from Scarfeather's skull as they could. Soon they were at the arch and started down the stairs carefully carrying their discoveries with them. Finally, when they were both as tired as they could ever remember, they were back at the entrance to the Stonekeeper's tunnel. Chandra and the other mice were still asleep and Starwhiskers crept across to wake them. After that though for once even mouse curiosity had to wait,

Sunfur and Starwhiskers were just too exhausted to tell their story then. So, reunited, they all made their way out of the cathedral and back to the old rectory where two very tired mice were at once asleep. Having laid the papers and the cloth in a safe place, their companions soon joined them, after all if they were going to have to wait for the story what was the point in missing out on a good snooze. By the time that the sun rose a few minutes later none of them was up to see it.

CHAPTER 12

Anju and the Heartstone

By mid-morning Sunfur and Starwhiskers' tiredness had given way to hunger and they both woke up slowly with thoughts of breakfast. In recognition of the adventure they must have had and in the hope of getting the story sooner, their companions had already made plans and arrangements. In other words Candletail had gone to find Martin. By the time that the two explorers stumbled bleary-eyed down the stairs, the rectory kitchen was filled with the tempting smells of hot bread and scrambled eggs cooked to perfection. Breakfast had the desired effect and, duly revived, Sunfur and Starwhiskers found themselves sitting surrounded by a semicircle of mice with Chandra and Martin behind. It was an attentive and eager audience which would put up with no further delay. Only after the entire story of the expedition had been told, talked about and re-told several times was there any question of moving. Then Honeymouse who wanted to hear the adventure at least once more suggested that they should all go and find the Bishop and show him what had been discovered. Having collected the cloth and the documents, they went over to the study and found the Bishop there. As they all settled themselves somewhere comfortable there was a moment's silence, they were all aware of Moonbeam's empty place and felt the loss.

Just as Honeymouse had hoped, the Bishop of course wanted to hear what had happened, so it was only after a further re-telling of the story that attention turned to what had been brought down. Everyone was just as excited as Starwhiskers and Sunfur had been at the cloth and, in the same way as they had done, nobody thought anything other than that it was what Sailvoyage had wrapped the Heartstone in all those years before. Chandra and the Bishop then spread out the papers that had been in the box with it and all the mice crowded round to have a look. They were in the same unfamiliar script as the directions for the map had been. One page was a letter in exactly the same paw-writing and with Chandra translating, they very soon realised that it was no less than Swiftclimb's last letter to Sandrace - the one that the elephant had brought. They then looked at the other two. These were in a different hand. It was too large for a mouse and yet too small to be normal for anything else, it was almost as if someone or something much larger had been trying to write for the mice or to them so that they would find it the right size to read easily. It was Hugbundle who realised first what they might be and as she spoke the thought, she left the others silent in surprise.

'These could be the other things brought by the elephant when he found Sailvoyage out in the heat near Madras.'

After the pause the Bishop answered her.

'I think you may be right but let's see what they say - then I'm sure we'll know.'

Chandra picked up the first and after a little difficulty found that it was an account of the predictions, including the one about their own arrival, that Moonbeam had told them about. Then she turned to the second, a much larger sheaf of pages, and read silently to herself for a minute.

'It's a story,' she said looking up, 'and quite a long one at that.'

121

'That's all right,' chorussed the mice who all loved stories, especially mysterious ones, 'we'll make ourselves comfortable and you read it to us.'

So in the Bishop's study with him, Martin and the mice sitting round her Chandra began to read a tale that had not been heard ever since the elephant had given it to Sailvoyage. Being in Tamil, only he would have been able to read it and then it had been forgotten and left in the archive of the Stonekeepers. The only other person or mouse who just might have heard it was Lavenderwhiskers, perhaps Sailvoyage told it to her whilst they were snuggled up together one cold night on their travels - a good time for telling stories. If Lavenderwhiskers did know it however she had not passed it on, Chandra's reading was a new discovery. This is what she found and what the mice heard as she translated what she read.

'Anju was a young girl who lived with her parents in a village by the sea in one of the kingdoms here in the South of India. Anju had been born with a deformed right arm which hung withered and useless by her side. Of itself this was bad enough, but what made it far worse was that her family were net makers for all the local fishermen and even some further away, all the way along the coast in fact. It did not seem that with only one good arm she could even help in the family trade and who, everyone thought with her problem, would ever want to marry her.

Anju's parents were always kind but if she was with them they seemed uneasy in the company of others, almost as if they were ashamed. This was not so bad in the village where they lived because everybody had got to know Anju. The sad result of it was though that she was never taken on any of her parents' journeys to the big city further up the coast to sell their nets. It was not right, all her sisters and brothers had been but in her entire life Anju had never left the village. The difficulty was that it was surrounded on all sides by dense forests

122

where leopards and other wild animals lived. One or two of the men had tried to find a safe permanent way through it but none of them had succeeded and some had not even returned. Leaving the village by land was restricted to rare and large expeditions with many men, some armed. The only real way of travelling was on the boats when they sailed off and into the distance, usually to the city. Those were the trips she was never allowed on, however, and Anju almost felt a prisoner in her own body and her own home. It just did not seem fair.

In the village there was a temple dedicated to the great god Shiva and his consort Parvati. It was at that temple that there was the only creature that Anju really regarded as a friend. When she had been very young the other children had largely accepted her but as they all grew older, the problem with her arm seemed to matter more and more, and who she really was to count for less and less. Her friend was the elephant that lived in the temple and accepted offerings of money and then blessed the giver by touching them lightly on the forehead with its trunk. She had always thought of this elephant as a friend for as long as she could remember and it was only later that a sad event was to bring them even closer together. As the elephant got older, old even for an elephant, the great gentle animal began to have problems with its right front leg. The joints seemed to have stiffened and it could no longer walk or stand properly. Some of those who were responsible for the temple began to grow angry with the elephant saying what use was it now that it could not go in procession round the village at the time of the annual festival. What was worse was that the other temple elephant was the daughter of the older, now disabled, animal. In all things this younger elephant was as gentle as her mother - all things except one.She almost seemed to sense her mother's difficulties and if anyone ever treated the old elephant harshly or impatiently for her slowness then she was there, ready to protect her mother with all her strength and considerable power.

Anju knew that the temple authorities were beginning to say that the elephants were a danger and a problem and should be driven out and up into the forest. That made Anju very sad and afraid. Firstly, she would lose her friend and then the elephants might be in danger as well. They were used to living in the village and with people and would have lost their skills of keeping safe in the wild. The forest leopards were said to be so fierce that even an elephant, especially one who could only move slowly, would have something to fear.

These worries and their hurt grew in Anju who sat for long hours alone on the beach desperately trying to think of something that could be done. Although she had never left the village, Anju did know a little of what lay across the water, she always listened to everything people had to say when they got back. It was after all her only way of getting news. Most of the nets, fish and other goods from the village were sold in the market in the city that was the land's capital and where the King lived. She had heard that in the city there was a very special temple with a huge statue of Ganesh, the elephant-headed God, who she knew from the shrine to him in her own temple was the great helper to those who overcame troubles. Ganesh was the son of Shiva and Parvati and Lakshmi, the goddess of good fortune, had blessed him with the power to bring good luck. Anju thought that if only she could make a pilgrimage to the city temple and make an offering, then surely Ganesh would help her friends, the elephants in the village.

Her make a pilgrimage though! She who had never gone anywhere, and her make an offering, she who had nothing. Anju did not even have the bangles and jewellery of the other girls, none had been given to her. It seemed that no one thought they would ever appear right on a crippled arm or that anyone with her problem

124

would be interested in how they looked and being pretty. If only they all knew how wrong they were. Despite these difficulties, the thought did stay with Anju and finally she did make a plan. If she was careful she might be able to stow away on the next boat sailing to the city and then she could make an offering of the only precious thing she had - a beautiful pink and white conch shell she had found on the beach one day as she wandered alone excluded from other children's games. No one else thought it of value but it was to her and surely the God would know that and accept it as the gift for which it was intended.

Finally, the day for the ship to sail came and very early in the morning Anju crept out of the house carrying her shell carefully wrapped for the journey. She had also helped herself to some food, rice and yoghurt wrapped in a banana leaf left over from the meal of the night before, to eat on the way. Anju was trying not to think of what her parents would say on her return. Unnoticed she passed through the streets just as the first signs of the day's activity could be seen. She found the boat and, to her great relief, there seemed to be no one on it or taking any notice of it. Anju slipped on board and hid herself in the bow beneath the deck by lying under an old sail that had been left there. The next few hours were to be some of the most tense of her life. Suddenly people did come and there was much shouting and banging as things were loaded onto the vessel. Anju expected to be discovered at any minute but she was not, who after all would pay any attention to the old sail that had been there for years.

Anju had never been to sea. As the boat got farther into the channel it began to lift and fall in the swell of the open water and she began to feel rather ill, cramped as she was in her hiding place. There was nothing Anju could do however and she just had to wait and hold out as best she could. It seemed like an age until finally the men's voices told her that they were approaching land. Soon the boat was secured against the quay at the city waterfront and was being unloaded. To Anju's dismay though not everyone left the boat with the cargo. Two men stayed on board whilst the others went into the city. How was she to get away? She did not know and for a full hour lay there hidden and helpless wondering what on earth she could do. Finally the men, who had spent the time talking, draped a sail at the back of the boat to form a shelter with some shade and lay down to sleep. After they had not moved for several minutes, Anju crept out from her hiding place and stepped silently onto the quay. With her heart in her mouth and not daring to run she walked slowly towards the city streets before her. She had broken her prison, she was free!

Her joy was shattered however by sounds of shouting behind her. Had she been seen, worse had she been recognised? Anju did not wait to find out. She ran as fast as she could into the safety of the city crowds which packed the streets in a way that, if she had not seen it with her own eyes, she would not before have believed possible. Strange sights and smells assailed her from every side but she did not dare to stop. Anju ran on until she could run no more still clutching tightly the bundle containing her shell, in her good left arm.

Although a stranger in the city, Anju had some idea of which way to go from the stories she had heard. The temple with the Ganesh statue was by the market and since this was market day and all the people seemed to be going in one direction, they had to lead her there which they did. When she saw the market it was beyond her wildest imaginings, a sight of unbelievable activity and colour but despite its attractions, Anju did not go and explore. Not only did she have her pilgrimage to think of but one of the men from her village might recognise her. Why, she thought, did her arm have to make her so conspicuous.

Beyond the market lay the temple with its four great towers or gopurams covered in sculpture rising on each side of the courtyard. Now feeling the strength and purpose of her mission Anju walked through the main gate, an arch in one of the towers, pausing only to leave her sandals as one should at the entrance. Inside she went straight across an open paved area and entered the central low building passing along its outer corridors towards the middle where she knew the huge statue to Ganesh must be. Doubts already touched her mind. Would the great God grant her prayer and help the elephants. Would he even listen to her a mere girl, a child and a cripple. She had heard the elders in her own village talk of such things however and knew that they were for the gods and fate alone to decide. All she could do was play her part.

Finally Anju reached the central shrine and there to represent the deity was a giant statue of Ganesh, the elephant-headed God, covered in ghee or melted butter and flower petals from the day's offerings. She knew that she should have first gone to the temple offices and given money but she had none and they would have laughed at her shell. She had to find a priest to help her. Then Anju saw one, an old man bent with age and walking slowly with the aid of a stick, surely he would be sympathetic. She ran towards him unable to contain herself any longer. Then Anju did not know what to do and stood uncomfortably in front of him wishing the words she wanted to say would come but failing to find them.

The priest was old, he had learned much and seen even more; mostly of people. So when the young girl, she must have been about twelve or thirteen, with a twisted arm ran up and then stood uncertainly before him he guessed at least a little of her needs. His thoughts that they were because of her disability or perhaps a sick relative although wrong did not matter. He could see that she needed to be understood and that meant someone spending time listening to her story. Still, he had the time, it was one of the few benefits of his age he could enjoy.

Anju and the priest sat and talked for a long time, well into the afternoon. Slowly he learned of her story, admired her bravery but feared for her in a way that, despite his wisdom, he was not quite sure of. He did however help her make the offering. The shell was placed at the foot of the statue and under his strict instructions it was not moved that day or for some months afterwards. After that, it had been there so long that no one questioned that it should just stay there, which it did for many many years. Anju prayed with all her heart to Ganesh to help the elephants and it was almost with excitement that she began to think of returning to her village to see what had happened.

The priest walked with her to the quay and waved goodbye as he left her beside what he thought was her boat. About this however Anju had not been truthful. She had no idea where that craft had come from or was going but she had not dared to return to the ship from her own village fearing that the shouts she had heard did really mean that she had been discovered. Anju had not told the priest that she had come as a stowaway. Her courage then for the only time that day failed Anju. She wandered about on the quay wondering how she could get back on her own boat and even thinking that perhaps the time had come to just go and own up for what she had done. The idea was not an attractive one though and Anju was still trying to think of an alternative when the choice was taken from her. To her dismay, she looked up to see that her boat had set off and was already well out into the harbour, she was marooned in the city.

Anju was to leave that night but it was not in a way that she would have chosen. When it had got very very late she was allowed on board an old and rather dilapidated fishing boat from a village down the coast from her own. The problem was that she was already going to be in trouble with her parents and this was going to make it worse. The village from which the boat came was not as well off as her own and was not thought of as very respectable. The people she knew and her parents tended to look down on anyone from there and they would certainly not like her being with them. Still there had been no choice, she had to get back that night or she really would be for it, far far worse than any trouble she was in already. Whatever her parents might think of them, Anju was very grateful to the fishermen for taking her and she sat quietly in the bottom of the boat as they talked amongst themselves. At least out in the open air she didn't feel sick as the boat moved.

The fishing boat landed at its own village and before anyone had the chance to offer her shelter, Anju thanked the people who had helped her and set off along the beach towards her home. Her mind was occupied with the single thought that she must get back as soon as possible. Her village was however some way down the coast and as Anju walked and ran along the beaches in the darkness, she passed the fringes of the forest that reached down to the shore. Anju began to get frightened and ran on faster, as fast as she could, but the sand at the water's edge seemed to stretch on in front of her forever. Then it happened; the sound she had feared so much carried to her from the trees turning her blood to ice and her legs to jelly. It was the low half-growl of a leopard hunting.

Anju froze not daring to move and with her back to the sea but the great cat had seen her. Slowly, almost as if it knew its victim was trapped, its menacing form padded out from the line of trees at the top of the beach to stand dark against the near white sand. Its eyes shone in the night like those of a demon forming two piercing points of a green and evil spark. Anju stood transfixed with terror and, with her whole soul and being remembering the priest and the temple, prayed to Ganesh for help. Her little shell would have to serve as the offering for both prayers now and even more Anju hoped that the God would understand. The leopard however began to advance a second growl breaking from its throat. It was at that very moment though that the moon, which, although full, had been hidden behind clouds, broke through casting a clear path of brilliant light across the sea from the beach far out to the horizon. The leopard stopped, was unsure, and stepped back a pace. The moon's rays shone full on a great white horse standing at the sea's edge with its hooves only just in the water and it was surrounded by what seemed to be a luminous blue haze. Anju looked round and ran towards the animal not knowing what else to do. The horse stepped up onto a raft that floated almost submerged and unseen beside it, and Anju threw herself on to the logs in the absolute relief of the terror she had escaped not caring what might happen next.

The raft moved silently from the shore, too fast to have been caught simply by a mere current, and slipped purposefully through the waves. Anju lost all sense of time, speed or direction and in all the voyage, the horse just stood there beside her staring out towards the horizon. Then the animal stiffened and became more alert, it had seen something. Anju strained her eyes to try and glimpse in the moonlight what it might be. At last she saw a faint outline, in the distance there was a small low island and the raft was making straight towards it. Anju could not remember ever having heard of an island like it anywhere along the coast and she was never with certainty to see that land again, so it was with some fear of the unknown that she watched the rapidly approaching shore before her. When the raft glided up to a beach in a small bay and touched the sand however she had no doubt what she should do, what it seemed she was meant to do. Anju stepped ashore and looked round her, she could see everything very clearly despite its still being night since in that place the moon seemed to shine more strongly than ever before and the night was now perfectly clear. In the silver light, she could easily make out a path running down to the top of the beach which ended where the sand began. Instinct from she knew not where took her to that path and she started to climb its slope as it led to the top of the small hill that was the island's centre. As she climbed she could hear no sound other than the gentle noise of the waves breaking on the coast behind her, otherwise all was silence. Near the summit the path turned sharply and as Anju rounded that bend what she saw remained the wonder of her life.

There in front of her, cut into a low rock cliff like a cave, was a temple of pillars and sculptures. All around the entrance hung hundreds of oil lamps and their light bathed the scene in a soft, warm orange glow. No people however were to be seen anywhere. Anju, fascinated, crept closer and peered inside and her heart leapt for joy. There standing happily in a new temple home was her elephant and its daughter side by side. The mother's leg was still bent stiffly but Anju at once saw that it no longer bothered her, the great animal was content and carried her weight easily and without fear. The elephants were however not alone. Beside them on a low platform of rock lay a wonderful gem of clear crystal that seemed to reflect light of any colour as it touched it and sitting beside the stone was a mouse. Anju felt that she could have gazed at that jewel for hours, it seemed so close to her own heart and the sadness of her life but she did not have the chance to see or notice much more. The back of the temple began to be occupied by a great light that filled the air beside a large carving of a beautiful yet strong image of a head with three faces looking outwards to the three sides of the cave around it. The light became too powerful for her to look into but with it was a sound that Anju knew well, the noises of a great elephant walking slowly and its breathing, a sound familiar but magnified a thousand times. As the light and the sounds of the elephant grew more brilliant and louder, the jewel began to pulse with an energy that seemed to Anju like fire that leapt up all around the temple in its cave.

'Ganesh,' Anju whispered out loud but a voice seemed to answer her.

'No I am older, far older.'

Then the mother elephant, her elephant, turned to the light, touched the jewel with her trunk and then stretched it out to Anju in the familiar blessing that she knew. When the trunk rested on Anju's forehead, the touch was like the flames of an inferno. It was as if all the rejection and suffering that Anju had ever felt was reflected back on to her and her withered arm felt as if a white hot knife had been plunged into it.

That was all Anju could remember clearly, she might have even fainted at that moment, who could tell. Later she had a vague recollection of stumbling down the path, of being back at the beach and finally collapsing on the raft from which the horse had now gone but that was all. Anju woke early the following morning lying on the beach below her village and just lay there until she was found. She would have been in terrible trouble and her story would have been dismissed as a child's silly dream or excuse if it had not been for two things. Firstly, the whole town was taken up with the mysterious disappearance that night of the two elephants from the temple. So taken up with this were most people that they did not even listen to Anju at all and secondly, Anju's arm although still withered had suddenly gained the strength and function that it had always lacked. Neither event however was without its problems. As far as the elephants were concerned, it was strange that in contrast to the general ill will and bad treatment they had been receiving many now seemed very occupied with their welfare and there were various accusations and counter claims made as to who might have been responsible. About Anju's arm there was also dispute. Since it was still twisted and small some refused to believe it was better, even when she showed them what she could do. Her family learned to trust her but that feeling was not shared by everyone and when it was known that she was now helping to make the fishing nets, some refused to buy them saying that because of her the nets could not be relied on. The situation continued uneasily for a year or two but mostly the problems remained.

Through her family's new respect, Anju did however begin to travel going frequently on the boats she had been excluded from before. One year she journeyed on from the city inland and came to a village where the silk weavers lived and worked. At once they were friendly to Anju and she stayed there for some time. As she watched the silk being made an idea formed in her mind. All right, if because of what her arm still looked like no one would trust her to weave the coarse fishing nets, she would show them how wrong they were and what she really could do, she would learn to make the finest and most delicate silks instead. So that is what she did. After some months with the weavers Anju had mastered the trade and then she went back to her own village. Soon her skill grew and she began to make some of the finest silks anyone could ever remember having seen. In her own small way Anju became quite famous and people would come for miles to the city market to buy her cloth when she took it there on the boat from the village.

To those with the shallow eyes of the surface, Anju was never thought of as a beauty and the prejudices that die so hard meant that she was never to marry. It was a good thing that she was so completely taken up with her new work and it was what she did for the rest of her life, right up to the day she died. When that time came she was old and had won great respect in her village. Her body was wrapped in one of the beautiful silks she had made and was carried to the beach where it was laid reverently to rest overnight. The following morning it was to be placed with due ceremony on a pyre of logs so that everything could be done as it should be. There was however one last mystery. By dawn the body was gone, it had disappeared without trace as the villagers were to recount for years afterwards. There was one account of Anju's passing but that was from a boy with a turned-in foot that would not straighten. He was always at the beach very early since he could not walk fast enough to keep up and go down with everybody else and the other children at the usual time. The boy's story was however given little attention, who could believe a child and a cripple after all. If anyone had listened though he could have told them of Anju's old frail body wrapped in the blazing silk drifting out to sea on a raft, a raft surrounded by mist and with the shape of a great white horse just visible standing beside her.

That boy became my father and on this the time of his own passing from this world I have done as he asked and written down all that he told me just as he saw it or heard it from Anju herself as he grew up in their village. She was almost like a second mother to him and I am sure that she would have only told him the truth just as I know he would never have deceived me. I pray the Gods have been kind to them both.'

CHAPTER 13

Hugbundle Understands

'What a beautiful story,' said Candletail.

'Yes but it was very sad,' added Jasminemouse.

'Life's like that sometimes,' replied Martin and they all nodded.

Their serious mood was not to last though, it was Honeymouse who changed the subject.

'Do they really wrap food in banana leaves in India?'

'In the South they do,' said Chandra.

'What everything, even chocolate biscuits?'

'No not everything, and not chocolate biscuits, they come in packets like everywhere else. Mind you when Anju was alive I don't think they had chocolate biscuits in India.'

'Oh, that makes the story even sadder,' said Honeymouse.

'Well they did have things to make up for it like Jangri and Ladoos,' said Chandra.

'What's a Jangri?' asked Snuggletoes.

'Not a Jangri, just Jangri you get lots of them together. It's, well it's a very special sweet a bit like toffee and honey all mixed up only not as chewy as toffee and they're very sweet and covered in sugar and syrup.'

'And Ladoos,' said Jasminemouse.

'They're a bit the same only they're not quite as sweet and they're made up into balls and they've got a special flavour.'

'When do you have them?' asked Sunfur.

'All the special times like festivals and weddings and parties, times when it's happy - and the smells when they're being made, they're fantastic.'

'You don't happen to have any do you,' said Honey-mouse hopefully.

Chandra shook her head.

'No, I'm afraid I don't but I'll get you all some if you like when we get back to London.'

'Oh yes please.'

'Are there really temples in caves in India?' asked Star-whiskers.

'Yes, just like the one in the story,' said Chandra. 'The temple is cut as a cave literally out of solid rock, all together with its sculptures.'

'I'd love to see one,' said Wanderpaws.

'Yes they are very beautiful and very special - if you can ever go you should,' said Chandra.

It was at this point that Hugbundle interrupted, up till then no one had noticed that she had been unusually quiet and thoughtful.

'Excuse me, I'm sorry to butt in but there's something that's beginning to bother me. Have you noticed that there seem to be rather a lot of elephants in this adventure?'

All the others stopped and looked at each other.

'First there's the one that carried the Heartstone North. Then there's the strange elephant meeting Swiftclimb and Sailvoyage. Now we've got a whole story full of elephants. Apart from the mice, us, and a few people, elephants seem to be what it's about.'

'Yes and remember what we heard down by the lake when Moonbeam's body disappeared,' said Sunfur.

'That's right, an elephant!' went on Hugbundle, 'You were sure weren't you Chandra?'

'Oh yes, there was no doubt about it.'

'Don't forget your guess that the story about Anju might have been what the elephant gave Sailvoyage outside Madras,' said the Bishop.

'No I haven't forgotten,' replied Hugbundle looking out of the window and into the distance, 'that's what started me thinking. Do you think I was right?'

'We can't be sure but you could well be,' said the Bishop, 'it would fit after all.'

'Yes, what better way to introduce yourself if someone doesn't know you than to tell or give them a story about you,' said Sunfur.

'That's right!' Wanderpaws cut in, 'After all we do it all the time so why not an elephant.'

'You don't think that the elephant that met Sailvoyage was one of Anju's friends from the temple,' gasped Snuggletoes.

'No I don't,' replied Hugbundle, 'I may not be an expert on science like some of you at the observatory but even I don't find the idea of an ordinary elephant sneaking up behind you unnoticed very easy to believe. Even less one with a bad leg.'

'Anyway there was only one elephant and I don't think Anju's friend and her daughter would have gone anywhere without each other,' said Jasminemouse.

'No I don't think it was Anju's friend,' repeated Hugbundle,' I think it might have been someone older, far older.'

CHAPTER 14

What is to be done?

The mice and Chandra spent the rest of the day after Sunfur and Starwhiskers had gone down the Stonekeeper's tunnel quietly. They all felt like a rest, too much had been happening all at once and there was too much to think about. The same instincts led them to an early night and they were to sleep very soundly.

The following morning they woke up feeling much better, well after they had had breakfast anyway. They were still sitting in the kitchen of the old rectory when the cathedral bells started ringing.

'It must be Sunday!' said Wanderpaws in surprise, everyone had quite lost track of the days with so much going on.

Just then Martin and Simon put their heads round the door and then they came in.

'Do you want to come to the service?' asked Simon slightly nervously.

'It's all right,' added Martin looking straight at Chandra, 'we know you wouldn't feel about it quite as we do, no one here would expect you to. To us in some ways it's what things are all about, after all it's not just our religion and faith, it became our calling and our work as well. Your life has been different and in Wellminster if not elsewhere no one would look for you to pretend to be anything you did not want to be, or look down on you for not being the same. There are some very beautiful parts of the service though and, if you would like to come, it would mean a lot to share them.'

138

'Yes I would,' said Chandra, 'I would like to very much.'

'And me,' said Hugbundle.

'Yes, of course, no one would leave you out Hugbundle or any of you, why don't you all come?'

'Will the candles be lit?' asked Jasminemouse.

'They always are,' said Simon, 'all of them.'

'And will there be singing?' asked Sunfur who liked choirs.

'Yes and anyone who wants to can join in,' replied Simon.

'And will there be lunch afterwards?' said Snuggletoes.

'Yes!' laughed Martin, 'but you don't have to come to the service to get fed, that would happen anyway. Just come if you want to.'

'Oh yes I do,' said Snuggletoes, 'I always did. I was just.... well I was just checking about later on, that's all.'

'I think we all want to come,' said Starwhiskers. 'We'd love to see what happens and what you do, it would be so much part of everything else here, but it's just fun to find out our favourite bits now so we can get even more excited.'

'Yes I should have known,' said Martin, 'Candletail always wants to know everything in advance for the same reason, only then she complains if something doesn't happen which is a surprise as well.'

'Oh yes we like surprises as well,' answered Honeymouse, 'of course we do, they're fun.'

So Chandra and the mice went to the service that Sunday morning in Wellminster. The cathedral was very full but they still found seats and sat and watched everything as it happened from a pew opposite the Heartstone window. There were candles, hundreds of them, and the singing was very beautiful and Sunfur loved it. The music was however not just provided from one source. Yes, there was the normal church choir in their place in front of the altar. They faced each other in two groups one on each side of the aisle and wore brilliant red cassocks and white surpluses but if you looked carefully at the carved wooden screens behind them, there was another group of singers. About twenty or thirty mice were there all holding tiny sheets of music in front of them and all singing with the main choir, except once when they even had a solo section to do by themselves. These were not the only mice involved in the service either. On the front of one of the pillars, fairly high up so you could see it, was a board which gave the numbers of the hymns so the congregation could look them up and join in if they wanted to. On ledges cut into either side of the board sat Dennis, Colourpaw, Whiskersketch and Rainbowtail and as each hymn was sung they would put up a new number for the next one using beautiful cards with the figures on that they had painted earlier. Mice were also busy helping to play the massive organ that filled one side of the building behind the choir. The organist sat in the middle and to either side of her were rows and rows of knobs that you could pull or push to change the sound that the organ made. These are called stops and beside each sat a mouse ready to operate their stop if it was needed for that piece of music. The best job was to pull on the stop that after you had done it made everything very very loud, so loud that you could feel the vibrations even through the great stone floor. The smallest mouse could work it and they all loved to hear what they had done.

In the middle of the service, the Bishop got up and went to the front to a special raised section called a pulpit to give his sermon. Now a sermon is where someone who is one of the clergy at a church talks to everyone who has come to the service about things that have been happening in a way that should make the people think more about what is going on and about what might be done to make things better. A good sermon can be fun to listen to and be something you can get a lot out of, even if you do not share the religion of the church. A bad sermon is one of the most boring things there is. Now as I have said, the main idea of a sermon is to make you think and that means that it must leave you time to do just that, which is why most of the bad ones are that way simply by being far too long. The Bishop knew this and wanted people to get something from what he said which is why he always got Candletail to help him. She would sit beside his notes with an egg timer, the sort where sand runs down from the top to the bottom, and when all the sand had run through and she thought he had said enough she would hold up her paw and he knew it was time to come to an end. The sand only took five minutes to run through though so if the sermon was interesting enough, Candletail would turn it over more than once so the Bishop could carry on. They had been doing things together that way for years and, as a result, the Bishop's sermons were some of the best and most popular in the whole area and that made him very happy as well.

After the service, they all went over to the Bishop's palace for Sunday lunch and, much to Snuggletoes' delight, Martin had remembered to make some chocolate cream sauce. After lunch, the Bishop had to go and visit another church in the area he was responsible for and Martin, Candletail and Simon went with him. Chandra and the mice all went into the study and sat there quietly for some minutes as if no one could think of the right thing to say. Then Sunfur broke the silence.

'Would I be right in thinking that we are all rather preoccupied with a promise that we made to Moonbeam?'

There were nods of agreement.

'And that however exciting all our new discoveries may be that the time has come to actually do something?'

141

'Yes but what,' said Wanderpaws, voicing the problem that had been on all their minds.

'We have a map that was kept just for us,' said Starwhiskers, 'providing the Professor's cracked the key so we can understand it that has to be a start.'

'Yes but a start to what?' asked Chandra.

'Well maps are usually the start of a journey,' said Honeymouse.

'But where to?' asked Jasminemouse.

'The prophecy said that the travellers, and that's us, would continue the work in London. Remember?' said Sunfur.

'That's right!' agreed Starwhiskers.

'Yes but we don't need Swiftclimb's map to get to London do we,' Wanderpaws cut in impatiently.

'No,' said Hugbundle, 'but we might need it once we got to India.'

'India!' the others chorussed in surprise.

'Why not,' said Hugbundle looking rather shy.

'Isn't why a rather better question,' asked Wanderpaws.

'It could be fun,' said Snuggletoes, hopefully.

'Yes but we've got a promise to keep,' Wanderpaws continued, 'and sometimes that can mean more than just having a good time.'

'But we would be keeping our promise,' said Hugbundle, 'once we had brought some more of the Heartstone back anyway.'

'Are you feeling all right?' asked Honeymouse.

'I think so,' said Hugbundle although she didn't sound all together sure.

'Now let's just slow down a minute,' said Sunfur turning to Hugbundle, 'You're saying that we should go to India, find the Heartstone and bring some more pieces of it back to England?'

'That's it,' said Hugbundle.

'You're not all right,' said Honeymouse and she would have said more only Sunfur held up her paw for silence so she could continue.

'Well Wanderpaws has asked the next question already - why? Can you explain?

'Possibly,' said Hugbundle looking rather nervous.

'Then if we promise to all keep quiet till you have finished I think you ought to try.'

Hugbundle swallowed hard and looked round the room.

'Well it's like this. Chandra you said that Wellminster was not like any other place you had been to.'

'That's right.'

'Now this adventure all started when some very nasty people tried to stop Chandra's show didn't it?'

There was a murmur of agreement.

'And I know how nasty they are because I met them with Chandra in the park that night down by the observatory.'

Hugbundle shivered at the memory.

'Now when you say that Wellminster is different, Chandra, does that mean that although some nasty things may still happen, at least it's as if someone cares a bit more than in London, as if someone or something is on your side.'

'That's right,' said Chandra, 'but I wasn't completely alone in London, not after I met you lot anyway.'

The mice all smiled.

'No, but apart from us Wellminster is different.'

'No doubt about it.'

'But the Bishop said that it hadn't always been that way so it must have changed when the Heartstone came.'

'What are you getting at?' asked Wanderpaws more thoughtful now.

'Just this,' went on Hugbundle, 'bringing the Heartstone to Wellminster changed things here so if we want

143

to make things different in London perhaps we should try and take some fragments of the Heartstone there as well.'

'You're right,' said Starwhiskers, 'but what an adventure that would be.'

'Yes but we promised didn't we,' said Hugbundle.

'We certainly did!' cried Snuggletoes.

'So you are saying that we go to India with Swiftclimb's map, follow the directions that may have been left for Sailvoyage, find where the Heartstone was taken in the mountains, bring some of the fragments back and hide them in London just like Sailvoyage did in Wellminster?' asked Wanderpaws in a tone of disbelief but with more respect than before.

Hugbundle hesitated for a second.

'Um..... yes that's about it.'

All the mice looked at each other in amazement. Only Chandra seemed to have understood what Hugbundle had suggested and she just looked at the little mouse in more wonder and friendship than she even had before.

'You do realise that there might just be one or two problems do you,' said Wanderpaws, only he sounded more as if he wanted to solve them than let them stop the idea.

'Oh yes,' replied Hugbundle.

'Little things like the fact that any trail left by Swiftclimb in India is now nearly two hundred years old.'

'That was one of them.'

'Problems or not,' said Sunfur, 'Hugbundle is right, it's the only thing we can do and I think we should start making plans right now. The first thing is who wants to be on this adventure?'

'Me!' said Snuggletoes emphatically.

'Right. Starwhiskers?'

'Definitely.'

'Honeymouse and Jasminemouse?'

144

They looked at each other for a moment then nodded.

'Wanderpaws? We need you, you're the only one with experience of this sort of thing.'

Wanderpaws hesitated.

'Yes I'm with you and I'm sorry that I asked so many questions earlier. Of course I want to come.'

'Hugbundle? After all it is your idea.'

'That depends if Chandra's coming.'

All the mice turned to look at Chandra.

'Well what about it Chandra,' said Sunfur, 'you know India which is more than we do and even if the Heart-stone is mouse business this is rather your adventure.'

'I know and I want to come, perhaps more than anything I've ever wanted to do before, but there is a problem.'

'Oh come on,' said Jasminemouse, 'we need you to tell us which sweets to buy, all those Ladoos and things.'

Chandra smiled.

'Yes of course but that's not what's wrong.'

'Well what is?' asked Sunfur.

'It's that whilst you may be able to go anywhere you want to, it's not so easy for people. We have to have tickets to go on aeroplanes and ships and to get to India they cost a lot of money, more than I've got. Dance isn't a very well paid thing to do.'

'Not that silly stuff money again,' said Honeymouse.

'I'm afraid so,' said Chandra.

'Dance like yours should be well paid,' added Jasmine-mouse.

'Well it isn't. It would take me years to save up enough to go.'

'I might be able to help,' said Snuggletoes.

'How's that,' asked Honeymouse.

'Well I know money is silly but there are one or two things it can be useful for so I've been saving some up. I was going to spend it on decorations for Christmas but Chandra can have it to buy her ticket to India.'

145

'How much have you got?' asked Starwhiskers.

'50p,' said Snuggletoes proudly.

'I don't think that's quite enough,' said Sunfur, 'but it's a kind offer and we'll keep it in mind.'

'Look Chandra,' said Wanderpaws, 'if you want to come you should start thinking of yourself as part of the adventure right now. The prophecy said 'when the mice shall come with the moon' and as far as that went, you were the moon. So if the mice should come with the moon then they should go with it, or in this case her, as well. Money is just another one of those problems we'll have to solve and the best person to ask about that is the Professor, he always seems to be able to put his paws on some when he needs it. Leave that to him, you're coming.'

'So Hugbundle,' asked Sunfur, 'that just leaves you.'

'Oh I'm coming if Chandra is, you're not going to leave me behind.'

And so the group for the new adventure was almost complete.

After their decision, Chandra and the mice went for a walk down by the lake and into the woodland beyond. They did not notice Screechfoot and Croakwing as they perched high up in the trees above them. By the time they turned to go back, it was beginning to get dark and when they reached the rectory night had fallen. They heard the bells but did not go to the evening service at the cathedral preferring each other's company at a simple meal they had prepared. Later in the evening, it was almost nine o'clock, Sunfur suddenly made a suggestion.

'I want to go and have one more look at the Heartstone window before we go to bed. After what we have decided to do, it somehow just seems right.'

The others agreed. Also because it seemed right, Sunfur took the cloth Sailvoyage had wrapped the Heartstone in, to be an additional link to the past. The side door of the cathedral was open and they slipped inside, there were still a few lights left on although all of the candles had burned down or been snuffed out. Together they stood and gazed up at the Heartstone where they knew it was in the window high above them. There was however no answering flicker or response, the sky was overcast and there was no light for the stone to feed on. Their arrival had been seen and Candletail, Colourpaw and some more of the cathedral mice came and joined them. After several minutes being with the stone, they all turned to go and began to make their way down the aisle and back towards the side door they had come in by. They had not taken more than a few paces however when the lights started to flicker and dim, then they went out all together.

'Power cut,' said Starwhiskers.

'I'll get some candles,' said Colourpaw.

Colourpaw did not have time however to fetch the lights. Within seconds a sickly luminous green glow began to spill into the blackness of the aisle in front of them. It was coming from between two of the pews on their left. They were all absolutely still, tense and silent. Then one of the cathedral mice shrieked.

'Wimptread!' and suddenly pandemonium broke out.

Mice rushed in all directions diving into nooks and crevices to try and find a hiding place squeaking frantically and tripping over each other as they did so. Honeymouse and Jasminemouse disappeared under the nearest pew, Snuggletoes with them. Hugbundle jumped up and hid in Chandra's coat and Wanderpaws dashed off to the right as they learned later to try and find a lantern. Starwhiskers and Sunfur stood their ground in front of Chandra and they all waited to see what would happen next.

Slowly the green glow got brighter and they thought they could hear a soft, a very soft, rubbing sound as if something furry was moving over the stone. Then the

147

spectral figure they had feared shuffled into view in front of them to stand in the centre of the aisle barring their way. They saw the outline of a rabbit, only this was a creature in which some horrible trick had been played its face and limbs were so twisted and deformed. That might have produced some sympathy if it had not been for the eyes however. These were sunken, blank and unmoving, expressionless, and seemed to look at you and yet through you dismissing your very existence as they did so. Chandra, Sunfur and Starwhiskers were looking at Wimptread, the ghost of Wellminster, and instinctively they recoiled in loathing and stepped backwards towards the altar. Wimptread however advanced. Sunfur dropped the cloth and they took two more paces backwards. Wimptread still came on towards them.

Wimptread had been a presence in the cathedral for many years. No one knew where he or she, no one knew that either, came from or exactly why. The first reports of the ghost's appearance were from the night before a meeting was held in the old rectory to decide whether Gandhi, the great Indian leader, should be invited to speak at the cathedral during his visit to England in nineteen thirty one. A new bishop had just been appointed and he was not a very strong man, preferring to avoid problems rather than confront them. There had been opposition to extending such an invitation from some senior church leaders in London and the meeting in the old rectory had been between them, the Bishop and others from the cathedral to resolve the issue. Wimptread was seen the night before in the room they were going to use. The following day against the advice of his staff the bishop decided that it would be best not to invite Gandhi to speak so as to avoid any possible trouble. It was only some weeks later when it was too late to change things that the Bishop asked for and was given a transfer away from Wellminster and to another cathedral. His close friends at the time who helped arrange the move were very worried about him since he kept on saying odd things such as there was a window in the cathedral that didn't like him. It had been that way with Wimptread ever since. Anything that the rabbit appeared at and in some way touched never took place. Not because anyone or anything stopped it but simply through a fear that Wimptread seemed to be able to give of what could go wrong. If you think about it, that is very silly since something could go wrong with anything you might do and if you thought about it in that way, nothing, even the smallest thing, would ever get done.

Chandra and the mice from the observatory did not know any of this however as she, Sunfur and Starwhiskers stood and faced Wimptread. Already the ghostly rabbit's spell was beginning to work on them. They wanted to find a light, make a noise, at least do something but fears they could not explain gripped them and held them where they were. Sunfur saw the cloth and took one step forwards to retrieve it from where it had fallen but at once dropped back to stand where she had been. Wimptread shuffled closer to the cloth, sniffing at it from a distance. Candletail who knew something of the story and had just been told the plans for the expedition to India called out from under a pew.

'Get the cloth, get the cloth! If Wimptread touches it the expedition will never happen.'

Sunfur, Starwhiskers and Chandra however still did not move, held as they were by Wimptread's presence. Seeing this, Candletail slipped out from her hiding place to try and help but as soon as she was in Wimptread's gaze she too moved no further and just stood where she was, helpless and afraid to even tremble. Wimptread took one more half shuffle, half hop towards the cloth. Two more paces and the rabbit would touch it, already it lay in the luminous green glow that spread out in all directions. If the omens that Wimptread had always brought before were true, the expedition was in great danger. Then a small figure stepped out from the shadows at the edges of the aisle and stood between Wimptread and the cloth, it was a mouse. The newcomer met Wimptread's full stare and returned it with an unflinching gaze.

'Be gone, you are not welcome here,' she said.

It was Magicnose.

'Go back! You will not touch this business and I will not let you taint it,' Magicnose continued.

Wimptread continued to look at and through her with those awful eyes, then made another shuffling movement forwards. Magicnose held her ground but those watching could see that she was trembling all over as she stood facing her adversary, their noses no more than an inch apart. If she moved there would be nothing between Wimptread and the cloth.

'Go, you will not touch this!' she said, but her voice was not as steady now and they all wondered how much longer her defiance could last.

Then a voice came from the darkness to the side of the altar.

'Quick Colourpaw come out from where you are hiding and get over here now! I need some help and bring someone else with you - it'll take at least three but whatever you do don't look at Wimptread, not even for a second, don't look back just follow my voice.'

It was Dennis. Colourpaw reached out and grabbed Snuggletoes by the paw and started towards the altar.

'Whatever you do don't look behind you,' Dennis was still saying, and they didn't.

Snuggletoes was very frightened but he and Colourpaw held on to each other in the darkness and listened to Dennis's voice ahead of them. They also noticed another sound in the air they had not heard before, a low quiet rushing noise which seemed to be coming from in front of them as well. At last they reached Dennis, from over their shoulder they could still hear Magicnose telling

150

Wimptread to get back, at least she had not fallen to the fears that the rabbit must have placed in her yet. Dennis was talking quickly.

Right, we haven't got much time. We've got to get up to the organ, I've switched it on and you'll see why later. Now Colourpaw I've brought two of our ladders, I'll lead, you follow up the first and then roll it up for the next bit whilst I get the second in place. You,' he turned to Snuggletoes, 'follow Colourpaw, right.'

'O K,' squeaked Snuggletoes nervously.

The three mice began the climb up towards the organ. Dennis led and would scramble up with a rope ladder or throw it skilfully in front of him to bridge a gap. He always seemed, even in the dark, to be able to get it to catch and hold on on the other side. Colourpaw and Snuggletoes followed. At last they hauled themselves over the last obstacle and collapsed in a heap on the floor of the place where the organ was, high up from the ground. Still they did not look back or down fearing the effect Wimptread might have on them even at that distance.

'All right,' said Dennis, 'this is what we do. You see that knob,' he turned to Snuggletoes as he pointed to one of the stops on a board to the right of the keys, 'get up there and get ready to pull it when I tell you.'

Snuggletoes nodded.

'Colourpaw come with me, I hope the two of us together will be heavy enough to make this work.'

Snuggletoes climbed up to the stop and Dennis and Colourpaw scrambled up to stand above the keyboard, beside the mice the keys looked huge, their white shadows being just visible with the tiny amount of light that penetrated down from the gloom to meet them.

'Right now pull,' shouted Dennis and Snuggletoes did pull as Dennis and Colourpaw jumped down onto one of the keys. The stop moved easily and stood jutting out from the board in its new position but the key proved

151

more difficult. For seconds that seemed like hours, it hovered only just down from its resting position as Dennis and Colourpaw frantically jumped up and down to try to get it to go further. Then slowly, ever so slowly, it started to sink under their weight and as it did so a great deep base note began to sound from one of the tall pipes which stood above and beside the organ itself. The note steadily got louder and louder still, Snuggletoes had pulled the stop which made it do that, and as its music filled the cathedral, Wimptread's spell began to weaken. The rabbit took one pace backwards and Magicnose advanced. Chandra bent down, grabbed the cloth and lifted Sunfur and Starwhiskers out of danger. For a terrible moment Dennis and Colourpaw could not hold the key in place and it began to rise under them but Snuggletoes dashed over and joined them after which it stayed firmly down. Below in the cathedral the music, even of that single note, was changing everything. Wimptread was now moving back down the aisle away from Magicnose. To the right, Wanderpaws appeared with a lantern which he lit and inspired by its light more mice dashed off and fetched lamps and candles which soon blazed in all directions. Wimptread finally turned and shuffled off to disappear in a remaining patch of darkness in a far corner. The mice had held Wellminster.

CHAPTER 15

Magicnose

The following morning the Bishop's study was the place for even more of a meeting than usual. The Bishop himself was there together with Martin, Simon, Candletail and Dennis. Then there was Chandra, Hugbundle, Sunfur, Starwhiskers, Honeymouse, Jasminemouse, Snuggletoes and Wanderpaws. This rather intimidating group was spread round the room whilst in the middle, on the edge of the Bishop's desk, sat Magicnose. To look at she was much like the other mice, although of course once you had got to know them you could have recognised her, but there was one very important difference. Compared to the others, Magicnose was very serious and sad, almost withdrawn, and yet this seemed to give her a power that no other mouse shared. Wanderpaws was asking her a question.

'So how could you stand up to Wimptread like that, none of the rest of us could manage to do anything!'

A flicker of regret passed over Magicnose's already sad face.

'That is a story that I would rather not tell now, probably ever for that matter. All you need to know is that once, it now seems a long time ago, I faced Wimptread for the first time, like you did last night. I was filled with all the doubts that you felt and they made me so afraid that I broke a very special promise I had made to someone. The person I let down was hurt very badly by what I did and as far as I know is still sad because of it. I only realised how wrong I had been once it was too late and

153

although ever since I have been trying to put things right, so far I have been able to do very little, practically nothing. When you have lived with something like that for long enough you do not give way to Wimptread a second time however scared you may be. I have a score to settle with that rabbit and one day I hope I will get my chance.'

'Yes but no one could blame you for what Wimptread made you do,' said Honeymouse.

'Couldn't they,' replied Magicnose, 'I'm afraid I think they should. After all I know now that Wimptread can be beaten if you really try, perhaps I could have done that the first time as well.'

'Yes but you are older now and learned from what happened then, nobody else has ever stood up to Wimptread at all,' said Chandra.

'Possibly,' sighed Magicnose, 'but all that Wimptread ever made me do was to be frightened of how I could be hurt. I didn't even think that I was doing something far worse to someone else. That's what makes it so bad - I didn't even think.'

'Well, you are trying to do what you can now for the person you wronged aren't you,' said the Bishop.

Magicnose nodded before she replied.

'Yes, but so far I haven't even been able to find them.'

'Is that why you travel so much?' asked Candletail, still in some awe of Magicnose from her reputation.

'One of the reasons,' was the characteristically guarded answer.

'What do you mean about a score to settle,' continued the Bishop, 'you should be careful, two wrongs don't always make a right.'

'True,' said Magicnose, 'and I've certainly done enough wrong already but I can't just leave that rabbit to go on wrecking beautiful things the way it does. Somehow it's got to be stopped. It doesn't just appear in Wellminster you know.'

The others looked surprised.

'No, there are tales of Wimptread to be heard all over England and in other countries too.'

'Well whatever you may have to say against yourself, you saved our expedition last night,' said Starwhiskers to Magicnose, 'and we've all been talking about little else since and we've come to a decision. Like you we are not just travelling for fun and it was not by chance that we were here for the third night of the blue fire. We are on an adventure, an extremely important adventure, and if you would like to, we would be very happy if you joined us.'

Magicnose looked round the room and smiled, it was the first time any of them had seen her do so since they met.

'That's very kind of you,' said Magicnose, 'and I would like to help in any way I can but I still have my own business to take care of, I could not leave that all together.'

'That's all right,' said Honeymouse, 'Perhaps we could help you at the same time.'

'That would depend on where you are going,' replied Magicnose, 'but if you want to tell me your story we might be able to work something out.'

'Then you should make yourself comfortable,' said Sunfur, 'because it's a very long story and to understand you will have to hear all of it.'

'That I had already guessed,' said Magicnose, 'perhaps you should get started.'

'Well it all starts with Chandra and some things that happened in London,' Sunfur began.

'And me,' said Hugbundle.

'Yes, and Hugbundle,' Sunfur continued, 'she was the first mouse to get involved, without her none of this would ever have happened.'

So it was that starting with Chandra and Hugbundle, Magicnose was told the whole story of everything that

155

had happened ever since that first day in Langley Park which for them all by then seemed a very long time ago. Being a lengthy story, it was only late in the morning when Sunfur got to the part where she explained why they had gone to the cathedral the night before and so had met Wimptread. When Chandra and the other mice had all finished telling their parts of the adventure, Magicnose sat quietly for a long time, obviously thinking about something.

'So you are going back to London and then off to India,' Magicnose finally said.

'That's right,' said Starwhiskers.

'Well I can't come in the same way as you can, or make the promise you have made but London and India suits me as well as anywhere so we could travel together.'

Wanderpaws looked hesitant but Sunfur nodded reassuringly.

'I think that that is all we would expect,' said Starwhiskers, 'welcome to the adventure.'

'One thing I must ask you though,' said Magicnose looking round the room at each of them in turn, 'have any of you seen any porcupines either round Wellminster or in London?'

'No and I'm rather glad I haven't,' said Honeymouse.

'Have you ever met a porcupine?' asked Magicnose.

Honeymouse looked uncomfortable.

'Well no I've never actually met one .... but I've heard a lot about them and they don't sound very nice.'

'Then I've got a suggestion for you,' said Magicnose, 'don't make up your mind till you have met one and when you do, try seeing what's in front of you rather than something you have been told to find. You could be in for a surprise.'

'I don't think any of us have seen any porcupines,' said Hugbundle trying to help, 'why are you interested, do you know any of them?'

156

'One or two,' was all that Magicnose would say in reply.

'So now we have a party of nine for our trip,' said Sunfur changing the subject, 'we'd better make some plans and get started.'

'Well there is still the little problem of the money for Chandra's ticket,' said Wanderpaws.

'Silly,' said Honeymouse meaning to say more but she was not given the chance.

'There I may be able to help,' said the Bishop, 'now you have made up your mind what you want to do there is something that you should know about.'

'What's that,' asked Starwhiskers.

'Simply that I have a fund of money in safe keeping which is now at your disposal.'

'Is it more than 50p?' said Snuggletoes.

'Yes it is quite a lot more than 50p,' replied the Bishop, 'in fact with all the interest that it has earned over the years it is now several thousand pounds.'

'Are you serious,' said Wanderpaws.

The Bishop nodded.

'Where did it come from?' asked Sunfur.

'That I'm not sure,' said the Bishop, 'the fund was set up by one of my predecessors way back, only just after Sailvoyage came to Wellminster. Moonbeam had an idea that it was started with money from the sale of a diamond Sailvoyage had brought with him but even he was not sure. The only thing which is certain is that the bishops of Wellminster have run it but strictly on behalf of the Watchmice and it has only one stated purpose, to be given to the travellers if they leave on a journey having seen the Heartstone, if they have need of it.'

'You see Chandra, I told you you were coming,' said Wanderpaws, 'that's that problem solved.'

'Yes there is certainly enough to buy Chandra a ticket to India,' the Bishop continued, 'but it now sadly falls to me to give you the advice which I know Moonbeam meant to say. You should give serious thought to buying tickets for all of you. There are people who will try and stop you from doing what you plan and your all having tickets will make it easier to stay together. Remember what you told me about what happened on the train when you came here.'

'We're not likely to forget that,' said Jasminemouse.

'The Bishop's certainly got a point,' said Hugbundle who liked the idea of having her own ticket on an aircraft even more than she had enjoyed having one on the train.

'O K we all get tickets to India,' said Sunfur who had seen the sense in the Bishop's suggestion from the beginning.

'Fine,' said the Bishop, 'now the money can be made available to you through a London solicitor, you can trust him completely. He's a friend of mine. He's got an office in Westminster close to Victoria and he's called Peter Hamil.'

'That's fantastic,' said Chandra, 'how do we get in touch.'

'I'll phone him now if you like,' replied the Bishop.

'Please do,' said Snuggletoes who also liked the idea of having his own ticket and the bishop went over to the telephone and dialled a London number.

Once the Bishop had spoken to Peter Hamil, he passed the phone over to Chandra who after a brief discussion arranged to meet the lawyer in St James' Park around one o'clock the following Thursday. The park was close to Peter's office and they both agreed they would rather meet somewhere where they would not be noticed. Peter knew about all the problems there could be for Chandra and for the plan especially in London. Following Chandra to his office and guessing something of what was going on would, as Peter had said, be far too easy. To make sure that she did not attract any unnecessary attention, the mice reluctantly agreed it would be best if Chandra went to the meeting in the park alone. Snuggletoes did offer to go and protect her but it was pointed out to him that there were not many places where you could buy ice cream in St James' Park in November and without it, there would not be much he could do.

Outside the study window Screechfoot turned to Croakwing, they had been hiding in the bushes.

'Did you get all that?'

'Yes I heard every word.'

'Good, so did I, and I managed to see the number that that bishop dialled, that could be useful.

Croakwing rustled his wings in agreement.

'Right, our friends should be back this afternoon. I got a message that they're on their way now even if they did need longer down there than they first said. I think we should go and wait for them, they will be very interested in what we have found out.'

'Good idea,' said Croakwing and the two birds hopped down from the bush and round the corner of the building before taking off to disappear over the city.

Back inside the study Magicnose looked round at the window.

'Did you hear something?' she asked.

Everybody shook their heads.

'I must be imagining things then,' and she settled down again in her place on the desk.

'So the time has come for us to leave Wellminster,' said Starwhiskers with a tone of regret.

There was a murmur of agreement.

'Yes but not forever, you will come back,' said Candletail.

'Oh yes we'll be back,' said Honeymouse, 'it's nice here.'

'And you will write and tell us what happens,' said Dennis.

'I promise,' said Chandra, 'we're not going to forget you.'

'So we'd better be off tomorrow,' sighed Sunfur, 'does anyone know what time the trains are?'

'There's a timetable in the office,' said Simon, 'I'll go and look them up,' and he slipped out of the room.

'If you're not going till tomorrow there was one thing,' said Martin.

There was a pause, Jasminemouse was holding her breath and looked as if she was making a very big wish.

'Well I was wondering.......'

'Yes,' said Hugbundle trying not to look too excited.

'I was wondering if you would all like to have a farewell dinner with me tonight.'

'With choc......,' Snuggletoes didn't get any further, Martin was already nodding and smiling at him.

Chandra tried to preserve at least some sense of being polite.

'Yes I think we would all love to come,' she said sounding very serious and correct but then she and all the mice burst out laughing.

They spent the afternoon looking round the cathedral one last time and then when it was early evening they all went down to Martin's cottage. Candletail, the Doodlemice and Simon were already there and the Bishop soon joined them. It was the start of a very special evening. In a car park in the city however, a safe distance from the cathedral and under the cover of darkness, two men sat in a battered van, the woman who had been with them was no longer there. The window in the front door had been wound down and Screechfoot and Croakwing perched on the edge looking in. On the top of the dashboard sat Smirkmuzzle. One of the men was talking.

'Now you're sure that this was the number,' the man pointed to some notes he had made on a pad.

'Completely,' said Croakwing.

'Good because we will need it. Smirkmuzzle how do you feel like being a telephone engineer again for a bit?'

160

Smirkmuzzle sniggered.

'Why that way?' asked the other man.

'Because they will never trust a straight call but if we get them to phone the number of that London lawyer they'll believe anything they hear. Only after Smirkmuzzle has finished, they won't be speaking to London at all, they'll have been put straight through to us.'

'But won't they know it isn't him?' asked Screechfoot.

'Yes they know his voice but I'm not going to pretend to be him,' said the man, 'just someone with a message from him who they will trust because I'm speaking from his number. Get it?'

The others nodded.

'Then what?' asked Croakwing.

'You'll see,' said the man and Smirkmuzzle sniggered again, 'but if it's going to work we had better get started.'

'All right,' said Screechfoot, 'we'll be off but remember what you said about the mice, they're ours when you get them. You promised.'

'Don't worry,' answered the second man, 'you've done your bit, now it's up to us but you won't be forgotten.'

Screechfoot and Croakwing took off and flapped lazily away to find a roost for the night. One of the men started the van and it swung round and out of the exit to the car park to disappear jerkily up the road which led out of Wellminster. They did not go very far however. After about two miles, just as they were reaching the outskirts of the city, they turned into a side road and parked beside a manhole cover in the pavement. The first man climbed out and looked round cautiously trying not to be noticed. There was nobody about. Then his companion got out and joined him and together they lifted the manhole cover and peered inside with a torch.

'Come on Smirkmuzzle, we've found it,' said the first and Smirkmuzzle jumped down and had a look.

'That's it all right,' said the rat, 'the main telephone cable out of Wellminster on the London side. Pass me down the stuff.'

Smirkmuzzle scrambled down into the opening and one of the men went back to the van returning with a small bag of tools which he passed to the grubby waiting paw that was held up for them. By the light of their torch the two men watched as Smirkmuzzle cut through some of the wires and then connected two new ones to a pair of the cut ends.

'That should do it,' Smirkmuzzle said with a snigger.

Then he clambered out of the hole dragging the two wires behind him and the men partly replaced the cover so it did not look so suspicious. They all got into the back of the van pulling the wires behind them. Smirkmuzzle unpacked a telephone from a battered box and connected it to the wires.

'All yours,' he said with a grin.

'Right,' said the first man, 'now let's see if it works.'

He picked up the receiver and dialled the number of the cathedral. In the office the choir master was just packing up after the evening practice. He answered the call.

'Hello, Wellminster cathedral.'

'Oh good evening,' said the first man signalling for his partner and Smirkmuzzle to be quiet, 'my name is Reginald Stephens. I'm an associate of Peter Hamil, the London Solicitor, and I was wondering if I could leave a message for someone who is staying at the cathedral. Her name is Chandra and it's rather urgent.'

'Of course,' said the choirmaster reaching for a pad, 'what is it?'

'Just if you could ask her to phone me at Mr Hamil's office number as soon as possible and it must be some time this evening. It's London so that's 01 and the number is 246 80444.'

162

'Right I've got that,' said the choirmaster, 'and don't worry I know where she is. I can get the message to her tonight.'

'Thank you, thank you very much,' said the man and he put down the phone.

Smirkmuzzle and his companion burst out laughing.

'Perfect, that was absolutely perfect,' they said.

Back at the cathedral the choirmaster walked over to Martin's cottage and left the note for Chandra. The meal was finished and she read it out to the others.

'Do you think it's O.K.?' asked Wanderpaws.

'Oh yes,' said the Bishop, 'that's definitely Peter's number and I know there are other people he works with. Although I haven't actually heard him mention Reginald Stephens before I'm sure it's all right.'

'Then I'd better see what he wants,' said Chandra, 'have you got a phone Martin?'

'Yes it's in the hall, help yourself.'

Chandra went out and dialled the number. In the van the telephone rang and the first man let it for several times before he picked it up.

'Mr Hamil's office, Reginald Stephens speaking,' he said.

'Ah yes my name's Chandra; you left a message for me.'

'Yes that's right,' the man continued, 'thank you so much for calling back, it's about your meeting with Mr Hamil on Thursday. I'm afraid a very urgent case has come up, that's where he is now in fact working on it, and he asked me to contact you to make some alternative plans.'

'Oh fine,' said Chandra, 'when would you suggest.'

'Well the case is a very important one, a black family having some trouble on their estate.'

At this Smirkmuzzle and the other man clasped their hand or paw over their mouths to stifle an outburst of laughter but the first man continued unperturbed.

'Yes they need an injunction as fast as possible to protect them and that's going to keep Mr Hamil in court all of Wednesday and Thursday so he was wondering if you could meet him after work on Wednesday night instead.'

'Yes that should be possible,' said Chandra, 'what time?'

'Right, now that's the tricky bit,' the man went on, 'courts have a horrible habit of running late so it would have to be more in the evening I'm afraid, but you do live in London don't you?'

'Yes,' said Chandra.

'Oh good that makes things easier. Well how about eight thirty Wednesday night and we'd better make it the same place, the pond at the South East corner of St James' Park. Just off Birdcage Walk and Horse Guards, can't be too careful with this one can we.'

'No,' Chandra replied although she did not like the idea of the park at night, but it was in the centre of London and she did still want somewhere secret for the meeting.

'Right that's fine then, Mr Hamil will meet you Wednesday night at eight thirty in the park and please accept his apologies for any inconvenience but this case is very important to him.'

'No of course I understand completely,' said Chandra, 'I'll look forward to seeing him then and thank you very much for calling.'

'Not at all, a pleasure to help,' said the first man and he put the phone down.

'Brilliant,' laughed Smirkmuzzle, 'you fooled her completely! Now let's get back to London and make the necessary arrangements. We're going to have some fun on Wednesday night.'

'We certainly are,' said the first man with a grin, 'how many of your friends can you get together at the London base.'

'For this, hundreds,' sniggered Smirkmuzzle.

'Good well we'll grab her in the park and then bring her over and you can all have some fun,' the man continued, 'and remember the first thing we want to know is where those mice are. We want them as well.'

'Oh she'll tell us that soon enough,' said Smirkmuzzle, 'and a lot more besides. Not that it will do her any good of course but she won't know that till it's too late. I'm looking forward to this.'

'So are we,' said the second man, 'and we'll be bringing a couple of friends, they had some trouble on a train and they want to get even.'

'The more the better,' said Smirkmuzzle, 'it's going to be quite a party.'

The three of them got out of the van and disconnected the wires they had used whilst Smirkmuzzle put everything back under the cover as he had found it so as not to arouse any suspicion. He carefully twisted the wires he had cut back together so there would not be any fault that could lead to an engineer coming and finding what he had been up to. Then they all clambered back in the van, turned it round and headed off up the road to London. Back at Martin's cottage, Chandra told the others about the change in plan and everyone agreed that she had done the right thing, saying that this way it was better since they could see Peter Hamil a day earlier than they had hoped. Finally, apart from Martin, they all made their way back to the cathedral where having said good night to the Bishop and Simon, Chandra and the mice disappeared towards the rectory and bed knowing that they had to be up early the following day to catch the train to London.

CHAPTER 16

Hugbundle and the Fudge

At the station the following morning, Hugbundle made the surprise announcement that she was not going with them straight to London. What she planned to do was catch a different train and go further South to somewhere very special and catch up with them all in a couple of days' time. At first Hugbundle would not say what she was going to do but after persistent questions fuelled by typical mouse curiosity, she finally told them that in a place called Earndel, near the South coast, there was a sweet shop which made the best fudge in the whole country and she wanted to get some for Chandra.

So it was that Hugbundle climbed on board an earlier train alone and waved goodbye to all the others as they stood on the platform. Once the train had left, Hugbundle made friends with a little girl who was sitting in a carriage in one of the seats by a window. Together they watched the countryside speed by until just after lunchtime they were in Earndel. Hugbundle scampered off from the station and into the narrow streets of the town. Very soon she came to the place she was looking for; it was an old style shop with windows that bowed outwards and small panes of glass. Inside there were bottles and jars with sweets of every description and stacks of bars of chocolate and other things, enough to keep any mouse busy for years. Hugbundle however went straight over to a side counter above which was a large sign that read:

and she quickly climbed up onto the top of the counter itself.

'Hello,' said Hugbundle.

An old woman with white hair and gold framed glasses who had been tidying some boxes turned to see who it was. Then a smile of recognition spread across her face.

'Hello Hugbundle, fancy seeing you here!'

'I've come for some fudge, some very special fudge for a friend, and to see you again of course,' said Hugbundle.

'Well you are always welcome as I've told you often,' replied Mrs Thomas, Granny Thomas as everyone in the town knew her, 'come round here and make yourself comfortable.'

Granny Thomas helped Hugbundle across onto a shelf behind the counter. In the middle, there was a pile of mouse cushions and Hugbundle made herself happy on these whilst Mrs Thomas found her some of the best fudge that she had for lunch. It was wonderful and had only been made that morning. They spent the afternoon talking and tasting fudge and comparing the results from different recipes and that night found Hugbundle tucked safely up in a cosy bed in Granny Thomas' flat which was above the shop.

The following morning, Wednesday, Hugbundle arranged with Granny Thomas for a large box of fudge to be sent to Chandra in London and then left with a small bag, as full as she could carry, that she could take back herself at once. When Hugbundle got to the station, she discovered that there was not a train to London for quite a long time so she wandered off to explore. Very soon she found herself down by a beautiful river and having walked along the bank for some distance, Hugbundle turned off into a thick bed of reeds that grew at the water's edge. The reeds were all very close together and down at the bottom where Hugbundle was you got occasional glimpses of the sun as it shone down through the stalks above. It was very mysterious and Hugbundle liked it and she went deeper and deeper into the reed bed to see what she might find. Then she stopped, off to her left she heard voices and they did not sound very nice. Hugbundle crept forwards and came to the edge of a clearing. In the middle of it sat two rats and they were arguing.

'You fool, you've made me miss the train and now I can't get there.'

'All right, all right, so it took longer than I expected but how was I to know. Anyway what have you missed that was so good in the first place.'

'Oh nothing much, just possibly the best party Smirk-muzzle has ever given, that's all!'

At the mention of Smirkmuzzle, Hugbundle's heart missed a beat but she crept even closer so that she wouldn't miss anything, thinking it might be important. In one paw she still grasped the bag of fudge that Granny Thomas had given her. The rats continued shouting at each other.

'O.K. so you've missed one of Smirkmuzzle's parties, so what? Once you've been to one of those you've been to them all.'

'Oh no, this one was different. It was at the London base and there was going to be some fun. They're going to grab a woman, one of those you know, and then make her answer some questions. It's all been fixed, they tricked her with a fake phone call and she's going to turn up at St James' Park tonight and walk straight into the trap.'

Hugbundle jumped back in horror realising that they were talking about Chandra. As she did so the bag with the fudge rustled, the two rats stopped arguing and looked round.

168

'What was that?'

'I don't know, I didn't hear anything.'

'Well I did, let's take a look.'

'No, let's get out of here, remember that dog we saw earlier on. It might be stalking us.'

Hugbundle wondered about trying to sound like a dog growling but decided that she wouldn't be able to make it very convincing. Perhaps that police dog Rex hadn't been so bad after all she thought.

The two rats moved off and into the reeds on the other side of the clearing. Desperate, Hugbundle sat down and tried to think of what she should do, she had to help Chandra somehow. But what could she do? The rats had been talking about having missed the last train to London and Hugbundle realised that it had been a very long time since she had left the station; the sun was worryingly low in the sky and she must have missed the last train too. Then she had an idea, she would get back to the shop and Granny Thomas would phone Chandra and warn her. Almost at once, however, Hugbundle realised that she did not know Chandra's second name or her phone number and it would be no good phoning the observatory. All that silly museum business would still be going on and by the time the Professor was back in charge, it would be too late. Hugbundle wished that Sunfur or Magicnose was with her, they would know what to do, but she wasn't coming up with anything. Hugbundle sat back dejectedly and watched the sun as it seemed to rush lower and lower towards the horizon making her feel even more how time was running out. Then she heard a voice above her. Hugbundle looked up and saw a tiny, tiny mouse, the smallest she had ever seen except a baby, hanging on to one of the reed stalks.

'Is something wrong?' the mouse asked.

'Yes,' sniffed Hugbundle, 'something's very wrong.'

'Hold on then, I'll come down,' said the tiny mouse, 'oh my name's Micromiss, I'm a Harvest mouse.'

169

The tiny mouse climbed down until she was on the ground beside Hugbundle.

'So what is it?' she asked.

Hugbundle told her the briefest outline of what was about to happen and that Chandra, her special friend, was in very great danger. Micromiss sat back and thought for a minute.

'Well I'm not sure what we can manage because I don't come from round here, I'm on holiday with my family you see. Normally, we live in the corn fields in the country but when the summer's over and all the crop has been cut, sometimes we come down here by the river. It's great fun and we can climb up and down the reed stems just like at home. Anyway that doesn't matter now, somehow we have got to get you or a message to London - and fast! Now just across the other side of this clump of reeds there's a whole lot of lakes and pools where hundreds of ducks and geese come and some swans too. There's people who like feeding them and watching them so they are very happy. It's called a wild-fowl sanctuary or something like that and a lot of the birds are on holiday like me, only they've flown for miles and miles just to be here. They're a pretty friendly bunch, perhaps one of them would take a message for you.'

'Do you really think so!' gasped Hugbundle.

'Come on, let's see,' said Micromiss, and she turned and scampered off through the reeds on their left with Hugbundle dashing along behind her.

Very soon they reached the water's edge. It was a big lake with an island in the middle and on it there were hundreds and hundreds of birds all swimming around. Micromiss put her front paws in her mouth and whistled. One of the nearby ducks looked round and swam over to where they stood at the very edge of the reeds.'

'Hello,' said the duck, 'nice day isn't it.'

'Yes it is,' said Micromiss, 'but not for my friend here. She's got a terrible problem.'

Quickly they explained what was wrong and asked the duck if there was any way that a message could be got to London. The duck shook his head and explained that if London was the place he thought it was, then it was far too far for him or any of his friends to make before night-time.

'What you need is one of the swans, they could do it,' the duck said.

'Would they help?' asked Hugbundle.

'Difficult to say,' replied the duck, 'they can be a funny lot. Just because they're big they expect to be left alone and don't always take kindly to being interrupted. Still, there's no harm in asking. If you want to I'll take you out to see one.'

'Oh please, I've got to do something,' said Hugbundle, 'let's hope they're in a good mood.'

With a little difficulty Hugbundle scrambled up onto the duck's back, she was still clutching her bag of fudge, whilst Micromiss climbed onto a reed that hung over the water and then dropped down beside her as the duck swam underneath.

'Right, hold on now,' said the duck, 'it's a bit choppy out there,' and they set off across the pond.

As they left the bank, the faces of the two rats poked out of the reeds behind them.'

'Quick,' one of them said, 'go and warn the others and get the boat.'

The duck was swimming quickly and soon they were in the middle of the lake and approaching the island. The water was quite rough and the duck bobbed up and down on each wave as Hugbundle and Micromiss clung on very hard to the feathers on its back. The duck swam round the end of the island and into a small bay behind it. The water was calmer there and ahead of them floated a massive bird with a beautiful curved neck. Apart from

171

its orange bill and some black markings round it, all the bird's feathers were pure snow white. It was a swan and it watched them as they approached but it did not move or try and drive them away.

'Excuse me,' said the duck slightly out of breath, 'but could you spare a minute.'

'Possibly,' replied the swan, 'what is it?'

The duck swam closer and stopped just in front of the swan, then turned slightly to one side so that Hugbundle and Micromiss could be seen.

'My friends here are in a spot of trouble,' began the duck, 'and we were wondering if you could help. It is all a bit serious.'

'Well what's happened,' said the swan.

Hugbundle told her story, the swan still did not look very interested.

'But I've got to do something,' Hugbundle continued desperately, 'those people, they're horrible with their drawings and their crow badges and things and I think they are really going to hurt her!'

The swan looked up sharply.

'Did you say crow badges?' he asked.

'Yes,' said Hugbundle wondering why this was so important.

'Silver badges and they wear them on their front here?' the swan pointed at his own chest with his beak.

'That's right,' said Hugbundle, 'how do you know.'

'I know because until I sorted them out there were two of them throwing stones at my family yesterday, that's why! They seemed to think it was funny!'

The swan looked very angry.

'Where did you say you want to get to?' he continued.

'London,' said Hugbundle.

'And all this is supposed to happen at eight thirty by that stupid people time?'

Hugbundle nodded.

'Right climb on my back, it's going to be close but we might just make it. I'll go as fast as I can, that's a promise, and we'd better get to know each other, I'm Rushwing.'

The duck moved in closer and Hugbundle climbed over and onto the swan's back. The larger bird turned to the duck and Micromiss.

'Can you go up that inlet there and tell my mate Tailgrace where I've gone.'

'Of course,' said the duck who knew that swans who are mates never like to be very far away from each other, especially if they do not know where the other one has gone.'

'Thanks,' the swan looked over his shoulder at Hugbundle who was nestled down in the feathers on his back, 'now hold on very tight especially for the first part. Take off is always the tricky bit.'

Hugbundle nodded but she had not needed any encouragement to hold on. The swan turned into the wind and began to swim forwards. Then he put out his wings and started to beat them downwards onto the surface of the water but backwards at the same time whist running with his feet as they lifted slowly, very slowly into the air. Before they had fully left the water, however, a boat shot out from behind the island and straight into their path. In it was a man and the woman who had been in the van with Smirkmuzzle the first time in Wellminster, both wore a silver crow badge. They stopped rowing and lifted their oars into the air to hit out at Rushwing as he sped towards them. There seemed no escape, he was going too fast to turn aside.

'We're still going to try!' he called out to Hugbundle, 'Just hold on this is going to be rough.'

Hugbundle felt Rushwing stiffen, his wings seemed to sweep down more and more powerfully and water streamed from them in sheets as they came back up for the next stroke. The swan had its neck straight out in front but still they were only inches above the water and

173

the boat was nearly on them. Then with only a few last feet to go, Rushwing swerved upwards and with one last surge of power almost threw himself into the sky. They skimmed over the tips of the oars which were now waved uselessly below. They were off.

Hugbundle buried herself deeper into Rushwing's feathers both to feel more secure and to keep warm. Underneath her, she could sense how hard Rushwing was trying to get them to London in time. Every beat of his wings seemed to have all his strength behind it and they swept forward faster than Hugbundle had ever thought possible. Rushwing flew with his neck out straight so conversation was difficult but every now and then, he would turn round to see that Hugbundle was all right. Below them, Hugbundle could see the countryside laid out as if it was a model with tiny fields and trees. Soon though it began to get dark and there were lights in the houses and cottages and around them the sky began to fade to a deep blue colour and finally an inky black in which the stars shone like a roof above their heads.

Hugbundle could feel that Rushwing liked the stars and she wondered if that was how he was finding his way to London. Sometimes he would look up and round and then make a slight alteration in their course. As he did so, Rushwing banked to the left or right and Hugbundle looked down the slope of his wing and over the tip where she could see the ground more clearly. If it had not been for the danger Chandra was in, Hugbundle would have loved that flight, once she had got used to being so far off the ground anyway, but as it was, she just kept wishing that they were already over London and was filled with admiration for the way Rushwing kept up his speed for mile after mile of the journey.

After some time, they began to pass over larger villages and some small towns and Hugbundle hoped that this meant they were nearer to Chandra. Rushwing however kept looking over to their left and Hugbundle could sense that he was getting nervous. Then she saw why. The stars were no longer visible and if you looked very carefully in the darkness you could see banks of thick cloud tinged a faint orange by the lights of a town below. Rushwing called back over his shoulder.

'I don't like it, there's a storm brewing.'

But then he returned to the work of flying as fast as he could, perhaps there was nothing else to do, Hugbundle thought, why did this happen now.

The storm finally caught them just as they began to pass over a large area of town lights which seemed to stretch for miles in front as far as they could see. As the clouds approached, the wind had also risen and now they were buffeted by great gusts that caught them from the left and seemed to toss even a bird as large as Rushwing to the side as if he was a single feather. Rushwing went lower so that they could see the ground but it was raining now and still they were driven off course.

'We should put down somewhere, but do you still want to try?' Rushwing called back.

'Yes!' Hugbundle shouted to be heard above the wind, 'Yes, we've got to.'

'All right, I'll do my best but this wind's driving us off course and slowing us down, I can't hold it completely.'

Hugbundle began to worry about Rushwing, his wing beats were getting ragged and were not so fast now, he had to be getting tired she thought, after all he had done enough even without the storm. The reassuring swishing sound his wings made as he flew had lost it's comforting rhythm and she wished for perhaps the first time in her life that she knew what hour it was by people time.

The minutes seemed to drag or race past, Hugbundle could not decide which, and below them all they could see was a dismal blur of lights and streets and a few dark spaces of open ground. It did not seem that even if they were in time, they would ever find St James' Park in this.

Then the weather eased and the clouds lifted a little, the rain stopping as they did so. Rushwing looked down and around them, he was flying much more slowly now and was obviously exhausted.

'We've been driven over to the East,' he called back, 'and the stars won't be visible again tonight. I don't know this part of London, do you recognise anything?'

Hugbundle gazed desperately round but she had never seen anything from the air and none of it made any sense.

'No,' she cried back sadly.

'O.K.' Rushwing said, 'we're lost. I'm going to circle and try and get some feel for where the North is. It's not very precise but it's all I can do.'

Even Rushwing's voice sounded empty now and it was only slowly that he began to turn above the city. Off to one side there was a dark band which must be the Thames but Hugbundle was too confused and Rushwing too tired to work out which way they were facing and which way to fly up it.

In the observatory, the coming of the clouds had put a stop to any further work that evening. Most of the telescopes had been put away and the Professor was in his study talking to a goose that had just arrived from the North and had come for the latest navigational sightings. In the main hall Cometpaw, one of the astronomer mice, was still at work trying to re-set one of the bigger telescopes that had been knocked out of place by a visitor during the day. As she gazed through it and focussed on the cloud, she saw a large bird, alone, circling over to the East. Cometpaw watched for a few moments then dashed up to the study.

'Professor! There's a swan still flying and I think it's in trouble. It's alone and circling and seems to be losing height.'

The Professor rushed down to the hall to see for himself.

'You're right,' he said, 'that bird really is in trouble. Heaven only knows why it would fly on a night like this but we've got to help. Someone go and get Fred and be as quick as you can, this is an emergency. Tell him to meet me in the dome.'

The Professor dashed off and out into the courtyard, down a path and into another building. He raced up a short flight of steps and stood in a dome which contained a giant telescope angled up to point at the roof. Cometpaw was just behind him.

'Get some others and bring all the candles you can,' he said to her and she disappeared on her errand.

Soon she and twenty or so mice were back each carrying two lamps and with them was Fred.

'Right,' said the Professor, 'sorry to drag you up here but we've got to open the dome, someone's in trouble.'

'Of course,' gasped Fred rather out of breath and he began to turn a wheel mounted on one of the walls. As he did so a crack appeared in the roof which widened to a slit immediately above the telescope.

'Good,' said the Professor and he climbed up to peer through a smaller telescope mounted on top of the main one. It was used to line up the instrument before making an observation and was just the right power for what he was about to do.

'All right now swing me round till I say stop,' he said.

Fred moved another wheel and the telescope and dome revolved on the giant platform it was built on. To the side, the goose who had come to see what was going on peered up at everything in amazement.

'Stop, back a bit, stop, that's it!' the Professor was saying, 'right I've got the swan in clear view; we're lined right up on them, now pass me that mirror.'

Cometpaw handed the Professor a small mirror which lay on a table. The Professor sat on top of the telescope and pointed it straight ahead. Then he told all the mice with the candles to stand in a group below him and he began to tilt the mirror rapidly backwards and forwards making a flashing pattern.

Up in the sky Hugbundle saw the light first.

'Look!' she called out to Rushwing who bent his tired neck round to see. Then he stiffened slightly and seemed to find at least a spark of new life.

'It's morse code!' he cried. 'Someone's trying to help us. Hold on I'll read it to you, I learnt it years ago so I could read all the light beacons and fog horns round the coast.'

Slowly Rushwing spelled out the message:

T-h-i-s i-s t-h-e E-a-s-t-w-i-c-h O-b-s-e-r-v-a-t-o-r-y. Y-o-u a-r-e f-l-y-i-n-g o-v-e-r W-o-o-l-w-i-c-h. H-o-l-d y-o-u-r p-o-s-i-t-i-o-n h-e-l-p i-s b-e-i-n-g s-e-n-t.

The message was repeated several times.

Back on the ground the Professor showed the goose where the swan was and the smaller bird took off with hurried wingbeats to intercept it. Soon the goose was alongside Rushwing and Hugbundle.

'St James' Park, guide me in, emergency,' was all that Rushwing said and the goose turned off to the West and they followed.

The contact had given Rushwing a new but last strength. His flying was still uneven but it had regained some of its power and together the two birds swept low over the river Thames giving Hugbundle a haunting sight of it in the silver and orange glow of the city at night. Soon they sped over Tower Bridge and then London, Southwark, Blackfriars and Waterloo bridges quickly followed. Rushwing seemed to be going flat out again now and Hugbundle could not imagine how he did it as she gazed out along his long white neck in front of her. Spread out below them on every side were the thousand star-like lights of the city at night. Then to their left there was a big building with huge windows all lit up and welcoming. As they came level with it, they veered right and left the water to pass what

178

to Hugbundle was frighteningly close to the tower of Big Ben. The goose had started to call and from either side they were joined by more birds, geese and swans, that began to form a formation with them. Four black swans fell in to their right, you could hardly see them in the darkness.

The whole flock swung and turned as one as they tilted sharply to look down on the park below them. There was a lake the surface of which was lit up by coloured lights and at one corner of it a figure stood silhouetted against its surface, it was Chandra. Behind her there were some very tall trees, stark against the sky, and to her right was a bridge across a small inlet of the water. From between the trees two men were creeping up behind her, she had not seen them.

'There she is!' cried Hugbundle in horror.

'Right,' said Rushwing and he swung downward and round leaving the others to follow. As he turned, Hugbundle could feel herself first pressed down against his firm back and then almost weightless and suspended in mid air as they began a steep dive. She held on tighter than ever. Rushwing skimmed the tops of some trees on an island and then aimed himself at the nearest man. Behind him the flock followed.

Chandra looked up in amazement at the sight of so many birds sweeping in towards her, then she glanced backwards, saw her attackers, and screamed. The first man was nearly on her but as Rushwing followed by the four black swans swooped round him he staggered off to the left trying to beat them away with his arms. After the first dive, Rushwing climbed quickly steering himself between two of the trees and then he turned through a tight half circle to make a second pass. This time they approached their target from the bank side and the lake was ahead of them. The man took several steps back in fear of the giant birds and fell straight into the water where he was at once surrounded by a group of five or six angry swans that lived in the park and had come to see what was going on. They gave him no chance of getting out again. The other would-be kidnapper did not fare much better. He was mobbed by the geese and ducks which, as smaller birds, were more manoeuvrable and circled again and again round his head, always just safely out of reach. Unable to see clearly where he was going, the man tripped and sat down heavily on a bush that grew near the water. It should have been quite a soft bush but as soon as he touched it, the man threw himself sideways yelling and clutching his back. He too fell into the water. From beneath the bush, an angry face appeared and then what looked like a giant hedgehog only with a lot of long spines that stuck out at the back stomped off across the grass and out of the park. The porcupine glared at everybody as he passed as if he wanted to shout at all of them for having disturbed his evening. He was carrying a sketchpad and some paints which he had laid in the top of a black bag. Attached to the strap of the bag was a label and it was this that caught Chandra's eye as the porcupine passed; she recognised it at once. It was a luggage tag for an airline and had been filled in for a flight the following day, the destination was India.

Both men were now surrounded by birds in the lake and helplessly they floundered about trying to stay on the surface whilst spitting out mouthfuls of muddy water. Chandra gazed round her in a state of shock and surprise as Rushwing glided down to land on the silver and gold surface of the lake. Then he swam over to the bank beside her and Hugbundle climbed out from her place deep between the feathers on his back. Chandra looked even more astonished and confused than ever but Hugbundle scrambled down and once on the ground put her paws round Rushwing's neck which drooped down under the invisible weight of his exhaustion and gave him a big thank you squeeze. Then she jumped up and into Chandra's arms and tried to hug her as well but since she really wasn't big enough settled for a cuddle herself instead. Several of the swans from the lake had gathered round Rushwing and gently they began to guide him out to the middle and safety. He was already asleep before they had gone more than a few feet and they had to push him the rest of the way.

Behind Chandra, there was the familiar sound of a London taxi drawing up and looking round she saw the Professor followed by Sunfur, Starwhiskers, Wander-paws, Snuggletoes, Jasminemouse, Honeymouse and Cometpaw all jump out and dash across towards them. The Professor waved in thanks to the driver who waved back. Another contact Chandra thought. There was no time for any reunion or explanations however. Just after the taxi had left, a large white police car screeched to a halt and a single constable got out. He ran across the grass and began to shoo the birds away from the men with his truncheon. At a sign from the Professor, the swans and geese fell back and the policeman helped the men out of the water.

'Now what's going on?' the policeman said in a very angry voice, he didn't sound very nice at all.

'These men, they tried to attack me,' said Chandra and all the mice nodded.

The policeman did not take any notice of them how-ever. It was strange - it was almost as if he knew about mice and what they could get involved in and so wasn't surprised by their being there and yet did not want them to have any say.

'Is that right?' the policeman asked the men.

'No, we was just having a walk like anyone else and then she started screaming, frightened all the birds and they drove us into the water,' one of them said.

'So you've been disturbing the peace have you,' he said to Chandra sounding even nastier than ever.

'No they tried to attack me, they were creeping up behind me and it was only when the birds flew down that I even noticed them. It happens all the time you know, you should do something about it. Sometimes it isn't very nice being an Indian round here, that's why they were attacking me.'

'Do you have any proof of that,' said the constable.

'What more proof do you need. Take a look around you!'

Chandra gestured to the scene about them and then to a sign which read 'KICK OUT SUB HUMAN WOGS' painted on a park bench close by. Underneath there was a crow symbol, the men were still wearing their silver badges.

'I'm sorry, that's not anything to go on,' the policeman said, 'and I'm warning you, don't let me catch you making trouble on my patch again.'

He waved his finger at Chandra as he spoke. Then he looked over to where the men stood dripping water onto the grass.

'You'd better go and get cleaned up and dry off.'

Quickly they walked away and into the night. Then before the Professor or anyone else had a chance to say another word, the constable turned his back on them and stalked back to his police car. He got in and wound down the window but did not look over towards them again. As he left, Wanderpaws gently reached up and took the lump of earth from Snuggletoes paw before he threw it.

'Nice one,' said Smirkmuzzle from the passenger seat of the police car and he sniggered just as the constable started the engine, put the car into gear, and pulled away.

The Professor, who like all mice had very keen hearing, swung round. Even at that distance he had heard.

'Right that does it!' he said in a furious voice and without waiting for the others, marched over to the edge of

182

the road where he looked both ways as if hoping someone would come. By the light of a street lamp the others
could see that the tips of his ears had gone very red and
no one dared to interrupt and ask him what he was going
to do.

A few cars passed but the Professor let them go and
seemed to be trying to think of something. Then in the
distance they all heard a motorcycle approaching. As it
got nearer they saw that the rider worked for a messenger firm, London Couriers was written on his leather
jacket and on the paniers at the back of the bike itself.
Without hesitation the Professor stepped out into the
road and held up his paw for the bike to stop. The rider
only saw the small figure when it was almost too late
but he managed to swerve to a halt just in front of the
Professor who unperturbed scrambled up to sit on the
handlebars in front of the rider's face. The rider lifted the
visor of his crash helmet and switched off the engine of
the bike and looked at the Professor in disbelief.

'Right,' said the Professor, 'I'm sorry I gave you a
fright but you've got to radio your boss. I need his help.'

'I'm not calling my despatch controller and telling him
there's a mouse that wants to speak to him, he'll think
I'm mad.'

'Not half as mad as I'm going to be if you don't,' said
the Professor, 'but I wasn't thinking of your despatch
controller, I meant Phil Andrews, he does own your
company I think. I know him you see.'

At the name Phil Andrews the rider looked worried,
then slowly he picked up the microphone of his radio.

'Bike seventeen to control, bike seventeen to control,
come in please.'

'Control. What's the problem,' the radio crackled.

'Er, you're not going to believe this but I've been
stopped by a mouse. Says he wants to talk to Mr.
Andrews.'

'You what,' the radio voice answered.

'That's right, says his name's Professor Watchmoon.'

'Chris if you want to keep your job just get back on the delivery and stop playing silly games,' the voice sounded angry.

'Give me that,' said the Professor reaching up and taking the microphone in his front paws, he could only just hold it.

'Hello,' he said, 'this is Professor Watchmoon and if you would care to take a look at your operational manual you will see that on the fourteenth of June last year Phil Andrews issued a memo that if you were ever contacted by me you should help me in any way you could.'

There was a delay as the controller looked this up in his manual.

'O.K. so there is such a memo,' the voice from the radio said, 'but it doesn't say anything about you being a mouse.'

'Why should it,' snapped the Professor, 'now you've got your instructions but if you need further clarification then phone Mr Andrews now!'

'All right,' said the controller, 'bike seventeen please await further directions.'

They all stood and waited for several minutes, nobody spoke. Then the radio crackled into life again.

'Bike seventeen. bike seventeen, this is control. Official instruction from Mr Andrews, please give any assistance requested to the mouse. Repeat any assistance requested.'

'Got it,' said the rider, 'what now?'

'Take me as fast as you can to New Scotland Yard,' said the Professor, 'do you know where it is?'

'Yeah, but wish I didn't,' said Chris, he'd been stopped for speeding the day before.

The Professor clambered round to the back of the bike and sat on the seat behind Chris whose leather belt he held on to with one paw.

'Right, let's go,' he called out and Chris swung the bike round and they roared off together into the night of the city streets. As they accelerated away, the Professor's short white fur was blown back in the wind and they could see that his ears were still very red and angry.

'I wonder what he'll do,' said Honeymouse.

'Who knows,' said Sunfur, 'but we'll find out eventually, you know the Professor.'

The following morning there was an item on the radio news in London.

'A police disciplinary hearing has been set up to investigate allegations of racism and complicity in a racial attack against a constable following an incident in St James' Park last night. A spokesman said that the constable would be given the usual right to explain his actions and that the events were not as yet entirely clear. Preliminary enquiries had however revealed that the officer was linked to a known extremist group which has previously been involved in racial incidents and that this was a matter of some concern. It is understood that the enquiry follows the intervention of a well known public figure and close friend of the Metropolitan Police Commissioner, the most senior officer in the London force, who by chance witnessed the incident. The public figure has however not been named and reporters have failed to discover their identity.'

CHAPTER 17

The Morning After the Night Before

'Trust the Professor!' cried Starwhiskers from his place on the windowsill in the sitting room of Chandra's flat.

There were murmurs of agreement from the others who were all present and perched somewhere comfortable as they listened to the radio.

'I knew he'd do something,' said Hugbundle.

'I think you only had to look at him when he left last night to see that,' said Sunfur, 'I don't think I've ever seen him so angry.'

'Oh, I don't know about that,' interrupted Honeymouse, 'don't you remember the day they wanted to put his records in the Central Nosey Store?'

'True,' replied Sunfur, 'but that was different. At least then you got the feeling that there was possibly some limit on what he would do; somehow I don't think there was last night.'

'And don't forget the time when that new museum manager wanted to make Fred redundant because he was too old, part of that silly efficiency drive or something,' added Jasminemouse.

'What's an efficiency drive?' asked Snuggletoes but nobody seemed to take any notice. Only Hugbundle who was sitting next to him on the sofa looked round but that was simply to shake her head to show that she had no idea either.

'No, that's true,' said Sunfur reflectively, 'he certainly did get pretty angry then. Not that it lasted very long of

186

course, we still don't know quite what he did but it was only fifteen minutes before Fred got his job back.'

'Well it doesn't matter to me whether he has ever done anything like that before, he really made things happen last night and that makes him a very very special mouse or person round here,' said Chandra, 'it's the first time I've ever seen anything effective done about something like that.'

The conversation did not continue any further however, just then they all heard small footsteps in the passage and in walked Magicnose. She hadn't been around long enough for any of them to have really noticed that she had been gone, even though it had been all night.

'Hello everybody,' she said looking round, 'quiet evening I hope.'

All the others shook their heads.

'Not quite,' said Sunfur, 'why don't you sit down somewhere. There are just a few things we should tell you about.'

So once Magicnose was settled, they all told her the story of the adventure starting from Hugbundle's journey South to Earndel. Magicnose listened intently to every word but otherwise showed very little reaction, even in the most exciting bits, until Chandra came to the part where the second man had fallen on the bush as he was trying to get away. As soon as Chandra described the figure that had emerged from under the shrub, Magicnose stiffened and stared at Chandra in disbelief.

'Like a Hedgehog only bigger?'

'Yes.'

'All the spines sticking out at the back?'

'That's right.'

'What colour were they, were there any markings?' asked Magicnose her eyes shining.

'I don't know, it was very dark,' said Chandra trying to remember, 'I'm afraid I didn't really see. All I can remember was the sketchpad and the drawing things.'

'Did you say sketchpad,' whispered Magicnose as if not daring to believe what she had heard.

'Yes that's right, it was in the top of a bag, I couldn't help noticing once I'd seen the airline label marked for India. It's silly I know but I always feel a bit excited when I see them, especially when they are new and that one was for a flight today.'

Magicnose just sat and stared as if she could not trust herself to believe what she was hearing.

'You don't think it was a porcupine do you?' asked Honeymouse rather nervously.

'Oh yes, that was a porcupine,' said Magicnose, 'but he wasn't just any porcupine. There's only one who paints that I know of and that's Speedybeard.'

'Who's Speedybeard,' asked Jasminemouse.

There was a moment's hesitation whilst Magicnose appeared to be trying to take hold of herself again.

'Oh, just a porcupine I met once, that's all' she replied and despite many further questions that was all they could get out of her even though her earlier reactions had suggested that Speedybeard was far more than just somebody she had met a long time ago. Enquiries as to where she had been all the night also failed to get any real answer and so it was that after those few moments of open excitement, Magicnose became her old mysterious self again. Sensing that it was perhaps best not to try and get her to explain and also just happening to see at that precise moment the clock on the mantelpiece, Hugbundle changed the subject in the most effective way possible.

'Excuse me but isn't it past breakfast time?' she said.

There was a moment's silence.

'She's right you know,' said Snuggletoes hopefully.

'Yes you could even say it's very past breakfast time,' added Honeymouse.

Everyone turned to look at Chandra.

'Well I'm not sure there's very much here, we haven't done any shopping since we got back,' she said sounding slightly worried.

'Yes you've got a point there,' said Wanderpaws, 'but would there by any chance be a bakery somewhere near here?'

'Yes there's one just round the corner,' replied Chandra.

'They don't happen to do hot bread do they?' asked Jasminemouse with anticipation.

'Oh yes, especially about now, they bake it every morning.'

There was a mass rush for the door.

'Right or left as we leave the house,' Starwhiskers called back.

'Right and take the first turning on the left,' Chandra said, and with that all the mice were gone before she had even had a chance to say be careful.

All the mice that was except Magicnose. Whilst the others were away she got Chandra to go back very carefully over the part of the story when the porcupine appeared. Magicnose was especially interested in the airline label for a flight to India that Chandra had seen on the bag and she was very disappointed to find that there had been no indication of where in India the aircraft might be going, at least none that Chandra could remember. After a pause in which Magicnose had been very thoughtful, Chandra asked her the question she had wanted to for some time.

'You know Speedybeard quite well don't you,' she said.

Magicnose nodded and then after a moment answered.

'Yes I know Speedybeard, perhaps as well as anyone although I'm not sure about that, but I don't think I know him well, I don't think anybody does.'

189

Chandra was about to ask if it was Speedybeard who Magicnose was looking for only she glanced out of the window and realised that she had lost her chance and would have to wait. What she saw at first sight looked like a French stick, one of the long loaves of bread that they make in France, running along the pavement. It was only on closer inspection that the cause for this apparent miracle was clear. Underneath several pairs of paws could be seen where the mice were trotting along holding the bread above them, at the back someone's tail even stuck out, whilst on top sat Snuggletoes and Wanderpaws calling out directions to the others. It was not a very effective means of navigation because the loaf swung from one side of the pavement to the other but very soon they were level with Chandra's house and they turned sharply and headed up the drive. Chandra went and opened the door for them and as they came in she saw that the bread was still so hot that it steamed in the crisp cold air of the November morning.

'Quick get some butter,' called out Honeymouse from somewhere underneath the bread as they came in.

'Yes and some jam,' added Snuggletoes hopefully just before he was thrown off as the end of the loaf ran into the edge of the doorway to the kitchen.

He wasn't hurt however and so the pressing business of having breakfast before the bread got cold delayed any further consideration of the more serious parts of their adventure.

It was later in the morning when Honeymouse tried to steer the conversation back to porcupines in the hope of getting some more information out of Magicnose.

'Do porcupines fly a lot then?' she asked.

'Sometimes,' replied Magicnose.

'Oh go on, you can tell us more than that,' Jasminemouse joined in.

Magicnose hesitated for a moment as if she was trying to make up her mind what to say.

'Well yes they do fly a lot,' she said, 'in fact sometimes they even fly the plane.'

The others all looked astonished but Magicnose took what she saw as their ignorance without comment and tried to explain. She of all mice had long since realised that porcupines could not be much worse at being understood by others even if they tried and so it was up to her to put things right if she could.

'Yes you see there are two things,' she continued, 'firstly they are very interested in technical things and so all the controls and actually flying fascinates them and then there's something else as well.'

'What something else?' asked Honeymouse guessing that it might be embarrassing.

'Well,' said Magicnose taking a deep breath, 'the other thing is that they don't really like sitting in the cabin with everybody else, you see there are some people on planes who try and have long conversations with the person next to them, even if they don't want to hear, and porcupines don't like that.'

'Oh, you mean like saying good morning and that sort of thing,' said Snuggletoes and he laughed.

Diplomatically Magicnose ignored the comment and continued on the safer theme of porcupines flying the aircraft.

'Yes it's quite well known, there's one porcupine, she's called Arrowback, who's always turning up on long distance flights, she especially likes Jumbo Jets you see, and it's said that she has flown more take off and landings in them than most senior pilots.'

'How does she reach the controls,' queried Sunfur thinking that although to the mice porcupines were very big, they were still smaller than people.

'Oh she's made some special computer controlled extensions and modifications that clip on to them,' Magicnose went on.

'And don't the usual pilots mind?' asked Wander-paws.

'No, they like to have her on board to help out, partly just to have another experienced pilot and partly because of the story about the hijack.'

'What happened?' asked Jasminemouse.

'Well someone with a gun forced their way into the cockpit and tried to take over a plane she was flying. Only what happened was that when the hijacker reached round the seat to point his gun at what he thought would be the captain, he rammed his hand straight into Arrowback's spines. He dropped the gun and then the real captain, who had been further back in the plane to talk to someone but who had followed the gunman through, overpowered him.'

'Do you think they will ever take over as official pilots?' said Sunfur.

'No, they'd never want to make the announcements,' interrupted Honeymouse before Magicnose had had a chance to reply, '"I don't want to talk to you and I'm not going to tell you anything" doesn't sound at all like the nice things they're supposed to say before you take off, like you see on the films.'

'What makes you think you would even get that,' said Jasminemouse.

Magicnose gave her a very dirty look and would probably have said something if it had not been at that moment, that they all heard the sound of a mouse coming in through Chandra's letter box.

It was Cometpaw from the observatory and she had brought a message from the Professor. They were all to come to the observatory at eight that evening because he had something very important to show them.

'It must be the map,' gasped Hugbundle.

'I don't know,' said Cometpaw, 'he's been far too busy to explain anything of what has been going on since he got back from Wellminster but he's certainly been working on something up in his study ever since then and he's had us making hundreds of observations and measurements and things.'

'Well we'll just have to wait till this evening to find out,' said Starwhiskers.

'Yes and I must be getting along,' said Cometpaw, 'I've got to go and pick up some things from the Indian High Commission for the Professor. Something to do with an observatory in Delhi, Jantar Mantar I think.'

'Oh well,' said Starwhiskers as he looked at Sunfur and they both remembered their adventure in the Stone-keeper's tunnel, 'we should have known he'd work that one out.'

Sunfur nodded.

'Right, I'll see you all later,' said Cometpaw and she scampered off but when she reached the door she stopped and looked back, 'oh yes, there was one other thing. The Professor told me to warn you all to be very careful when you come tonight. I don't know what it is but I think he expects some kind of trouble.'

'I think we will be anyway after last night,' said Starwhiskers, 'but thanks for the advice.'

After Cometpaw had left, Chandra phoned Peter Hamil and told him about what had happened the previous evening. They both agreed that it was no longer worth any attempt at secrecy and so it was arranged that they should all meet at Peter's office rather than in the park and that the mice should come as well. At that meeting, Peter gave them the necessary papers to withdraw money from two bank accounts, one in London and one with The Central Bank of India in Delhi. He had made the papers and arrangements in Chandra's name which, he explained rather apologetically to the mice, was because banks could be a bit awkward about paying out large sums of money to them directly. Wanderpaws looked a bit upset and angry but Honeymouse just shrugged her shoulders and said;

'Who cares, it's all silly anyway once money is involved.'

The bank accounts did indeed contain several thousand pounds, there was no doubt that they would all be able to buy tickets, and, as the Bishop had said, they had been in existence for nearly two hundred years, dating from just after the time when Sailvoyage would have arrived in England. Beyond this Peter had no details though and so the rest of the story remained a mystery. At least however there was some hope of learning more about one of the puzzles surrounding the Heartstone. News of the events of the night before had reached the Bishop in Wellminster and he had phoned Peter to ask him to pass on a message to Chandra and the mice that he would be coming to London the following day to see that everything was all right. Also, he would be bringing with him some very interesting details about Giles Benson that he had discovered that he thought they would all want to know.

'That's the lieutenant whose medal was in Sailvoyage's tomb isn't it,' said Snuggletoes.

'That's right,' agreed Sunfur, 'perhaps it will all start to make sense now.'

'Yes, there's still too many secrets,' said Honeymouse, 'it can't all be to do with elephants.'

Hugbundle however did not look too sure.

After they had stayed on at Peter's office for lunch, they all went down to St James' Park to see if Rushwing was still there. Not only was he but he had been joined by Tailgrace and when they saw Chandra and the mice on the bank, they both swam over to meet them.

'I've got something for you,' said Tailgrace looking at Hugbundle, and she reached over to a safe spot on her back between her wings, 'this, you left it behind with Bernard the duck.'

Tailgrace held out Hugbundle's tiny bag of fudge in her bill and she bent down so Hugbundle could take it.

'Thank you, thank you, I thought I'd lost it,' cried Hugbundle who reached up and put her paws round Tailgrace's neck in a big squeeze to show how grateful she was. Even this she did not feel was enough however and before they left the park, Hugbundle borrowed a soft small brush that Chandra had with her and she very carefully combed all the feathers on Tailgrace's and Rushwing's heads, where they could not reach, as the two great birds floated on the lake with their necks bent down to her on the bank. The two swans then took off together and flew South back towards Earndel only at a rather slower pace than Rushwing's previous journey. About that it was to become the talk of the swans everywhere in England all that winter. Many said it had to be an all time record for a single flight.

Chandra and the mice started to make their way home from the park happy that they had had a chance to say goodbye to Rushwing and thank him once again. What should have been a quiet journey however was not as untroubled as it might have been. They had started to walk down a backstreet as a short cut to get to the underground station when after only a few yards, they noticed the first of the drawings. It looked very new and read:-

THE ONLY GOOD PAKI IS A DEAD PAKI

beside it was a crow symbol.

'Smirkmuzzle!' hissed Wanderpaws in disgust.

'Not necessarily,' said Starwhiskers coldly, 'but one of his friends for sure.'

'Right let's get them!' said Snuggletoes looking all round for any sign of the vandals responsible.

Since they were nowhere to be seen, none of the others took the trouble to point out that, even with all his determination, Snuggletoes might be hard pressed to take on anyone capable of reaching up to write a message five feet off the ground. Now in subdued silence they continued further down the road, only as they did so they found that the same message of hate, sickness and fear had been repeated on almost every wall they passed, always with the crow symbol beside it. It was only when they reached the buildings at the end of the street that the writing changed. Firstly they came to a sign which said:-

JUST BECAUSE YOU WERE LUCKY LAST NIGHT
PAKI DON'T THINK YOU CAN ESCAPE US
FOREVER

then after they had taken a few more paces they came to what felt like the final disgrace of all their adventures. There in front of them was a picture, if you could call it that, scrawled in the same thick black pen as the other offerings. Its outline was a crude caricature, a drawing which is a distortion of the truth but only so much, so that it can still be identified. They all recognised it at once despite its cruel perversion of the real beauty it was taken from. It showed Chandra dancing, only here she had been made ugly and imbalanced, twisted, bloated and coarse, almost, but just not quite, beyond recognition so as to preserve the intended hurt it would carry. It was not even this however which made them all stand staring at it in disbelief with a cold feeling down their spines and a shaking in their legs. In the drawing you could quite clearly see a hand holding a knife behind Chandra's back, a knife raised ready for a final blow.

'Pretty isn't it,' said a harsh voice behind them.

They swung round to find themselves staring into the cold dark eyes of a crow perched on some railings on the other side of the road. Then before they had a chance to say anything in reply, or even think of one, the great black bird launched itself forwards into the air and dived down at the mice where they stood scattered on the pavement round Chandra's feet. Small bundles of brown fur shot in all directions as they all dived for cover, all that was except Snuggletoes. He stood his ground and faced the crow in its oncoming dive as, within him, an anger such as he had never known before swelled up and swept through his mind in a way that no sense or reason could have ever stopped. He had seen enough he told himself, not just up till then but in that road alone, and he was not going to wait, not going to let one more thing happen and no one and nothing would stop him now. However mad it seemed to all the others as they watched in horror, Snuggletoes looked with an unflinching gaze straight into the eyes of an attacker who would surely leave him dead in the first seconds of their unequal struggle. To Snuggletoes at that moment it made sense, perfect sense, and he knew of no other choice to even consider.

It was only a well aimed kick from Chandra that saved him. The crow had already guessed that she might try and intervene and so had begun to swerve round in a path that with any normal person would have left it safely out of reach. What the crow had failed to take into account, however, was that a dancer who has trained from the age of five has much better balance and is much more supple than most people are by the time they have grown up. Chandra's foot lashed out to reach both higher and further than Woundbeak had anticipated. Even so, it did not manage to hit her but she was forced to pull out of the dive and swerve upwards to pass harmlessly over Snuggletoes' head as he shook his paw up at her from below.

'Come back,' and 'Coward!' he yelled but all she did was look down over her shoulder and laugh at him.

'All in good time, all in good time,' she called back and laughed again as she flew off behind some buildings and was lost to view.

'You fool, you absolute fool!' shouted Wanderpaws at Snuggletoes as he emerged from the safety of a gap underneath a nearby doorstep.

'Yes he certainly is that,' said Sunfur, 'but before we try and teach him how to stay alive we'd better get back to Chandra's flat before anything else happens.'

'Yes,' said Starwhiskers firmly looking round at all the others to stop any further argument, 'now let's move whilst we are still all here to get back.'

So they set off at once and with some relief arrived at the comparative safety of the underground train station. It was only once they were on the train that they started talking again and by then even Snuggletoes had realised that he had gone a little bit too far. It was on that journey however that Sunfur raised the subject of Snuggletoes' name.

'I don't think that he can keep it much longer,' she said, 'I think he's growing out of it rather fast.'

The others nodded and Snuggletoes felt excited. He had liked his name so far but it was his first and all the mice got at least one more once they had grown up and started to do important things.

'What about Stupidhead,' said Wanderpaws with a scowl only even he didn't sound really angry any more.

The others all laughed, even Snuggletoes, and they never got any further than that and so Snuggletoes had to wait for a while at least before he would finally get his new name.

CHAPTER 18

Fire at the Observatory

The Professor's warning and the events of the afternoon were still fresh in their minds so when the time came to leave for the observatory, Chandra telephoned for a taxi. Magicnose however did not come with them, the news of Speedybeard had dispatched her on another of her night time errands. Even with this familiar absence something had changed though. Ever since Chandra had seen the airline label for India none of them had any doubt about Magicnose's commitment to the adventure, now they were truly travelling in the same direction. That she would continue to do that in her own way and often on her own was something they would just have to accept.

After a short ride they approached the buildings from the South, from the side that faced away from the hill down through the park. Superficially everything looked in order but that was only to someone who did not know the site and its night time activities well. Starwhiskers was the first to notice;

'That's odd,' he said, 'why has someone put all those lights up at the front? They've never been there before.'

The others turned to look and saw that all the way round the front of the building there was a row of flood-lights which lit up the whole scene almost as brightly as if it were daylight.

'It wouldn't be much use if they had,' said Sunfur, 'with all that light around you would never be able to see stars properly through the telescopes.'

'I'll bet the Professor's a bit mad about it then,' said Snuggletoes, with a note of hopeful anticipation at seeing another unthinking act fall under the influence of one of the Professor's contacts.

'No, we would have heard earlier on from Cometpaw if there had been a problem. Anyway if the Professor wanted them gone then they would have at least been switched off by now,' said Sunfur, 'my guess is that he had them put there.'

'Well that's silly if we can't see the stars,' said Jasmine-mouse.

'Yes, well I think Sunfur's right,' said Starwhiskers, 'and that means that the Professor isn't even planning to try and do any observations tonight. Now if that is the case, it would be the first night like it I can remember so there really is something going on and we should go and find out what it is right now!'

The taxi drew up as close to the building as it could go and they all got out; Chandra paid the driver. As they went through the main gate they saw that the whole courtyard was lit up as were both sides of the buildings, only a small section of the back was in darkness. They all felt more than a little afraid at the strange feel that the unaccustomed light gave to the place. As Hugbundle said later, it was like one of the frightening films, the sort that it's best to see with someone bigger who you can hide behind in the worst bits, that are sometimes on the television. The parts it reminded her of were when all the main people are caught together in one place and there's something outside waiting to get them. It wasn't a very happy thought. As they stood there that was indeed the problem, the circle of light gave some security round the entrance but it also served to make the night beyond its boundaries seem even darker, more absolute, and something in which anything or anybody could hide.

Sunfur disappeared through the small side entrance that the mice used only this time she did not reappear with a key but to everybody's surprise the main door was immediately opened by a man in an Air Force uniform, an American Air Force uniform.

'Hi, come on in,' he said, 'the Professor's waiting for you.'

More curious than ever, Chandra and the mice went inside where they found that everything was as different, or even more so, than it had been at the entrance. Instead of the usual candles, all the lights were switched on but there were blackouts at the windows so you could not see them from the outside. Only some of the sky-lights had been left clear. The floor was criss-crossed by what seemed like hundreds of enormous cables running out to the lights. In the main hall it was the same and all the telescopes had been pushed to the centre of the room. To one side stood a group of men and women dressed in strange protective clothing with military insignia on their arms who carried fire extinguishers and other pieces of equipment. On the other a telephone had been set up on a table. It was the sort with push buttons rather than a dial and several mice sat on and around it practising dialling a number as fast as they could, one mouse pushing each button in turn. The handset had been laid on the table beside them with a mouse sitting at either end, one to listen and one to speak, and a further two sat on top holding down the cradle for the receiver but ready to let it come up when a real call was to be made. In the middle of this curious scene, beside the telescopes, stood the Professor and Steve, the pilot who had flown him to Wellminster, together with an older man, also an officer. Perhaps he was Steve's boss thought Hugbundle but she was too shy in the strange atmosphere of that night to ask for herself at once. All the unusual things going on made her feel nervous.

They went across to meet them and Steve smiled as he looked round and saw Chandra.

'Hi,' he said, 'it's nice to see you again.'

'Hello,' said Chandra, slightly surprised that he even remembered her from their first brief sight of each other which now seemed like ages before.

'Yes, well there will be plenty of time for hellos and stories later,' interrupted the Professor, 'I'm afraid that first I have some very worrying news and all of you, but Chandra in particular, have some very hard decisions to make.'

Steve looked at the Professor slightly surprised.

'Is there something that you haven't told me?' he asked.

'Not about what might happen here, no. About Chandra's link to it and her own particular danger, yes. But that's only because it's her business first.'

Steve looked a little hurt, as if he understood and accepted what the Professor had said but somehow his feelings still didn't agree.

'If you all go up to my study I'll be with you in a minute,' the Professor continued, ' I've got to tell you about tonight and what has been going on, but there may not be much time. Sunfur you know the way, show Chandra up in case she has forgotten.'

So with Sunfur leading they all went up to the Professor's study. There at least things were slightly more what they expected. The fire still blazed brightly in the grate, the piles of books and papers continued to occupy every space and the Professor's desk still looked as untidy as ever, in fact if anything there were even more notes than usual. All this familiarity felt strangely reassuring, even to Chandra who had only seen it once before, and the only thing that was really different was a new large computer set up to one side of the desk. Beside it stood a printer and in this there was a roll of paper with what seemed like endless figures on it, line after line of them. They all stood there staring at them, baffled.

'Mean anything to you?' It was the Professor standing in the doorway.

Starwhiskers and Sunfur looked embarrassed and shook their heads.

'Well don't worry; it took me long enough to crack it, and yes it is the key to the map, but it will have to wait whilst I tell you the plan for this evening.'

'Yes, just what is going on!' asked Honeymouse sounding slightly annoyed at all the disturbance.

The Professor gave her one of his looks that said that this was not the time to argue and then told them all to sit down so he could fill them in on what had been happening.

'Well I'll come straight to the point and get it over with. I have information that it is possible that the observatory will be attacked tonight, conceivably even bombed.'

'What!' they all gasped.

'Yes that's right, just fire-bombs that is, nothing explosive unless my data is not complete.'

To Hugbundle at that moment the difference between fire and explosive bombs seemed slightly academic.

'Can I just ask something then?' said Honeymouse nervously.

'Yes,' replied the Professor slightly impatiently.

'Well it's just that if someone is going to throw bombs in the building tonight, why are we still here?'

'Because we've got to look after everything and because we don't have much choice,' said the Professor sadly.

'What about looking after ourselves?' asked Jasmine-mouse.

'That I'm afraid is the 'not having much choice bit',' the Professor replied, 'the people we have to worry about would simply follow us if we went anywhere else. I've done the best I can and I do have some sort of plan to

203

deal with what could happen but I can't pretend it's perfect.'

'Never mind perfect, I just hope it's even good,' said Wanderpaws.

'Is that what all the lights are for?' asked Starwhiskers, trying to be more constructive.

'That's right,' said the Professor, 'now if you will all be quiet I will try and explain.

After last night, I guessed that there would have to be some more trouble and that it would be best to know what it was going to be before it happened. Whilst you have been away I've been working on a few things other than the map and with a little help from some friends and a lot of hard work, I've found out where the head-quarters of the group that has been causing so much trouble to Chandra is.'

'What, the one with the crow badge,' asked Sunfur.

'That's the one,' continued the Professor, 'so this morning at about the time I thought they would be having their meeting to come up with some new nasty ideas I went down there to join them.'

'You don't mean you know someone there as well!' exclaimed Wanderpaws in some disgust.

'No I don't know someone there,' sighed the Professor trying not to get angry at all the interruptions, 'but I do know a way into the building and I just sneaked in and hid under the table and listened.'

'But wasn't Smirkmuzzle there? It must have been very frightening,' said Hugbundle.

'Oh yes they were all there, Smirkmuzzle, some more rats, a few crows and about the most unpleasant group of people you could imagine. The only good thing was that they spent so long shouting at each other and arguing and the place is so filthy and such a mess that it wasn't too difficult to stay unnoticed.'

'Professor you shouldn't have taken the risk, it must have been very dangerous,' said Chandra.

'Possibly, but it had to be done. If I hadn't then all of us, including me, would be in even more danger now. So I didn't have much of an alternative.'

'Aren't you a bit old for that sort of thing,' said Snuggletoes.

The Professor drew himself up to his full height at his desk.

'You would do well to remember that I have been taking care of myself for a very long time now, far longer than you have and, from what I hear, with far more success. I am several times your age and no one has yet started making plans for my funeral. As far as you are concerned, however, I'm sure that quite a few people have begun to think of yours just to make sure that they are ready in time, which at the present rate will be in the all too near future.'

Snuggletoes sat down again and was silent but Chandra touched him lightly on the shoulder to show that even if he had been a bit stupid, she at least cared that he had tried to do something whatever the risk. It was not the first time they had shared such a moment and both their minds went back to the occasion in Wellminster when last Chandra had shown her gratitude in the same way. Snuggletoes had already realised that the biggest danger to Chandra and anyone else the thugs threatened was everybody else simply doing nothing, either because it was too easy to look the other way and pretend they hadn't seen, or by so wrongly convincing themselves that there wasn't anything they could do.

'Still,' he secretly thought to himself, 'he had got it a bit wrong that afternoon, why was it that he never seemed able to get the balance right?'

'So,' continued the Professor, 'once in the meeting I heard everything that was planned. They were very upset that they failed to kidnap Chandra yesterday and they were quite determined not to leave it at that one attempt. Their intention is to try again but if they fail, to use some other form of attack instead. Then came the frightening bit. I'm sorry Chandra and I don't know how they got it, but they know your address. Most probably Smirkmuzzle or one of the crows followed you. They may have even known it for some time. They will be watching your flat tonight, that is why I still let you come here, not however as I have said that even this observatory will be safe. Two men reminded the others that you were walking up through the park the other night when they attacked you. They put two and two together and guessed that you might well come back here and that we would be waiting to meet you.'

The Professor looked round at all the other mice as if to check that they were becoming aware of at least some of the seriousness and danger of what was going on. Then he continued.

'Just to be certain however, in case we had somewhere else planned, a hundred crows are watching this part of London tonight to make sure that Chandra can't give them the slip. For her, this evening nowhere is safe and it's just a question of where she wants to take her chances.'

'So they don't know we are here all the time?' asked Starwhiskers returning to the theme of the observatory.

'No, they just think we come on odd occasions and the longer they believe that the better. Anyway it was at that point in the proceedings that one of the more charming of them came up with the idea to wait till you all arrived here or anywhere else you might go to and then fire-bomb the place, only going on to Chandra's flat if you don't show up. They have put crow lookouts in the park and on the top road to see if you come and then pass word back to them. If they stick to what they planned, then they will wait until it's sufficiently late for them to feel safe or until there is some sign of your leaving.'

'That's a shame because up till now that is exactly what I was thinking of doing,' said Honeymouse.

'So what's the problem? Get Sergeant Randel up here and let him arrest them,' said Wanderpaws.

'That's what I thought of at first,' said the Professor, 'but arrest them on what charge? They haven't done anything yet and I'm sure the fire-bombs would disappear fast enough if the police showed up. At best they would only be held till tomorrow for questioning and then have to be released. Next we'd have to try and deal with something else tomorrow night and the night after and so it would go on until finally we would make a mistake and get into real trouble. The chances of you lot getting off to India would not be very good to say the least. You have to remember that however right we think we are, Sergeant Randel has to operate within the law and that means he needs reasonable proof and evidence.'

'At least have him on site then, get him up here to wait with us, that's got to be worth it,' said Sunfur.

'There I agree with you. The problem is that he's away tonight, he has been posted to another part of London where they are short of officers. I've sent him a message but I'm not sure he will get it in time.'

'Well surely we can fight them somehow,' said Wanderpaws.

Snuggletoes nodded in agreement but the Professor sighed.

'Yes, I might even be able to arrange for some sort of ambush to meet them but I won't do it. First it makes us almost as bad as they are. Any issues of right and wrong will simply be reduced to whoever puts together the biggest army for a given night. Secondly, you don't understand why sometimes people help me. It's exactly because I don't do that sort of thing. If I did, then I would become too dangerous and someone would want me out of the way and soon enough, it would happen and everything we have here would be gone. I have never asked for or used that kind of force against anyone and I never will.'

'But someone is going to attack us like that right now,' said Snuggletoes, 'why can't we do something now they've started it?'

'No. That's not for us to do. As far as the people world is concerned, it's up to the police to stop it and the courts to decide who is right.'

'O.K., back to the police, so where are they, we know what could happen, let's tell them and leave it to them as you say,' said Wanderpaws.

'I wish I had the perfect answer to that,' replied the Professor slowly, 'I have sent a message to Sergeant Randel as you know and I was going to contact Eastwich police station despite my reservations about them not being able to make any arrests, just as you suggested simply to have someone here. That, however, was before I saw the new Sergeant, the one who's on duty tonight in place of Sergeant Randel, at the meeting I went to this morning.'

'Just how many policemen are there who are members of this horrible set up?' asked Honeymouse with some force remembering the Constable in the park the night before.

'Full members like that, I'm glad to say very few; and by tomorrow there will be one less. That so called officer will be suspended by lunch-time, I promise you that, and I hope will not be in the force at all soon after. These days people like that are neither wanted or tolerated by those in command. Policemen who need to learn a lot more to understand problems like Chandra's and do something about them are I'm afraid rather more numerous but that's as much up to us to make sure they do learn as it is to anyone else. No, tonight we are on our own and will just have to hope that nothing too bad happens. The petrol bombs are the worst we are likely to face and so it's those I have made preparations to deal with. We have put lookouts on all approaches in the park with strict instructions to come back and bring the others with them as soon as any stranger is sighted coming this way. I'm not leaving anyone out there once our 'friends' are on the scene, I don't want one of the observatory mice having to face Smirkmuzzle on their own in the dark. Then, as you saw when you came in, the US Air Force has kindly arranged a little extra lighting round the place so that only one large window is not exposed. Anyone wanting to attack the observatory would be almost certain to pick that darkened window because they will not be seen.'

'What you mean the one round the back into that silly exhibition on 'Time',' said Jasminemouse thinking of the one part of the observatory the mice found some difficulty in relating to, 'well if that's all they are going to burn then good riddance.'

'They are not going to burn that or anything else if we can help it,' said the Professor sharply, 'From the outside the window looks perfectly normal but inside it's been sealed off with sandbags leaving only a few small holes open. Through those the people who you saw in the main hall will pump fire extinguishing foam into the space to put out the burning petrol.'

'Who are they?' asked Hugbundle.

'They are one of the special firefighting teams from the air base Steve is stationed at, they have a lot of experience and training in how to put out burning fuel very quickly. It's exactly the sort of problem you get when an aircraft crashes. And let's get one thing straight, although we will all need a sense of humour before tonight is over, fire is a very dangerous and frightening thing. If that gallery caught fire properly very little could save the whole building and quite possibly us with it and that is exactly what the thugs out there would like. We will probably never understand what hate drives them but it makes them murderers and there is no other word for them. Last week whilst you were in Wellminster, petrol was poured through the letter box of an Asian family in Bromswood and someone set fire to it. Their house was burned down and the whole family, father, mother and three children were killed and it's very likely that the person who did it is one of those out there right now with his or her petrol bomb ready beside them. So Chandra, I can't promise that you will be safe here but I have done what I can and I must to warn you; unless you think you can lose the crows out watching you there is no place that will be really safe tonight. So do you want to take your chances with us?'

'Professor, I think what you have done is incredible and I would not want to be anywhere else because nowhere is there anyone who cares as much as you all do, but what about you taking your chances with me, and what about the risk to your beautiful observatory? It must have all been so quiet and perfect before I came.'

'Chandra, we are your friends, and remember it was a mouse who brought you here. If you want to stay then together we make our stand with you. As for the observatory, I won't pretend I don't care but remember the spirit of the early astronomers and scientists who built this place and who my predecessors so admired. They wanted truths, they wanted a better world. Would I really be serving them or their memory to think of bricks and mortar and the past before the future?'

The others listening to this became very quiet, no one made any more jokes about it being no loss if the time gallery were burned down and they all felt very afraid at the situation they found themselves in. It was Snuggletoes who broke the silence first.

'I'm scared and I don't mind admitting it.'

'That makes a change,' interrupted Wanderpaws.

'No seriously,' continued Snuggletoes, 'I think there is something we should all remember. Whatever the Professor said earlier about having no choice, if we wanted to we could all go away and after a while they would forget about us and leave us alone. But what about Chandra? They won't leave her alone, they will find her just because she is Indian. Here we all sit frightened because for the first time in our lives we might be attacked with fire. Don't you realise that Chandra has gone to bed every night for years knowing that even if the chances are small that anything will happen that somewhere out there, nearby, there are people who would like to kill her and any night might just be the one when they will do something. I can think of things I'd rather have to remember when I go to sleep.'

'There's hope for you yet,' said the Professor who had been watching Snuggletoes with increasing surprise as he spoke. 'Has anybody said anything about your name?'

'Yes,' said Sunfur on Snuggletoes' behalf, 'but we didn't get very far.'

'Well not now, too much is about to happen, but remind me to give it some thought later,' said the Professor and Snuggletoes felt proud but a little embarrassed, it wasn't often that the Professor got involved in new names.

'Anyway,' continued the Professor, 'we must hope that Sergeant Randel gets here in time but, just in case, since we can't rely on Eastwich, if there is an attack we will have to call on another station. Bromswood is the nearest and it's still fairly close so they should be here very quickly to pick up our 'friends' as they try to leave. That's what the phone is for in the main hall.'

'Isn't there a risk that they will get away through the park?' asked Wanderpaws.

'Yes there is a risk but we'll just have to hope they don't. Anyway, that's about it and since I think it will still be a little while before our watchers out there think it's late enough for them to make their move, why don't I tell you about the map.'

'Oh yes!' all the others said almost in unison, very grateful to change the subject and take their minds off what was about to happen.

'Well I have to confess that it wasn't easy but I have finally come up with the answer, with the help of my new toy that is,' the Professor nodded in the direction of the computer.

'At the time when Swiftclimb first drew the map it would probably have been fairly simple to follow. It was intended for someone who knew the area and who would have been familiar with the appearance of the stars there. In addition, Sailvoyage of course knew where the Heartstone cave was and so where they were starting from. All that however is now a very long time ago and some of the observations and notes are not totally precise, in astronomical terms at least, probably relying on local knowledge to make them mean anything. In addition, there is the complication for those of us used to working in this country that all the sightings are made from much further South, almost at the equator and into the Southern hemisphere. The only thing that helped was knowing that the map and the directions give the location of a temple, and, since it had at least one elephant living at it, a fairly big one, or so my sources at the Indian High Commission tell me anyway. The final key was when I realised that the astronomical system from which the sightings were written down was that linked to the Jantar Mantar observatory in Delhi.'

'We found a drawing of Jantar Mantar in the Stonekeeper's tunnel at Wellminster,' said Sunfur.

'Well why didn't you tell me!' exclaimed the Professor.

'Because this is the first chance we have had!' said Starwhiskers, 'Ever since we got back to London someone has been attacking Chandra or you have been off trying to sort things out.'

'All right, this time I'll forgive you,' said the Professor with a wink.

212

'Now having adjusted to the location next I had to allow for the difference in time. On its own either would have been simple but of course each adjustment to a degree depends on the other since we do not know exactly where they set off from or when, to us that's the whole point of the map, and I don't expect there are many mice left who could tell us the position of the old Heartstone cave. Still, I made a few estimates and educated guesses and started to try and fit everything together. With the help of the computer, it did all begin to make sense and at least once I had an answer, I could check it against itself using more accurate star maps built up for the date. Fortunately, of course, we have at least a rough idea of the year in which the Heartstone was broken. Before I go on however, remembering your earlier comments, there is one thing I would ask you to think about. Without time astronomy means very little, in fact all time is is a sort of astronomy......'

Honeymouse looked increasingly doubtful.

'......And so is rather special. It's only the stupid things that people do with it like making themselves run round in circles all day and only thinking of it and not the stars and planets it comes from that make it silly. Still enough philosophy, now to the exciting bit.'

The Professor went over from his desk to the computer and climbed up onto the keyboard.

'Right, watch this,' he pressed a few keys and a map of the Southern part of India appeared outlined in green on the screen.

'The initial estimates and data for the point where the Heartstone cave was, put it in this area,' he pressed some more keys and a circle appeared on the map around an area close to the Eastern side of the country.

'Now if we superimpose the main towns and cities things start to get interesting,' again the Professor pressed a series of keys and all the major places appeared on the map with their names shown in a different colour so that they stood out.

'Look there's Madras where Sailvoyage got the ship to England!' said Hugbundle, 'It must have been very close to there that he met the elephant.'

'And look there's Kanchipuram right in the circle of where the Heartstone cave was,' Chandra gasped. 'It's the place where all the silks are made, like the one Sailvoyage wrapped the Heartstone in and where Anju went to work.'

'Well we can do better than this circle,' said the Professor pointing at the screen, 'further calculations and use of the star maps let me narrow down the site of the cave to this area.'

More keys were pressed and before their eyes the circle shrank down till it was a small ring between the towns of Kanchipuram and Chingleput.

'As you can see, it lay in an area of open countryside and what is very interesting is that Chingleput was a place of activity by the British army at the time of the occupation.'

'The gun,' whispered Sunfur.

'That's right,' said the Professor quietly, 'the gun. So now we have the point where Swiftclimb started her journey. From this, if we interpret the markings on the map and the notes we can begin to see their route as they travelled rather surprisingly South. I say surprisingly since of course they really wanted to take the stone North, but, as we know, the journey started with an elephant taking them to its own temple. I suppose that could have been in any direction for a short way at least.

From the site of the Heartstone cave they went South East till they reached the coast, just a little bit further down than Tirupporur.'

Again the Professor made an entry into the computer and a red line appeared on the map to show the route that Swiftclimb had taken. It ran down and to the right until it reached the sea. Then it continued almost due South actually along the coastline until it came to the mouth of a river called the Palar.

'Now this was the first place where I had real problems, not in fact because the map is that complicated but because for a long time I simply didn't believe what it was telling me. The story you heard from Moonbeam was that Swiftclimb and the temple elephant made the map and the notes just after they set out for the temple. That would mean it would basically show the route they intended to take, not the one they would have been forced to follow if there had been any hold ups. When I went over the data again and again, however, every time it gave the same answer which was that having reached the river, the route turned back and they went due North again till they came to a place called Mamallapuram on the coast that they had already passed through. Now why a planned route should include a section doubling back on itself I can only guess but I am now absolutely sure that that is what the notes say.'

'What's at Mamallapuram?' asked Sunfur, struggling slightly with the unfamiliar sound of the name.

'It's a fishing town on the coast,' said Chandra, 'and there are some very old temples and carvings in the rock but they haven't been used for years, as far as I know even at the time of the Heartstone being broken they'd been abandoned.'

'So the elephant didn't live there,' said Hugbundle.

'No I don't think any elephants have lived there for a very very long time, if ever for that matter,' Chandra answered.

'No, well there's no real question of Mamallapuram being where the elephant lived,' the Professor went on, 'because the directions quite clearly start the journey South again. Perhaps you will find out more when you get to India but at present we can only guess and mine is that this backtrack was put in to draw Sailvoyage's

215

attention to Mamallapuram in some way. Perhaps show him he had to find something there.'

'How exciting,' said Honeymouse.

'So,' said the Professor, 'having gone back they set off again and, as you can see if I put the route into the computer, they travel South and this time cross the river and keep going. Now if before we go any further I enter the places where there were large temples operating at that time, you will understand what happens next.'

The Professor pressed a series of keys and a number of the major towns shown on the map were underlined in blue.

'There you are. These are the possible destinations. Now if we extend the route according to the directions we see they passed inland of Pondicherry, perhaps to keep out of the way of any British troops there, and then virtually straight towards Chidambaram where the journey stops, and yes, there is a temple there, as you can see it is one of the places underlined as having one.'

As they watched, the red line of the route extended slowly down to end at Chidambaram just in from the coast.

'And so I'm as sure as I can be that it was in the temple at Chidambaram where the elephant lived and that it is there you should start your hunt.'

With that the Professor sat back, still on the computer keyboard, and looked at them as if waiting for one of them to say something. It was Chandra who spoke first and at once they all noticed the emotion in her voice.

'Yes Professor but Chidambaram is not just any temple. Do you know what it is?'

'Yes Chandra, I think I do,' said the Professor with a gentle smile, 'but why don't you tell us. It's more your special part of the discovery than anyone else's.'

Chandra hesitated for a moment while they all looked at her expectantly.

216

'Well,' she said in a voice that trembled slightly, 'Chidambaram is a large temple like some others but it has a very special association especially for someone like me. It is the temple of the God Shiva in his incarnation as Nataraja, the God of dance, and it is the temple of dance itself with thousands of sculptures showing all the poses and movements. Some say it is the place where Nataraja brought the dance to earth, think of it as the link between dancers like myself and the Gods who it came from.'

'Yes but there's more, isn't there,' said Hugbundle gently, sensing from how well she had come to know Chandra that something was being held back.

'Yes there is more,' said Chandra her voice still unsteady, 'and you would be the one to spot it Hugbundle because you seem to have understood more of all this in some ways than any of us. It's something that I'd forgotten, it all happened so long ago, but as I watched that red line go towards Chidambaram on the map it came back as if it happened only yesterday.'

'What happened,' asked Sunfur.

'Well it was when I was seven, just after my mother had died. I knew my father was going to bring us to England and because I was so mad on dance and thought that I might never go back, I pestered him until he promised to take me to Chidambaram before we left. He kept his word and we went one beautiful day late in the year, before it gets too hot to enjoy things. Everything at the temple was just as it should be and we both went to the priests to be blessed and then the time came for us to leave. I was very sad, I was finding it hard not to cry. I really did believe that we would never go back and having the dance all round me had been making me think of my mother all day. Once we were outside, my father told me to wait by a shop whilst he went to do something, I can't even remember what it was, saying he would only be a few minutes. Well like most seven year olds, by the end of the first minute it felt like hours and

217

I started to look round for something to do, especially because I felt so sad. Even then I had no intention of going anywhere however, I was just looking for something to play with, someone to talk to. Anyway, just as it seemed that there was absolutely nothing and nobody, it happened. I had a small cloth bag on my shoulder and in it were two sets of gungurus, the bells I wear when I dance. My mother had given them to me and at that time they meant almost more than anything else in the world. I had taken them because I wanted them to have been in the temple simply because it was the temple of dance. Then, suddenly I felt a tugging at my arm and looked round to see a monkey with its hand in the bag. I screamed at it and it jumped away but it had taken one of the sets of gungurus with it. Monkeys can be like that in the South, give them a chance and they'll grab anything. Well it was terrible, there was the monkey running off with my precious gunguru, so I chased after it as fast as I could go hoping there would not be any trees for it to disappear in to. I followed the monkey down a few turnings but it was getting away from me, it was just too fast for me to catch. I rounded a corner though and there in a deserted street as quiet as it could be on the edge of the town lay my gunguru, right in the middle of the road where the monkey had dropped them. I just caught a glimpse of the horrid animal disappearing into the dust and the distance. I was so relieved I dashed forwards and grabbed them before anything else could happen. Then, as I stood up, I had this strange feeling that there was someone or something behind me. I turned round very slowly and not a little afraid to look straight into the eyes of a large elephant only about ten feet away. I was so surprised that I just stood there rooted to the spot. The elephant looked at me and then took one pace forwards and reached out it's trunk to the gunguru. I should have snatched them away but I just couldn't move. It touched the bells, then touched my forehead and then each of my feet in turn. It was like the normal blessing that they are taught to do in temples but not quite, for one thing no one would ever teach them to touch your feet. I knew what it meant to me then, I was being told that whatever happened I must go on dancing because it was important. Not that I needed much convincing of course, and everyone laughed when I told them, said it was wishful thinking.

After the elephant had touched my feet it stood aside and I ran off to find my father. Fortunately, when I told him what had happened, he wasn't too angry and I didn't get into trouble. Before we left we asked about the elephant but strangely, despite the fact we thought that it must have been trained, no one seemed to know anything about it and no on else appeared to have seen it either, even a man who we met on the road coming in from that side of town. Still, nothing bad had happened and it seemed like just one of those odd things that occur sometimes. After a while I forgot all about it, forgot about it till now that is.'

'You mean that an elephant blessed you and told you that it was important to go on dancing,' said Hugbundle in awed tones, by that time for her anything that was associated with elephants became twice as special, however important it had been before.

'That's certainly what I thought when I was seven,' Chandra replied, 'and even if I doubted it, when I got older after what has happened since we went to Wellminster it's what I believe again now.'

'I think that an elephant who blessed the dance like that would get very upset with anyone who interfered with it later,' said Hugbundle.

'You and your elephants,' said Jasminemouse.

'No, give her a chance,' said Starwhiskers, 'there really have been rather a lot of them in this story and I don't think that they are all there just by luck.'

'No, neither do I,' said Chandra, 'it's strange that I had forgotten what happened that day for so long but it was something special, something very special, and I don't think it was an accident.'

'So just where do the elephants fit in?' asked Sunfur.

'Everywhere,' said Hugbundle.

'Oh come on,' said Honeymouse, 'you've got to say more than that.'

'I'm not sure I can,' said Hugbundle, 'it's just that for a long time now I've had this feeling that it's the elephants who are at the bottom of all this.'

'Well they certainly wouldn't be at the top, they'd squash everything!' said Jasminemouse.

Hugbundle looked a little upset and it was Chandra who came to the rescue.

'No, be fair, there really have been too many elephants for it just to be coincidence.'

'All right so what are we supposed to make of them?' asked Wanderpaws.

'That I think you will have to wait till you get to India to find out,' said the Professor, 'but one thing I agree with Hugbundle about is that they are very important and I don't think that any of us have heard the last of them.'

'Thank you,' said Hugbundle and no-one took the subject of elephants any further since at that second they heard the sound of a mouse dashing up the stairs as fast as it could. Seconds later Cometpaw burst into the room.

'They're coming, they're coming, the lookouts have seen them!'

The Professor looked very serious and sad for a moment.

'All right it seems we are going to have to face something tonight. I'd better go down but anyone who wants to can stay here, it might be safer.'

Fearing that they might be the only one to stay and then be left alone, nobody took up the suggestion.

Quickly but without panic, the Professor led the way down the stairs and back into the main hall. There everyone had heard the news and was quiet, waiting with their own fears for what might be to follow. The fire-fighting team and the older officer had gone into the 'Time' gallery and positioned themselves around the sandbagged window with their extinguishers pointing into the gaps left in the protective screen. The mice at the telephone had stopped practising and were tense and alert, sheltering behind the phone on the side away from any windows, but waiting to put their new skills into effect. The Professor went over to the middle of the hall where a low display case had been pushed to keep it out of the way. He climbed onto it before he spoke.

'Right, I know you have heard that our lookouts have spotted some people they don't entirely like the look of coming this way. We can only assume that something is going to happen so if you have not already done so, please now go to your positions exactly as we did in the practice this afternoon and stay there till whatever is about to take place is over. Chandra, if you ask Steve he will show you the safe areas we have worked out, please stay in one of them from now on and everybody, you must keep very quiet, not a sound that might give anything away.'

Steve gestured to Chandra and she joined him in a doorway which was partially sheltered from all the windows. Hugbundle, Honeymouse and Jasminemouse went with her but Starwhiskers and Sunfur accompanied some of the astronomer mice under one of the telescopes. Wanderpaws hid behind a large metal box in which the firefighting team had brought part of their equipment whilst Snuggletoes stood defiantly in the middle of the room as if to say that even if everybody else was going to take cover, he was out there ready to fight, whatever happened. He would have probably stayed there but Wanderpaws reached out and dragged him behind the case. Only the Professor remained out in the open and no-one dared argue with him.

An absolute and heavy silence fell on the hall and all the other parts of the observatory. Every man, every woman, and every mouse could hear the beating of their own hearts and feel the chill which seemed to run up and down their spines with no way to stop it. Somewhere one of the younger mice started to cry but two others quickly found him and squeezed in on either side so he felt safer and was quiet again. He would not have been the only one to have given in to their fears if it had not been for the sight of the Professor standing calmly in the open and full view. Perhaps that was why he had stayed there, even if it wasn't it was certainly what made the difference then. The silence deepened and in the uncertainty of what might be to follow, everyone began to imagine that the observatory must be completely surrounded with enemies on all sides and at every window. They all pushed deeper into their hiding places. The suspense and the waiting was becoming unbearable when they heard the sound of someone or possibly more than one moving at the back of the building. Then for a moment it was silent again followed by some muffled whispers that none of them could make out. Anything had to be better than this they thought and it wasn't just Snuggletoes who had ideas of rushing out to find their tormenters and fight a more direct kind of battle. It was more than ever only the quiet, firm presence of the Professor that held them there and still they had to wait and pray.

Suddenly it happened, there was a scraping sound, an instant's gap and the shrieking voice of glass as it is shattered and broken.

Immediately following came a ghastly wave of smell, of fire and burning, fumes and heat, that swept over them all, even with the protection of the sandbags. There were more sounds of breaking glass as two further petrol bombs followed and outside came shouts and screams of hideous triumph.

'PAKI ANIMAL, COME OUT AND WE'LL KILL YOU!'

Then there was laughter followed by more threats and shrieks. Steve and Snuggletoes who had broken free from Wanderpaws started for the door but the Professor was ready for them, and faster, and he stood there and barred their way. They went back to their positions and the Professor to his own place.

The firefighters reacted at once, their training being beyond any fears, and the extinguishers pumped foam under high pressure into the window bay where the fire was raging. All the others however, apart from Steve and Snuggletoes with their thoughts of retaliation, were terrified by the proximity and sheer presence of the fire however well controlled. All that was except the Professor. He remained on the display case and anybody who saw him then was in no doubt that whatever might be said about museums during the day, this was his observatory, he was in charge, and anyone who wanted to take it from him or damage it had better think again. From his place he was giving calm instructions as his plan unfolded.

'Phone group send your message now.'

The mice hiding behind the telephone sprang back to their places and dialled the number they now knew so well. The mouse at the mouthpiece frantically squeaked the message, perhaps too frantically since she had to repeat it several times before she was understood. Their task finished they all dived for cover under the table the phone was standing on.

Outside, the six attackers were taken aback by the limited results of their assault. They could hear the extinguishers working and even though they had not guessed exactly what was happening, could see that the flames were already dying down and being brought under control.

They looked at each other in confusion and one of the women cursed out loud. The man next to her however gave a sickening smile and pulled one last petrol bomb from inside his jacket. He lit it and tossed the blazing missile high up and towards the roof. It arched momentarily in the air and then crashed as he had intended it through a skylight in a passageway between the 'Time' gallery and the main hall. Inside, Chandra, had a terrifying glimpse of the fireball before it struck and then all was chaos as she screamed, the skylight shattered and blazing petrol seemed to fly everywhere accompanied by a nauseating stench of burning hot fumes. Part of one wall of the main hall became a sheet of flame and worse burning fuel splashed across onto a group of sheltering mice who now scattered screaming, some with patches of their fur on fire. The bottle finally exploded as it hit the floor sending out more splashes and two rivers of burning petrol which rushed across the wood to surround the case where the Professor stood. All those who were not injured or in complete panic looked on to see his small outline silhouetted against two sheets of crimson flame. Fire was also actually around him now where pools of petrol had fallen on the top of the case as the bottle had disintegrated. Still he did not move. Then they heard his voice, clear amongst the shouts and screams of terror and confusion.

'Smother the flames on anyone hit by fuel! Get some extinguishers over here now! Sound the main alarm!'

The Professor's voice had a power even in that dreadful moment and at once his orders were obeyed. Sunfur, Starwhiskers and Wanderpaws with very little thought for their own safety threw themselves on top of the mice whose fur was burning, rapidly followed by several others until all that could be seen was an untidy heap of squirming bodies on the floor.

Steve jumped across a blazing pool of fire and grabbed a spare extinguisher at once releasing it at the flames surrounding the Professor's station. Almost instantaneously, he was joined by two firefighters who had left the window and clouds of white fumes shot out as they advanced together towards the heart of the blaze. On the other side, Chandra was beating at the floor with an asbestos blanket she had found in an adjoining passageway and two mice dived down a corridor and raced up ladders that had been left up against the alarm control box. They threw themselves at the switch and suddenly all the alarm bells in the building went off at once, the noise was deafening. It was then that the lights went out.

Damaged by the heat or the flames the electricity supply had failed. With the loss of the lights, their friendly bright illumination was replaced by a lurid orange glow from the fire against which the smoke stood out as terrible black wraiths floating on the air. The fumes were choking but at least the firefighters were still all right protected by their masks and breathing equipment. They had offered a set to Steve and Chandra but since there was no way that the apparatus could be adapted for the mice, both had refused saying they would take their chances with their friends. The extinguishers of Steve and the two firefighters brought the blazing section of the floor under control and together they turned their attention to the wall behind them. Chandra struggled forwards and pushed the fire blanket down round where the Professor stood putting out the patches of flame that threatened him. Two more firefighters left the window bay where the fire was now out and joined the group at the wall. With the combined power of all their foam the flames flickered, drew back and finally died and all was blackness and silence since the alarm batteries had by then failed as well.

In the swirling fumes and smoke, mice struggled and coughed as they groped their way trying to find where they were, their friends, and help the injured. From several points there were cries for help and sobbing that demanded immediate attention. From the 'Time' gallery the older officer was shouting instructions.

'Use your torches but be careful how you move, don't step on any of the mice.'

The firefighters fumbled for their lights and as they were switched on, eerie beams cut through the swirling fumes, stabbing in all directions. From outside they heard the most welcome sound of all, approaching sirens.

The attackers had felt a wave of triumph as they saw the skylight shatter and then heard the screams of pain and fear that they had inflicted. Despite it being their last petrol bomb, they stayed to watch what to their perverted minds was fun and enjoy the suffering they had caused. Also in accordance with their plans, they still hoped that Chandra would be forced to run from the building straight into their trap. This idea particularly pleased Smirkmuzzle as he stood beside them. He had not given up thoughts of his schemes of the night before. The alarm bells however had, as the Professor hoped, frightened them and when they started ringing, the cruel group withdrew down the slope into the park and the shelter of some trees where they would not be so easily seen. As soon as they heard the police sirens on the top approach road, they had had quite enough and began to run down through the park and towards their own van. Above them there were shouts and torches and they quickened their pace to a flat out sprint. It and the slope of the hill gave a momentum which made it difficult to turn as fast as they would have wished as in front of them at the bottom entrance to the park three police vans screeched to a halt and Sergeant Randel, four constables and four dogs, including Rex, jumped out.

226

The tables turned, the attackers, now the hunted, swung off to the right back up amongst the trees and scattered. Behind them they could hear the dogs and feel them getting closer. Rex was in the lead when he first saw Smirkmuzzle. The rat was racing off as fast as he could go, dodging past trees and bushes as he sped across the grass. Rex put his head down and ran. He might be a police dog and duty was all very well but this was almost getting personal, he had seen that rat once too often. There were only inches between them when he heard Sergeant Randel's voice telling him to go left and stop the man who had thrown the last petrol bomb. Rex hesitated, his training had been extremely good and Sergeant Randel was his friend, he knew he should change direction at once. He glanced round and saw the man, Rex certainly could not leave it very long or he really would get away. Perhaps duty did come first after all. Still there was just going to be time for one last gesture at least. Rex took two long leaps forwards and snapped at Smirkmuzzle's back.

Smirkmuzzle was running as fast as he could. As soon as he saw the police vans he had needed no further encouragement. He knew all too well how to spot which ones carried dogs. As he took off at top speed through the grass, he could hear their barks and cries behind him and the sounds gave him the extra energy to keep going. Very soon however he realised that one of the dogs was on to him, following his every move. Smirkmuzzle risked a backward glance over his shoulder.

'Oh no!' he thought, ' it's that great big dog, the one I've seen before. I never did like the look of him.'

Smirkmuzzle threw himself forwards with all the speed he could manage but still the dog seemed to be gaining on him till he was sure that he could feel its breath on his tail. Smirkmuzzle rushed on swinging wildly from side to side to avoid obstacles and try and throw the dog off. Then he heard Rex take two long fast strides and sensing real danger he twisted and jumped to the left. Even so, the dog caught a fold of skin and fur on his back and gave him a very painful nip before he could break away. He was sure he was done for but the dog jumped right across him, took two enormous bounds up a bank and threw itself onto a man on his left bringing him down sprawling on the ground.

'Good,' thought Smirkmuzzle who never had had very much sense of loyalty, 'right now it's everyone for themselves, this gives me a chance to get away.'

Behind him he heard shouts of 'hold him Rex, good dog,' and Smirkmuzzle dived down an inviting and very smelly drain to get his breath back and lick his wounds.

Back at the observatory it was definitely not a case of everyone for themselves. By the limited light of the firefighters' torches, all those inside were trying to come to terms with what had happened. All the mice who were injured had been found. Fortunately, although several had suffered real burns, with most who had been affected it was more a case of singed fur than anything else. Those who were really hurt were quickly carried to an upper attic similar to the Professor's study where by torchlight they were made as comfortable as they could be. After a few more minutes of groping round in the smoke and fumes of the fire extinguishers, Steve and two of the firefighters managed to repair the damage to the main fuse box and the lights were restored. A quick search was made to see if there were any more casualties and when everyone was sure that no one had been left without help, the Professor went outside to see what was happening whilst the firefighters started to pack up their equipment. Sunfur, Starwhiskers, Steve and Chandra went with him. Snuggletoes also followed but Wanderpaws would not let him go until he had made a very solemn promise not to throw anything or attack anyone in any way. Even then Wanderpaws insisted on staying right beside him just in case.

Outside, the situation was beginning to come under control. Behind the observatory there were four or five white police cars all with their blue flashing lights still running. Beside them was a fire engine only it was not brought any closer once it was clear that it was not needed. On the slope in front of the buildings all six of the attackers had been caught and were being taken up towards the vehicles in handcuffs. Behind them the police dogs sat on the grass obediently watching now that their job was over. As the attackers passed Chandra, one of them spat on the ground at her feet.

'Filth, you haven't heard the last of us,' the man said.

The detective at his side pushed him forwards towards the police cars.

'All right, that's enough, you're in sufficient trouble already without making it any worse for yourself.'

The group was lost to clear sight as it entered the aura of flashing blue around the vehicles and the attackers took on more of the image of demons from the depths of hell in the strange colour. It was then that another of the men craned and shouted back at them over his shoulder.

'At least we stopped your Paki show the other night!'

Chandra started.

'So it was them!'

'I'm afraid so,' said the Professor, 'it's been them all the time.'

'Well at least they're going to where they belong; prison and hopefully for a very long time,' Steve said with some emotion.

'Yes, I think we can be sure of that,' replied the Professor, 'but I'm afraid that that man, if you can call him that, was right. We haven't heard the last of them, at least not of people like them. The sooner you all get off to India and try and find the Stone the better.'

Just then, Sunfur began looking round as if she had suddenly remembered something.

'Has anyone seen Hugbundle?'

'No,' answered Starwhiskers, 'I thought she was still in the observatory.'

'Well she's not,' said Wanderpaws, 'we were the last out of the hall and she wasn't there.'

'I hope she's all right,' said Snuggletoes, slightly surprised at the unusual situation of one of the other mice being the cause for concern.

Then they heard a muffled voice from inside Chandra's anorak.

'Yes I'm all right, is it safe to come out now?'

And the tips of two brown ears followed by a nose very slowly emerged cautiously looking in both directions to see that everything was over. They all laughed.

Sergeant Randel came over and spoke to the Professor.

'Is everyone all right?' he asked.

'Some hurt but hopefully no one very seriously, I'm still waiting to hear,' said the Professor all at once sounding very tired.

'Anything we can do?'

'No, I've got some medical help on it's way otherwise just take care of those specimens, that's the best thing you can do.'

'Oh don't worry about them, they're not going anywhere except with us. Not for quite a long time I should think.'

'I know it sounds uncharitable but I'm afraid I'm going to say good to that,' said the Professor quietly.

'I'm sorry I wasn't here sooner,' said Sergeant Randel, 'I came as soon as I got your message.'

'That's all right, I knew you would. You couldn't help being away. Don't worry we'll talk about it some other time.'

'What about all this,' said Sergeant Randel gesturing towards the observatory, 'that's going to take a bit of explaining.'

'Ah yes you've got a point there,' the Professor answered, 'I think even I may be a bit out of my depth this time. Still even if I am, it will all have been worth it.'

'Well anything I can do to help let me know, but I'm afraid that you are going to need more than the influence of a mere sergeant to get you out of this one.'

'Thank you,' said the Professor, 'and don't underestimate yourself, I'm going to need all the help I can get.'

Just then a big unmarked car drew up beside the police vehicles and an older policeman in a uniform with different and more impressive markings got out. At once all the other officers stood to attention and the watching mice guessed that this had to be someone very senior indeed.

'Well I think you might just have it,' said Sergeant Randel in a tone of some surprise.

Together, he and the Professor went over and spoke to the senior officer. Not knowing quite what might be going on the others decided to stay back. They all knew that the Professor could be in a lot of difficulties about the damage to the observatory and they certainly didn't want to make things worse. They could not see the group very clearly and as they spoke, the Professor and the policemen moved even further away from them making it still more difficult to follow what was going on. As the group talked, the senior policeman kept glancing down the hill as if he was expecting something to happen. After a few minutes, a large and highly polished black car drew up alongside the Professor and both the policemen stood back. A chauffeur got out and opened the rear door and the Professor climbed inside. As the door swung back they all got a glimpse, but only a glimpse of the face of the figure sitting in the back. It wasn't a good enough look to recognise the person, even if you knew them well, and yet despite not being able to see it clearly they all found the face in some way familiar as if they had seen it before. The funny thing was that when they

231

had a chance to talk about it later, all those watching found they had been left with the same thought; that they had had a glimpse of someone they saw in the news programmes on television, and not once but often.

After a few minutes the door opened again and the Professor got out, for once even he looked a little surprised and he slowly came back to join them whilst the big car pulled away.

'Who was that!' they all asked.

'Now that I've been asked not to say, let's just say a friend, a new friend, and in some ways a rather surprising one. It seems some people have been taking notice of what I have been up to in the last few days.'

'But everything is going to be all right isn't it?' asked Snuggletoes nervously.

The Professor sighed.

'Well that depends what you mean. We've got some people hurt so that's not all right. There's the future and we're going to see plenty more problems then, so that's not all right either. But if you mean have I got one or two worries less than I had a few minutes ago, then I'm very glad to say that the answer is yes. Now let's go and see what we can sort out at the observatory.'

CHAPTER 19

Clearing Up

With the Professor leading they all made their way back into the observatory. At the entrance they met the fire-fighting team carrying their equipment.

'Sorry we made a bit of a mess,' said the officer.

'You dare make one more apology and you will see some trouble compared to which the evening so far will seem very tame,' replied the Professor, 'only this time it will be from me. I'm still trying to think of a way to thank you!'

'Well, now, I wouldn't worry too much about that,' the officer continued, 'let's just leave it that it was our pleasure, especially after it was you who decoded that incomplete satellite data and found our crashed aircraft last year. Without what you did the crew would have surely died.'

'Oh that was easy, I'm just glad that Steve brought the information down for me to have a look at, your people were along the right lines, they were just making it too complicated. Anyway that was fun, you can't have enjoyed yourselves much tonight.'

'No, I won't say we have, but I don't think we would have wanted to be anywhere else. You're quite a popular guy down at the base and I for one would not want to face the parade this morning and tell them something happened up here without our at least having tried to help. Still we'd better be getting back, but you can stay on if you want to Steve, I'll clear it with your flight commander.'

233

'Thank you sir, I'd like to.'

'Easily done. I'll leave you my jeep and you can come back when you're ready. Anyway we'll bring the truck over and get our stuff out of your way. Then you can start to clear up, it's going to be quite a job.'

The firefighters made their way across the courtyard and over to a lorry which had been hidden behind some trees. It was brought as close to the entrance as possible and all the remaining equipment and the lights with their miles of cable were carefully loaded into the back. The crew climbed in as well and with a wave from the officer, those left at the observatory watched as he and the men and women under his command to whom they owed so much disappeared slowly down the drive. Only when they were finally out of sight did the tired group finally turn and enter the building.

In the passage, they were met by one of the mouse doctors who had arrived earlier. Medicine for the mice was a bit like astronomy. It had all started when they lived alongside people in the early laboratories and hospitals many centuries before. The mice watched and learned from what they saw, in a few places they even worked with the people doctors as together they fought what to all of them felt like a war against disease and suffering. The following years had seen many mistakes and blind alleys and there had been some very bad things done by the people doctors which the mice could not agree with but, somehow, together the overall direction had been maintained. Then for the mice things started to go wrong. As bigger and faster advances in medicine were made, the people doctors seemed to care less about what their patients actually felt and lived and more about seeing them as scientific problems and a game. For a while, a very short while, one or two of the mouse doctors had tried it on their patients as well thinking it must be a new form of treatment. What happened to the first mouse doctor who told some sick mice that they shouldn't see their friends, or wake up when they wanted to, or try and look after the things they felt were important is not recorded but whatever it was, it was sufficiently bad that no others ever made the same mistake again. The mouse doctors very rapidly returned to listening to what their patients wanted and then trying to help them achieve it rather than deciding what they should want and telling them that was all they could have. The doctor who stood in front of the Professor now with a tiny stethoscope still round his neck knew exactly who he was supposed to be looking after and how to go about it.

'Well you've all been fairly lucky. Some of the burns are serious and will be very sore for a couple of weeks but I think everyone will make a full recovery.'

'That's what I wanted to hear,' said the Professor in a tone of great relief.

'Yes but that's only if we work for it,' the Doctor mouse continued. 'We've done our bit, all the wounds have been cleaned and dressed and we'll look in tomorrow to check that everything is O K. Those who wanted them have had some painkillers and we've left a supply with instructions as to how many pills they can have and when and how to use them. So that's a start but there are a number of things which as a doctor I must insist that you organise at once.'

'Don't worry,' said the Professor, 'just say what should be done and I will personally see that it happens.'

'Fine,' said the Doctor mouse, 'from you that's as good as a guarantee which is nice to have. Now the first thing is breakfast.'

'Oh that's all right,' said Chandra, 'we can make sure they don't have any if it will interfere with the treatment.'

The Doctor mouse looked at her with a strained expression.

235

'As I was saying, breakfast. This doesn't have to be rigid if anyone has any great preferences but most of our patients seem to get on with this regime quite well. Try hot waffles and scrambled eggs as a first course followed by croissant with jam and cream, oh yes and plenty of coffee, the real stuff if you can manage it, and that should be with cream as well.'

'What does that do?' asked Steve.

'Scientifically not a lot but it certainly makes you feel better and that's further than we get with the drugs most of the time. Anyway let's carry on. Lunch; get hold of as many special cheeses as you can, and some hot bread. Afternoon tea; strawberries and cream. You should still be able to get strawberries in a few of the bigger shops even at this time of year, it's one of the advantages of being in London, but just in case you can't, I've written you a prescription for some. You can go and pick them up at St. Wellpaws Hospital, at the pharmacy, when you get there just ask for the fruit section. We'll have called in again by tomorrow afternoon so we can discuss the evening meal then. Now I want to see a television up there when I come back and, if you haven't already done so, please send messages to their friends so they can come and stay and cheer them up. I've got one of my students making a list now of who they would like contacted. The other thing they mentioned was that the main lights are still on up there and could they have some candles instead to make it cosy and some hot water bottles if you've got them. When they all feel up to it, you should arrange a party as soon as possible, if you have any problems with that I'll send one of our physiotherapists down to help you, that's their speciality after all. Now one last thing - ice cream; day and night on demand. Get as many flavours as you can but if after a while any of them are getting bored with what you've managed to come up with, give me a ring. Our research laboratory has discovered several new varieties recently and would probably like to have some patient tastings so I'll be able to get tubs sent up for you. Right, well if you'll excuse me that's about it and I must get off and sort out a problem at the hospital. They called me earlier on, it's a bit of an emergency actually, something about the videos on C ward not being exciting enough. I just hope I can remember enough of my film studies course at medical school to sort it out. Bye, call me if there's anything you need!'

And with that the Doctor mouse dashed off and headed out into the night on his rounds.

'That much at least is the same as people doctors,' Chandra thought, 'always in a rush.'

After the Professor had made sure that the Doctor mouse's instructions were being carried out, they all made their way into the main hall and looked at the destruction around them. One section of the wall was burned and charred, so was a large patch of the floor surrounding where the Professor had stood, and everywhere was black from the smoke whilst the unmistakable smell of burning still hung in the air. On top of the black scorched coating, puddles of foam remained from the extinguishers and above them a cold chill wind blew through the shattered skylight. Next door in the 'Time' gallery it was almost as bad and an even bigger draft swept through the demolished and now re-exposed window but as they explored further, they were pleasantly surprised to find that the remaining rooms were almost completely unaffected having been sealed off from the area of the fire by the doors. The firefighters had put the blaze out so quickly that the fumes had not had time to seep into the rest of the building. Even so, back in the central hall in the grim light of that early morning, things were not very cheerful. Steve left them for a moment and found a mop with which he started to clear up the foam whilst Cometpaw, Sunfur and Starwhiskers got together a team of astronomer mice who fetched their

237

ladders and began to clean off the soot and dirt from the telescopes. The small areas of glass and polished brass that they uncovered however only served to show up even more clearly how bad the rest was and Steve's efforts with the mop merely revealed more and more scorched areas. The Professor wandered dejectedly over to the display case he had occupied earlier and sat on the edge, Chandra went over and joined him.

'It would have been better if I hadn't come here the first evening wouldn't it,' she said slowly, 'perhaps I just wasn't meant to have a show that night. Instead, you tried to help me and now look at your beautiful observatory, this is all the thanks you get.'

'Is it?' asked the Professor lifting his head, 'I'd rather hoped it meant enough to you for at least that not to be true.'

Chandra hesitated for a moment.

'Of course it meant a lot to me, it still does, more than I can ever explain. But that isn't enough, one person can't justify risking this.'

'And you're suddenly just one person,' replied the Professor, 'what about all the other people who are threatened and attacked, are they all just single people who don't count? And what about all the men and women and children who were looking forward to coming to your show, do they not count either? And what about us when you brought the moon back for us, I suppose that's a nothing now as well is it?'

'No, of course not, and I know you're right and you wouldn't have had it any other way but I just can't stand seeing you in all this destruction knowing how it must make you feel.'

That much at least the Professor knew he could not deny. He was feeling very sad at what he saw around him and he was sure that it must show, which it did. Chandra sat with him sharing his depression for a few minutes but then thinking that any action, however ineffective, would make them both feel better she tried to suggest something constructive.

'Still if we don't start then nothing will ever be put right, what should we tackle first?'

Chandra looked round and so did the Professor, but from the general mess and confusion no really meaningful task stood out that they could put their effort in to. Neither of them moved.

'All right, I'm sorry,' Chandra said, 'it would take an army to put this straight quickly, perhaps I was being silly.'

When she reached the word 'army' however the Professor jerked upright and his eyes shone.

'Of course, you're right! Why didn't I think of that - it will take an army so let's get one, let's get the Army; don't go away, I'll be right back!'

With that the Professor jumped up and dashed off towards his study. A few minutes later he returned with a beaming smile right across his face.

'Great, that's all fixed, they'll be here within the hour.'

'Who exactly will be here?' asked Chandra with a tone of some doubt at what might be about to happen.

'Why the Army of course,' laughed the Professor, 'don't you remember? After all it was your suggestion.'

'No, Professor I said an army not the Army. Which one do you have in mind?'

'Well, the British Army, they're the only one close enough to get here quickly.'

Chandra sat and thought for a moment and looked rather sad.

'Professor, I know it would be fantastic to get the observatory straight as soon as possible but how could you involve the British Army after what happened to the Heartstone, surely that can't be right.'

The Professor smiled.

239

'Chandra that was a very long time ago and you have to give people credit that they might have changed but I can understand your feelings all the same. Can I just ask you to trust me till they get here and then I would like you to talk to the Commander of the unit that is coming. If he can't convince you that they should be trusted then be as nasty to me as you like. Till then, just accept that they can't be all bad because of what they are coming to help with.'

In her mind Chandra knew that the Professor was right but somehow her heart could not accept what was about to happen. She stayed in the main hall for a bit but she did not talk much and soon wandered off into another part of the building to think. Steve came and found her and asked if she was all right and if there was anything he could do to help, but she sent him back to carry on with the clearing up saying that she needed to be on her own for a while. Some time later, as the first grey streaks of dawn were beginning to spread across the sky, she heard two trucks draw up outside and a lot of shouts and sounds of men jumping down and coming into the building. Next, she heard the Professor and two other voices in the hall discussing the damage and giving directions so work could start on clearing up. All Chandra felt however was an even greater sadness and emptiness that the successors to those who had broken the Heartstone were so close and now part of her adventure which had promised to change so much. The feelings were not happy ones and she went even further into the upper galleries of the observatory to get as far away as she could. Then she heard footsteps coming up the stairs and entering the room behind her. She did not however look round.

'Hello,' a voice said, 'I'm Major Summers, Nat Summers, the Professor said you might want to have a word.'

Chandra drew back for a moment feeling that there was no way that she could go through with this. How could she face this British Army Commander that represented so much she wanted to forget. She had already formed a picture of him that the perfect accent he spoke with confirmed. Chandra very slowly and reluctantly turned round to look into the face she did not want to see. Only then did Chandra realise how wrong she had been. Nat Summers had the firm handsome face she had imagined but he was as black as his birth as a native Nigerian would lead you to expect.

'The army's changed a bit you know,' he said.

Chandra swallowed hard and hoped that her feelings had not shown too much.

'It's all right,' the Major continued, 'I can guess how you feel, I saw things the same way once. Then my family moved here and despite a lot of bad that happened, I knew things were changing even if only slowly. I'd always wanted to be in the army for as long as I could remember so I kept an eye on what was going on there in particular. Before I had time to make up my own mind though my grandmother saw an advertisement for a scholarship for anyone who was from Africa or India who wanted to train as an officer. She wrote off, I went for an interview and an exam, got the grant and now here I am. And before you ask, no it hasn't all been that easy, just worth it in the end.'

'Yes I'm sure, or at least I hope so,' Chandra stammered, 'look I'm very sorry about what the Professor told you I said, I just didn't know you see.'

'The Professor?' Nat replied, 'He didn't tell me anything, just suggested I should come and find you, I guessed the rest. Never underestimate him, he's quite a little character.'

'No don't worry,' Chandra said, 'I'm learning very fast never to underestimate the Professor. Where did you meet him?'

'Right here, out there in the park. I'd been beaten up and called a 'nigger' once too often in training barracks and I'd got a day's leave so I came and sat under the trees to think. I was just getting round to giving up the whole scholarship and everything when I heard this little voice behind me. I turned round and there he was. All he wanted was to ask if I'd help him move some parcels that had just arrived up to his study before any of the museum people saw them. But we got talking and I stayed till the evening and looked through some of the telescopes and let's just say that the rest is history. By the time I left, I'd changed my mind and somehow things never seemed as bad again. I came up here quite a lot for a while, then I graduated and was posted round the country and overseas but I never lost touch completely.'

'That's quite a story,' Chandra said, 'tell me who provided the scholarship?'

'I don't know really,' Nat said, 'my grandmother handled most of the paperwork. It was some sort of trust, you know one of those funds set up years ago for some good purpose or other. This one was just to help anyone who was Asian or Black be an army officer. Odd sort of cause if you think about it but it suited me. All I can remember was the name because I had to keep putting it on forms and papers and that sort of thing. It was called the Giles Benson Trust, must have been after the person who started it I suppose.'

Despite her surprise, Chandra was not quite ready to share her knowledge of the name Giles Benson. She did not know how much of the Heartstone story Nat knew and she remembered their promise to Moonbeam only to ever reveal anything if they absolutely had to, even to someone who was so obviously a friend. Together they went back down to the main hall where all around there was frenzied activity as groups of soldiers, each accompanied by two of the observatory mice to tell them how things had been, worked at top speed to put the

242

damage right. Soot was washed away from the ceiling as fast as one team could move its ladders whilst on the floor the blackened top surface of the wood was being sandpapered away to leave fresh new grain. Burned paint was being stripped off the walls and at the window in the 'Time' gallery the charred remains of the frame had already been removed and lay on the floor. Nat looked round and gave a few instructions to the men but he did not join in.

'Officer's privilege,' he said to Chandra and winked.

They went down a passage to the alarm control where Steve and the Professor were completing more permanent repairs to the system.

'Professor,' Nat said, 'one thing I was going to ask, where's the circus?'

'Circus, what circus?' the Professor said after a pause as if he was only half listening.

'The circus, the one the elephant comes from.'

The Professor looked round quickly and behind them in the main hall Hugbundle nearly fell off the telescope she was polishing.

'Yes, the elephant, the one I saw silhouetted against the skyline as I came up through the park. You must know about it, it was only a few yards away from the building.'

Starwhiskers and Sunfur stopped work and came over with Hugbundle right behind them.

'Nat,' the Professor said, 'there isn't a circus anywhere round here, never has been as far as I can remember.'

'Well, I know an elephant when I see one, you forget I've been back to Africa quite a few times and I got a good look at this one. I can even tell you what kind it was.'

'What do you mean?' asked Sunfur.

'Well there's two different types of elephant, one from Africa and one from India. The main difference is that the African ones I'm used to have bigger ears.'

'But this one?' asked Hugbundle.

'No, this one was definitely Indian, no doubt about it.'

'Nat, I can honestly say I have no idea how the elephant got there,' said the Professor, 'but I have to admit to knowing a little more about why. For the moment don't ask, there's a very special and secret mission about to start and for a while, it's best if it's talked about as little as possible. Sometime we'll tell you the full story.'

'That's all right Professor, I can understand a secret mission, you forget what I do, but if I can ever help let me know.'

'Nat, you already are.'

Behind them, still thinking about the visitor, Hugbundle and Chandra looked long and hard at each other hoping for confirmation that they were not dreaming.

Back at the telescopes the mice returned to the work of polishing and cleaning. With most of the cloths getting very dirty, Snuggletoes wandered off to find a new one. All the available bits in the hall were in use or too soiled to be of any value so he went further and up into the Professor's study. The flash of brilliant purple at once caught his eye and for a moment he had doubts about using it but he told himself this was something of an emergency and everything had to be pressed into service. The square of fabric could always be washed later. It was only after he had been back in the hall and working on a telescope for a full ten minutes that he heard Sunfur shriek behind him.

'You idiot! That's the Heartstone cloth, the one Sailvoyage wrapped the Stone in!'

Snuggletoes stopped rubbing and all the mice gathered round to look.

'Give me that,' said Sunfur holding out her paw, 'it must be so filthy by now that it could be ruined.'

Snuggletoes gave her the square of purple cloth and hung his head. Sunfur took it from him and turned it over again and again in her paws with an increasing look of disbelief.

'How long have you been using this?' she asked.

'Not that long,' said Snuggletoes trying not to make it sound too bad, 'only for the last ten minutes. All I've done so far is clean one side of this telescope.'

'But there isn't a mark on it!' gasped Sunfur in amazement and round her the other mice nodded in agreement.

'Isn't there,' said Snuggletoes hopefully, still not realising the implications of what Sunfur had seen.

'No there isn't,' Sunfur repeated, and she went over to another telescope and rubbed a large area of soot off with the fabric.

The mice all crowded round as she turned it over, still there was not a mark on it and those watching looked at each other in confusion and surprise.

'Well,' said the Professor, 'science does seem to be taking a back seat tonight. Give Snuggletoes back the cloth, it would appear that he might even be meant to be using it.'

The work of clearing up continued throughout the morning. Fred arrived at six and stood for a moment staring at the damage and shaking his head. Then at the Professor's suggestion he went and made everybody a cup of tea. Since, with the soldiers, there were so many people around it took him quite a long time and kept his mind off what was going on and what might be said about his not having been there. He need not however have worried. Whoever it was the Professor had been speaking to in the big car had obviously been busy. No one from the museum turned up for work and by eight o'clock a van arrived with signs saying that the museum was closed for the day which were placed at all the entrances and approaches. Behind them, the Professor and his helpers were not bothered and after some of the soldiers had gone to get supplies of paint, glass and other

245

materials, the observatory began to look more and more like it had done, only in some places rather cleaner. By mid afternoon everything was finished and all that was left was for the final coats of paint and varnish to dry. From a safe distance Nat and the Professor looked at the result.

'Not bad for a bunch of amateurs,' Nat said, 'after all it's not exactly what we are trained for.'

'Nat, it's incredible,' replied the Professor, 'thank you, thank you very much.'

'Don't thank me, after all what are friends for. All I still want to know is who on earth did you get to speak to my commanding officer. After I got your call, as I told you, however much I wanted to help I needed permission and I was ready to have to argue for quite a bit to get it. By the time I got to his house, however, the C.O. was out of bed and waiting to see me, almost demanded to know why I hadn't left yet.'

'Now that,' said the Professor with a grin, 'you really shouldn't ask. Another friend, someone else who cares, that's all I can say.'

By four o'clock the soldiers were gone and most of the observatory mice had also left or disappeared upstairs to find somewhere to sleep. Only Sunfur, Starwhiskers, Snuggletoes, Wanderpaws, Honeymouse, Jasmine-mouse, Chandra, Steve and the Professor were left in the hall as outside the light started to fail and darkness approached.

'Do you want a lift back?' Steve asked looking at Chandra.

'Oh yes please,' she said and began to collect her things.

The mice also started to find their belongings but whilst Chandra and Steve were looking the other way, the Professor signalled to all of them, even Hugbundle, that for once they should let Chandra go alone. Starwhiskers held out his paws in a silent question 'why?' but all the Professor did was smile. When Chandra looked round to see if they were coming, Sunfur told her that they would stay on to finish sorting things out and would join her later at the flat. Together the mice watched as Steve and Chandra walked over to the jeep and then slowly drove off down the drive. A short time later in the beam from the same headlights that had lit that departure, fresh but familiar slogans of hate in Chandra's road confronted the man and woman who the writers believed should not even talk to each other. The lettering was so new that it had to be far less than a day old, it had been done even after the attackers at the observatory were arrested. Not everything was over by a long way.

CHAPTER 20

Speedybeard

Steve went in and had a cup of coffee with Chandra at her flat before he set off back to the the base and some well earned sleep. Whilst he was there he asked about Chandra's family and she told him that her mother had died all those years ago and her father had gone back to India in the spring that year, so apart from the occasional letter she now had very little contact with him. Steve also learned that Chandra had no brothers or sisters and that she had not kept in touch with her aunt because they never had got on very well. Chandra knew there were other aunts and uncles in India and that she had a lot of cousins there but, since she had not been back for many years, she could not say she really knew any of them at all, let alone well. It was however thoughts of Chandra herself that filled Steve's mind as he drove West through the London traffic, not her family. It had been the same the first night he had seen her in Wellminster, somehow her image just stayed with him.

About half an hour after Steve had left, Sunfur and the others arrived from the observatory having been brought by the taxi driver the Professor knew, the one who they had first seen in St James' Park. Five minutes later came Magicnose. They first heard her open the letter box and climb through and then as she walked in to the middle of the circle of faces seated round the lounge, they somehow knew what she was going to say.

'Quiet evening I hope.'.

'NO!' replied eight angry voices in unison.

'All right, all right, I was only joking,' said Magicnose, 'I heard you had a spot of trouble last night.'

'A spot of trouble!' exclaimed Snuggletoes.

'No, a lot of trouble, I'm sorry I wasn't there to help.'

'Just how do you know?' asked Wanderpaws.

'News travels fast.'

'Not that fast, unless of course you are on good terms with any of the rats who got away.'

'Hold it right there,' interrupted Sunfur, 'before this goes any further I think it's time we changed a few things.'

Wanderpaws sat down and folded his front paws angrily.

'Like what?' asked Magicnose.

'Like if we are going to work together we should know a little bit more about what everyone is doing. After last night, there's no room for confusion between those who are supposed to be friends.'

'That's fair,' said Magicnose, 'what do you suggest?'

'Well we have got to tell you about the map and what happens next but I think you should tell us where you went last night, and just what it is you are up to. It's the only way we will ever be able to help each other.'

Magicnose looked at Sunfur for a full minute before she spoke.

'Go on then, after you.'

Wanderpaws appeared as if he was going to object and ask why it had to be that way round but something made him change his mind.

'Very well,' said Sunfur and with the help of the others she told the full story of the events at the observatory and what the Professor had told them.

'Now it's your turn,' she said when she had finished.

Magicnose hesitated.

'Go on, we won't tell anyone. Just like our adventure yours can be shared and remain a secret too.'

'All right, on that understanding I'll tell you. Not everything, some of it's personal and doesn't change anything, but enough so we can trust each other.'

'That's all we ask,' said Sunfur, 'now where were you last night?'

'At Westminster.'

'You're going to have to say more than that.'

'No, at Westminster, not the borough, Westminster itself, the Houses of Parliament.'

'And who were you seeing?'

'If I could avoid it absolutely no one. I wanted to look through the notes of the Committee of MP's for International Conservation. The committee room is deserted and locked at night, but there is still a way in.

'Who?' asked Honeymouse.

'Like I said, the Committee of MP's for International Conservation.'

'All right, why?' said Sunfur.

'To find out what the major projects in India are at the moment.'

'Look we're not going there on a botany trip!' Wanderpaws exploded.

'Yes and who wants to get involved with those silly conservation people,' said Jasminemouse, 'why don't they just leave us alone and let us look after ourselves. It's not much of an offer is it. First one lot of people come along and mess things up completely and then another bunch turn up, put a tiny part of it right and expect to be told how wonderful they are.'

'Well it's better than doing nothing at all,' said Magicnose, 'people aren't all the same, the ones who try and help deserve some thanks.'

'Fine, but why check up on them now?' asked Starwhiskers.

'Because I want to find Speedybeard.'

'What, the porcupine in the park?'

'Yes, that's what I'm trying to explain.'

250

'So are the Conservation Committee looking after him then?' asked Hugbundle.

At this suggestion even Magicnose had to smile, the thought of the Committee looking after Speedybeard was, to anyone who knew him, rather funny. If they ever met, it would be far more likely that he would be taking care of them.

'No!' said Magicnose, 'Now if you will all wait a minute I'll tell you why I went there. Speedybeard is a porcupine that I met a long time ago. He cares a lot about looking after the special bits of the world and he gets very upset when anything beautiful is destroyed, especially the natural things like hills and valleys and with them the plants, flowers, lakes and other things they have kept safe. I know you all think porcupines aren't like that but some of them are different, Speedybeard's different. He's so different that he is hardly accepted by the other porcupines any longer, he just spends his time wandering on his own like some sort of outcast, that's why he's so difficult to find.'

'Why don't the porcupines like him?' asked Hugbundle.

'Basically just because he's not like the rest of them, cares about different things, cares about them more than he's supposed to.'

'So what does he do on these wanderings?'

'That's the strange part, not what he does but what has now happened to it. He paints, paints the land and the flowers, the lakes and everything else he sees, sometimes even people. The pictures are very, very beautiful but for a long time he never showed them to anybody. Then a particularly wild and special valley was threatened by a mining operation. It didn't have to be dug up to get at the rocks underneath but it was going to be cheaper than extending a shaft from an existing mine nearby. No one was prepared to spend the money to save it. Speedybeard knew that valley and loved it. He

251

went up there one night and painted it by moonlight. The painting was one of the most beautiful he had ever done and the following morning it went on show in the city where the mining company was based. There was a public outcry at what was to happen and the plans were changed. More than that, however, the painting was sold for a lot of money which was used to help make the valley a nature reserve. As an artist Speedybeard became famous and everyone wanted his paintings, not that they knew who he was, the picture appeared under the name of Brian Ekips, and everyone thought and still thinks that it's a person.'

'O K,' said Wanderpaws, 'we've got this itinerant porcupine who paints things which everybody else thinks are done by a person. Now just what has this got to do with India, us and you last night.'

'Just bear with me a little longer and perhaps you will begin to understand. Brian Ekips is now a famous artist. His pictures are shown all over the world and there have been several times when he has painted something that was threatened and managed to make people care enough to save it. About a year ago however a new series of pictures started to emerge. They were more magical, more ethereal, and seemed to capture something beyond what could be simply seen if you looked at where they were of. The colours were stronger, things seemed to shimmer, and almost everyone who sees them has the same thought, that they show not just the land but its spirit, its soul. No one however noticed a tiny black dot on the horizon of the first two pictures but by the time the third was put on show, the speck had become larger. It was someone or something walking into the landscape of the picture. Since then the figure has become bigger with each painting, but still not clear enough to recognise, always it is too small or it is lost in haze or mist. The more it has been seen though the more sure people are that they know who the figure is, they think it is the land spirit itself, some call it the God or Goddess of the land, others the life force it holds. What everyone can't wait to see of course is if the figure will ever be large and clear enough to see. Each time a new picture is released, everybody gets very excited in case this will be the one. There is a new picture due to go on show in London next week but it is being very carefully guarded so no one can find out what it is. After I had been to the Houses of Parliament last night, I went to the gallery and succeeded in finding a way into the room where it is kept. It wasn't easy, the alarms are so complicated that even a mouse could set them off if they were not careful. Still, I did see the picture and I even managed to take one of the press releases which are being kept there for the opening and there's a photograph of the painting on it.'

'And can the land God be seen?' asked Sunfur.

'Yes,' said Magicnose, 'and I think you should all have a look, I'll go and get the photograph. The painting is a strange one, it is even more magical than the last but the God is there.'

Magicnose went out into the hall and came back with a rolled up leaflet which she carefully put on the floor and uncurled so they could all see. Beneath the heading;

'BRIAN EKIPS - Major New Work. Is this at last the spirit of the land revealed?'

there was a picture. It showed a valley with the viewpoint at its base so that to either side of the scene the two steep sides rose up to reveal a jagged edge of rocks at their top. At the back was the head of the valley where the two sides came together. Banks of cloud or mist seemed to pour down the sides of the slopes forming downward waves or streaks towards the base where there was a river flowing towards the viewer. Everything was lit by a ghostly blue and silver light and in the sky there was a full moon shining down. In the foreground, standing beside the river and filling two thirds of the height of the picture, was the magnificent form of an elephant, with huge tusks, which gazed out and to its right, almost as if it was staring over the left shoulder of anyone looking at the painting. From somewhere high up in the slope of the head of the valley two shafts of silver light shone out and over the elephant's head in the direction in which it was looking.

'It's beautiful,' whispered Hugbundle.

'Yes but it's more than that isn't it,' said Sunfur.

The others nodded.

'I'm glad you think so,' said Magicnose, 'so now the two adventures come closer together. For my own reasons, I want to find Speedybeard and we know he has gone to India. After I had been to the gallery I went and looked up a few things in the British Library and the Natural History Museum. Since mice are banned from both libraries, I could only go there at night and work by torchlight. Putting what I found together with what I saw at Westminster, I now know the location of all the elephant conservation projects in India. Having seen the painting I'm sure that Speedybeard is headed for one of them and we can start in the South where the Professor has shown you to look. After that, I somehow don't think that my quest for Speedybeard and your search for the Heartstone will be in entirely different directions.'

CHAPTER 21

Giles Benson

After the strange story of what Magicnose had found at the gallery and the events at the observatory, they were all quite exhausted. Jasminemouse was the first to suggest it was time for bed and the others all very gratefully agreed. Almost at once, they were asleep and it was only the postman ringing the doorbell the following morning that disturbed them. Chandra put on her dressing gown and went to see who it was. She returned holding a parcel wrapped in brown paper with an Earndel postmark. With the mice eagerly watching, except Hugbundle who stayed at the back and smiled, Chandra tore off the paper. Inside was a large box of Granny Thomas's finest fudge. They had already tried the small bag that Tailgrace had brought for Hugbundle but, although it had been good, they had had to agree it had not been improved by a night out in the rain. The box that had arrived now however was something different. Everyone was sure that it was some of the best sweets they had ever tasted.

After a rather small breakfast to compensate for all the fudge they had eaten, they left for their meeting with the Bishop who was travelling that morning from Wellminster by train. They met him at Paddington Station and then went to a restaurant for lunch. Afterwards the bishop took them to a small flat that the cathedral owned in a block close to Regents Park which the Wellminster staff used whenever they visited London. Once they were comfortable, he began to tell them what he had discovered and what it was they were waiting to hear. All their other news had already been shared over lunch.

'Well,' the Bishop began, 'as I think Peter has already told you, I have some more information on the mysterious Lieutenant Giles Benson. Without giving anything away, I happened to mention the name to one of the church wardens who retired last year. He has always had a fascination for the history of Wellminster and I wanted to see if he would come up with anything. Anything turned out to be rather a lot as you can see.'

The bishop reached down and brought out a large sheaf of old looking papers and some notes.

'You can have a look for yourselves in detail later but the main points of the story are these. Giles Benson was born in seventeen seventy five in Chelmsford, Essex. His father was an army colonel and, as was the custom of the time, Giles, as the eldest son, followed him joining his regiment at the age of nineteen in seventeen ninety four. He served in Europe which was where he won his first and only medal. In seventeen ninety eight he was posted to India, stationed with the garrison at Hyderabad which was by that time under British control. Still a lieutenant he must by then have been coming up for promotion. One night in seventeen ninety nine news reached the garrison commander of lights moving and activity in a nearby valley. Fearing some sort of uprising, he sent a scouting party of ten men under the command of Lieutenant Benson to investigate and report. Here I would actually like to read you the entry in Giles Benson's diary which has survived.'

The Bishop searched inside one of the files and pulled out a slim battered volume.

'Right, here it is, now just let me find the place.'

The Bishop flicked through the pages of the diary and then stopped at the part he wanted and started to read.

256

'I now come to a most difficult thing to record. If it was not that ten good men of the regiment who were my companions shared the vision which I saw, I would surely now think myself mad and beyond hope. We were despatched by General Banks to investigate reports of movements in a valley West of Bhongir, some twenty miles ride away. Having stopped to rest and water the horses, it was only after midnight that we approached the area. Since the first report was now some hours old, I had already chosen a course which would bring us out on the Western summit at the valley side some leagues North of the original sighting to allow for progress by whoever it was we would encounter.

As we neared the top of the ridge from the side away from the valley, I gave orders to the men to tether the horses with two of them remaining on guard whilst I and the others went ahead on foot in order to present the least chance of our being seen. The closer we got to the edge the more we could see a strange light, a mixture of orange and silver yet with a trace of blue. Not knowing what we might encounter, we crawled the last few feet and then looked out on the land below. At first it was difficult to perceive the scene clearly in all its detail but at once we were aware of a great elephant walking North along the floor of the valley and to the side of the river that flowed along it. On the back of the giant animal there were many tiny lights and from the centre of these shone a silver glow. A full moon hung in the sky and since the glow was like none I had ever seen before, I surmised that it must be some form of reflection of the rays. All around the elephant however were thousands more of the miniature lights and these, like flowers in a spring field, formed a carpet which stretched as far as you could see in every direction. My first thought was that some great army surrounding its king was on the march but none of us could see the men, the soldiers who had to be carrying the lanterns. Even with my field

257

glasses I could make out nothing save the pin points of the lights themselves. Still thinking it to be a military force however, I knew that I must discover more. I instructed two of my men to wait on the ridge whilst I and the remaining six tried to get closer to see what was happening. My orders were that if we were discovered and captured they should not try to help us but ride as if the devil himself was chasing them back to the barracks and tell their story. This done, I and my companions began the descent of the slope, half crawling, half crouching and always trying to remain unseen to the great army below us. During the difficult scramble, we all at any moment expected to hear shouts that told we had been spotted followed by shots or pursuit, but nothing came. Occasionally, a ghostly beam of silver light from the elephant's back swept the hillside and rested on us and when this came we froze, scarce daring to even breathe, but almost as if it sensed our tension it always moved on just when it seemed we could stay still no longer.

Finally we reached the bottom of the slope. All the way down I had scanned the scene time and time again for some clue as to what might be taking place but still all I could see were the myriad lights flowing like the river along the valley floor. When at the base we could still see no scrap of additional detail, I determined that whatever the risk we would know the secret of this marvel. Accordingly, we flattened ourselves upon the ground and squirmed like snakes upon our bellies to approach unnoticed. After we had gone some thirty yards and when we were only a few feet from the nearest light, I had my first glimpse of the miracle. Each gleam was a tiny lantern carried by a mouse and there were score upon score of them, all marching in the same direction and as an escort to the elephant. Unable to contain himself, one of my companions let out a muffled cry and I can scarce blame him, by then I hardly knew what I

258

was doing myself, such was the strangeness of the scene. The nearest mouse looked round and we half stood to a crouching position since no further attempt at concealment was possible. At once, tens and hundreds of mice broke away from the main procession and surrounded us, blocking our path and any possibility of progressing towards the elephant. The men raised their rifles but feeling we were in no threat if we stayed where we were, I ordered them to lower their arms, which reluctantly they did. On some strange impulse I then joined my hands as if in prayer in the way I had seen Indian people greet each other and bowed to the mice before me. They put down their lights and returned the greeting. I ordered the men to follow my example and again the mice reciprocated the signal. Then, sensing that whatever contact had been established, our presence was in some way still not welcome, I saluted in military fashion towards the light in the distance carried by the elephant and turned to go. In front of us, the mice stood back and left a path towards the ridge. Once we had regained the slope, they turned and rejoined the main body of their party.'

The Bishop closed the book and looked round the room. No one spoke.

'So,' he said, 'now you know why I wanted you to share this.'

'The Heartstone being carried North,' Chandra whispered.

'Yes,' the Bishop replied.

'What happened then?' asked Jasminemouse, slightly annoyed that the Bishop had stopped the story half way.

'Well,' the Bishop continued, 'Giles Benson and the others rode back to headquarters and reported what they had seen to the General. Despite the fact that nine of them had seen the lights and seven the mice themselves, they were not believed and were all promptly placed on sick leave and relieved of their duties. General Banks

sent out a larger party of hundred soldiers and four officers, heavily armed, with orders to intercept whatever
sort of procession it was that Giles Benson's unit had
seen and, if there was an elephant carrying a strange
light, to capture it using as much force as was necessary
and bring it to Hyderabad for investigation and display.
That party was never to return and no trace of it was ever
found. Meanwhile back at the garrison, Giles Benson was
still suspended from his duties. In the eyes of his fellow
officers, ever since the night of that patrol he had been
behaving very strangely. Not only did he stick to his
story about the mice but he even began to question
whether what the army was doing there was right.
Worse still for the authorities, he became friends with
several Indian families and was regularly seen talking to
them and sharing meals at their homes. He learned the
language and at times even adopted Indian dress. For
one or two months this was just about tolerated, he had
been a good officer and well liked, but the closer he
became to the local population, the more his actions were
suspect. He was confined to barracks but even there he
spent most of his time with the Indian servants. Finally,
word reached the General and Giles Benson was dis-
charged from the army as medically unfit and mentally
unstable, a judgement in which his own father partici-
pated and approved. Whilst they were waiting for a ship
on which he could be sent back to England, Giles was
allowed some extra freedom since, now being out of the
army, he was seen as less of an embarrassment. His use
of it was to go back to his Indian friends and then write
a pamphlet on the dangers and wrong of the growing
British influence. What had changed his mind from the
time when he first arrived in India we can, of course,
guess and it is born out in his diary where he constantly
refers to nothing he saw being the same since his eyes
first rested on the light carried by the elephant. Initially
even he doubted his own sanity but he seems to have

become increasingly sure of himself as he spent more time with the Indian families who welcomed him. There is also reference in the diary to one special friend, most of the time he uses the Indian name but then at one point, perhaps as a practice of his learning the language, he has tried to translate it. The nearest he got was Lotuspaw, so I think we can safely guess it was a mouse. Anyway, she was to become very important since after he had written the pamphlet, the authorities had had quite enough and arrested him on charges of treason and rebellion. The few copies that existed were burned and Giles Benson was thrown into prison where he was to remain until he was forcibly put on to a ship bound for London. Whilst he was in jail, his diary makes frequent references to Lotuspaw spending time with him despite the fact that he was allowed no visitors. He even says at one point, '.....they can never stop my last true friend from reaching me. For all their guards and bars she is the stronger for they do not even see her let alone have a way to block her path.'

So Giles Benson arrived back in England in disgrace. Rather than try and redeem himself in the eyes of his family however, he promptly returned to writing about the British in India, and in none too complimentary terms, whilst he travelled the country. Looking at the sort of places he went, it's my guess that he might have been following news of Sailvoyage and Lavenderwhiskers, trying to meet up with them. Since he only came to Wellminster in eighteen forty, two years after Sailvoyage had died, presumably he never succeeded. Perhaps he was finally drawn by the stories of the moon nights of the Heartstone. He must have met Lavenderwhiskers or Stonechild of course since only they could have put the medal in Sailvoyage's tomb. Also, it can only have been them who gave him details of what had happened from which he drew this.'

The Bishop reached down and pulled out two sheets of card tied together, from his briefcase. He undid the knot and inside they saw a pencil drawing in very intricate detail and shading. It was a scene high up on some scaffolding beside a church window. A workman in old fashioned clothes was looking very intently at one place in the lattice of glass fragments and making some fine adjustment. Beside him stood another workman holding out his hand on which sat a very old mouse wrapped in a blanket who was pointing to the right as if giving directions.

'Sailvoyage!' they all gasped.

'Yes,' said the Bishop, 'drawn only two years after his death and with the help of mice who knew him. It could be a very good likeness. So Giles Benson settled in Wellminster. He wrote articles and spoke on the dangers of England taking colonies the way it was and in a small way became well known for it but, because of the times, not well liked. It seems that he even spoke in the cathedral on a few occasions, the Bishop of the day got into all sorts of trouble about it. In order to support himself, Giles started a small wholesale food company specialising in cheese. It did rather well, apparently he seemed to have an unerring knack of knowing just where to go to buy the very best at just the right time when it became available. Some of his rivals said that he must have had spies in every dairy and cheese factory in Britain and Europe. When he died, Giles Benson was prosperous if not rich and in his memory at his own request in his will, the Benson family endowed a trust to help anyone who was from Asia or Africa become a British Army officer. Presumably at least something of what had drawn him to the army had survived and he wanted to offer funds for the only real way to change things. It seems to have been a rather idealistic gesture however. The trust specified that the candidates would have to be allowed to join full regular regiments of the army, not special so called 'native' sections. The army at that time was not going to let that happen and so there were no successful applicants and the trust became dormant and unused. Giles Benson was buried in the cathedral churchyard and, if we had known to look for it, we actually carried Moonbeam past the grave.'

'Bishop,' said Chandra, 'the trust, it may have been dormant for a long time but it did survive. We met someone the night before last who had been given one of the scholarships. Nat Summers, he's from Nigeria.'

'Really? Well perhaps things do change eventually, even if it does take a long time. Tell me, have you had a chance to look at Sailvoyage's diary yet? I was wondering if there was anything in there which might confirm my suspicion that Giles Benson tried to meet up with him.'

The mice and Chandra all looked at each other in some confusion; with so much going on at Wellminster they had quite forgotten the diary and no one could remember having seen it since Moonbeam gave it to them.

'Has any one got even the slightest idea where it is?' asked Starwhiskers.

Hugbundle looked uncomfortable.

'Well, I might know,' she said.

'Just what does that mean?' said Sunfur.

'It means I've got it in the other room, I've been reading it before I go to sleep each night. It's a really beautiful story, I think Sailvoyage and Lavenderwhiskers loved each other very much.'

'Yes, but does it mention Giles Benson?' said the Bishop.

'No, they met a lot of people and a lot of mice, but I don't remember seeing anything about Giles Benson.'

'Then that means I'm probably right,' said the Bishop, 'I somehow think if they had got together, Sailvoyage would have made reference to it. So now we know at least a little bit more about what happened. One other thing that's turned up concerns the fund the Watchmice set up for you, the one that's going to pay for your tickets. I was looking through the original papers and I found the receipt for the initial bank deposit that set it up. It was the proceeds of the sale of a diamond and there was a valuation certificate. It refers to one small but flawless stone clearly from the newly discovered sources in South Africa. I've looked it up. The British took control of South Africa in seventeen ninety five although it then returned briefly to Dutch influence for a while. The major diamond discoveries only came in the middle of the next century but there were some early small finds before that. The question is of course what was Sailvoyage doing in, or at least, with a diamond from there.'

'I think as Moonbeam said, there are parts of this story that no one will ever know completely,' said Chandra.

After they had finished talking about the discoveries the Bishop had made, they went to collect the airline tickets for the flight to India. Chandra had already telephoned the airline office to reserve them and they were expected. The mice decided to go in Chandra's shoulder bag, partly because it would save time since they couldn't walk as fast as she did and partly because it was raining. The bishop said that he would like to come too and they all got a feeling that he was hiding something. When they arrived at the offices, Chandra went up to the counter and gave her name whilst the Bishop stood a little behind her. In order not to cause any problems, the mice had agreed to keep out of site. The clerk went over to a file and came back with an envelope with Chandra's name on it containing nine tickets. Chandra handed over a banker's draft for the cost drawn on the account that Peter had arranged for them. The clerk checked it and put it in a drawer but she still did not hand over the tickets.

264

'Can I see your passport please?' she said to Chandra who fumbled in her bag whilst being careful not to hurt any of the mice until Starwhiskers gave it to her.

'Thank you,' said the clerk, 'and the passports of your companions please.'

Chandra's face fell and inside the bag the mice looked at each other in worry or confusion depending on whether they understood what was going on. The Bishop however did not look concerned and calmly stepped forward.

'Ah, I think I have those,' he said, 'I'm the Bishop of Wellminster you see and the party is travelling on cathedral business, I'm sure you will find everything in order.'

The Bishop handed over eight brand new full British passports and the clerk took them and put them on the counter. It was only two minutes later when she opened the first to be confronted with a picture of Honeymouse taken at the farewell dinner at Martin's cottage that she lost the air of efficient thoroughness that till then she had given to the transaction. She called over to a man in a suit who sat at a desk behind her.

'I'm sorry Mr. Perkins,' she said pointing to the passports, 'but this man claims to be a bishop and he's just given me these.'

Mr Perkins looked at the Bishop.

'Aren't you the Bishop of Wellminster?' he said, 'I've seen you on the television.'

'Yes that's right,' said the Bishop smiling, 'is there some sort of problem?'

Mr Perkins who didn't think it was right to argue with a bishop looked embarrassed.

'Well we can't accept these,' he said pointing at the passports.

'Why not!' said Magicnose sticking her head out of the bag.

Half an hour, some argument and a telephone call to the passport office later, they got their tickets. In the process, the Bishop insisted on speaking to the airline's manager to make sure that there would not be any similar problems at the airport the following week. Once they were outside, Snuggletoes asked the question he had wanted to for some time.

'Excuse me, what's a passport?' he said to the Bishop.

'Well, it's something that each country gives to one of the people who lives there so they can take it with them when they travel to say where they come from. You have to show one when you leave the country and when you enter another one.

'Why's that,' asked Honeymouse.

'It's so a country doesn't let anyone they don't like arrive or leave.'

'I can understand the arriving bit,' said Jasminemouse, 'but why would you want to stop someone leaving if you didn't like them.'

'Well it's so you know where they are,' said the Bishop but Jasminemouse didn't look very convinced.

Honeymouse, meanwhile, was having a good look at her passport. She had just found the blank pages where all the visa stamps are supposed to go.

'Hey this is good,' she said, 'there's space here to stick postcards and pictures of your friends in, and for their autographs.'

The Bishop shook his head.

'I'm afraid not,' he said, 'I'm not sure you are all going to get on very well with these, they're a bit too official for you to like them, but you had better take care of them. Chandra has to use one and if you want to stay together, it would help if you kept yours safe and left them the way they are.'

Snuggletoes put down the pencil with which he was about to try and improve the photograph in his.

266

'You mean that Chandra has to have one of these and it's not just for fun?' he said.

'I'm afraid so,' the bishop replied and all the mice looked at Chandra as if they should be trying to find a way to cheer her up.

CHAPTER 22

The Airport

The last few days before the flight seemed to rush by with scarcely a moment to even think about what they were about to begin, a search driven by desperate need but based on a mystery and clues centuries old. Despite there being so much to do, they went to the observatory almost every night where they found that things were almost back to normal. There was the procession of astronomer mice up to the building after dark, all the telescopes were back in use, and those hurt in the fire were well on the way to recovery. They had even held their party one evening just as the Doctor mouse had ordered.

The night before they were due to leave, they made one last visit to see the Professor. He was really happy since it was a cloudless night and the moon was nearly full so he could look at it to the fill of his heart's desire. Hard as they found it to believe, it was almost a month since the third night of the blue fire. Just as she had when they left for Wellminster, Chandra asked the Professor if he would go with them but he just smiled and said that he was too old, which really meant that he didn't want to be away from the observatory that long and thought they could take care of themselves. He did however promise to see them off the next day.

The following morning they left Chandra's flat early to make sure they would catch the plane and, knowing they would be away for a very long time, locked up very carefully and checked that everything was secure. As an additional precaution, Chandra had left a set of keys with Fred who had promised to look in and see that the flat was all right whilst they were away. Then they caught a train to London Bridge Station and went down to the underground to travel on to Heathrow airport. To their surprise and delight the Bishop, Martin and Simon were waiting to see them off at the check-in desk where they had to present their tickets. There was however no sign of the Professor. They waited as long as they could but he still did not arrive and reluctantly they had to make their way through into the emigration hall to present their passports. Chandra also looked round to see if Steve had come but there was no sign of him and she felt rather disappointed for reasons she could not quite explain.

No question was raised about the Passports for the mice and Chandra wondered if it was the Bishop or the Professor who had been busy, or perhaps it was both of them together, with people like them you never could be sure. There was however one unfortunate incident. A woman who had arrived on a flight from Africa was being questioned by officials in uniform. They were being very kind in the way they spoke but there were obviously difficulties about her passport and letting her into the country and she was very upset. Seeing this, Snuggletoes dashed across and said that if it would help she could have his and he would manage without for a bit but he was turned away and they had to leave her there. The Bishop and Martin, however, stayed to try and help and Simon was not allowed to accompany Chandra and the mice past the passport control so he very soon went back to join them.

Once they were through all the checks, Chandra and the mice followed signs to a departure lounge where they sat on plush seats and drank orange juice until the time came to board the aircraft. Then they went down a short walkway that took them onto the plane where they

269

were greeted by a steward who showed them to a group of nine seats where they could all sit together. Hugbundle rapidly claimed the one next to Chandra but it didn't make much difference, all the mice could easily fit onto any of the seats and they very soon all ended up in a row on the back of one of them so they could see out of the window.

After a short delay, the airliner taxied out onto the runway and the pilot announced that they were going to take off. The engines roared and they all felt the push backwards as the aircraft accelerated and soared into the sky. Then it made a sharp turn to the left and they got a view down along the wing of London laid out below them like a toy city. They all wondered how long it would be before they saw it again. After they had been in the air ten minutes, the Captain made an announcement.

'Good afternoon ladies and gentlemen, I have received a request from a military aircraft that wants to fly alongside us for a minute to check its instruments. It will come up quite close on the left side but there is no need to be alarmed.'

Chandra and the mice who were on the left hand side all looked out of the window. From the distance, a small aircraft slowly converged till it flew beside them and at the same height only a short distance away. The wings were swept back and a single glint of sunlight reflected off the canopy. Underneath there were several pods and projections and four large missiles. The impression was of a great and slightly sinister power waiting to be unleashed. Then they looked into the cockpit. A pilot sat in the front but the seat behind appeared to be empty only when they looked again they saw that they had missed a small figure in a tiny helmet who was waving to them.

'It's the Professor!' said Sunfur and they all laughed, 'Typical! He only said he'd see us off, not be at the airport, we should have known he'd be up to something.'

Chandra looked again at the pilot and at just that moment he turned and raised his hand in salute. Even with his flying helmet on she recognised Steve at once. Then the fighter aircraft swung sharply to the left and two jets of orange fire appeared in the engines at the rear as it shot upwards in a steep climb and was lost to view.

Chandra and the mice, happy that they had not been forgotten after all, settled back in their seats to enjoy the journey. Going all that way and, in so many senses, into the unknown, it was strangely reassuring to know that someone left behind was thinking of you. It would have been an even more welcome comfort if they had known of the airmail letter to a particularly nasty cat that lived in Madras which was in one of the sacks of mail in the aircraft's cargo hold. The address on the front was scrawled in the unmistakable ugly writing that Smirk-muzzle used whenever he wrote a letter in the hope of causing some trouble. The excitement at the harm he might do always seemed to affect the way his paw gripped the pen.

The airliner roared on and in a very short time, they were crossing the eastern coast of England and all that lay before them was the sea and new lands on their way to Bombay and then Madras itself. They were so high that they could see nothing but the most general layout of the countryside below which appeared as fields of green with a band of pale sand before the blue of the sea. Down on the beach beneath them, however, a lone elephant looked up into the sky at the silver shape of the jet and raised its trunk in its own salute to the travellers as they began their quest. The great animal stared after the aircraft as it continued onwards to the East and then turned and slowly made its way along the deserted shore to disappear into an enveloping cloud of a fog that had blown up from the South. The final traces of its footprints in the sand were lost to the fast incoming tide.

The story will continue in Book 2:
THE HEARTSTONE ODYSSEY - INDIA AND
BEYOND

and in Book 3:
THE HEARTSTONE ODYSSEY - MOONRISE OVER
FIVE CONTINENTS

ARVAN KUMAR

Arvan Kumar is a pen name designed in the heritage of that tradition to conceal the identity of the author. For once however the primary reason is not one of secrecy but is to prevent the Heartstone Odyssey being judged on any prejudices which could be ascribed to a real name and the origins that can be linked to it. This book is about the breaking of divisions, not their enhancement and that means not only divisions between cultures and races but also those within countries, a form of tension and segregation which can still be seen in England, India and throughout the world. It is too easy to see a name, attach a stereotyped view that such a person must hold and then not see the words which are really before you but only those which your fears have told you must be there.

Many people have asked whether Arvan Kumar is from India. It is sufficient to say that he has been taken for an Indian in India but has also been seen there as being from Europe. In England in the same day he has been racially abused in the street for having Indian origins and then later invited to join a group in a pub made up of people with identical sympathies to those who had yelled their insults earlier since they now judged him on his appearance to be one of, as they saw it, their own. In many ways Arvan Kumar belongs in both worlds and yet the irony is that in the terms of the separatist mind strictly he does not fit in either or, for that matter, any other group among the long list that have tried to claim to be an island in what should be the ever flowing sea of humanity. As to his true origins, no doubt there could be a note of them in a Central Nosey Store somewhere but, if truth be told, it is far more likely that you will find the details of what he had for breakfast on the day

275

that he started to write this book, and, as any mouse will tell you, that is far more important to know.

So why Arvan Kumar? The answer to that is very simple. 'The Heartstone Odyssey' was first told on a train journey from Bombay to Madras in 1985. Arvan Kumar was the best name anyone in the carriage could think of! The passenger who suggested it however had thought very hard before speaking. Arvan is not a first name in use in India, although it sounds as if it should be. Arvan is from Hindu mythology and means one of the horse messengers of the moon. All writers hope to be messengers and the name was suggested after the telling of the 'Anju and the Heartstone' section of the story, where not only is the theme of the moon present as in so much of the book, but also the horse as a presence linked with the Spirit of the Land appears. Kumar is not a surname in the European sense but is more a suffix denoting a man, rather as Mr is used as a prefix in England. Hence, Arvan Kumar is a very special name not only given by someone from the South of India but created in response to the story as it was told. People tend to think of connections and meanings like that more in India than the West; perhaps that's why the mice like some of the names they find on their journey with Chandra so much, but that tale must wait till the next book to be told.